The Sailweaver's Son

Kyle and Esben,

May the winds
be kind to you ...

Jeff Minerd

4/12/16

THE SKY RIDERS OF ETHERIUM

The Sailweaver's Son

By

Jeff Minerd

HOLLISTON, MASSACHUSETTS

THE SAILWEAVER'S SON
Copyright © 2016 by Jeff Minerd

Cover Art by Silviya Yordanova.

First printing September 2016
10 9 8 7 6 5 4 3 2 1

ISBN # 1-60975-139-6
ISBN-13 # 978-1-60975-139-5
LCCN # 2016946752

Silver Leaf Books, LLC
P.O. Box 6460
Holliston, MA 01746
+1-888-823-6450

Visit our web site at www.SilverLeafBooks.com

For my son, Noah

Acknowledgements

I wouldn't have written this book if it weren't for my son Noah. It never would have occurred to me to try writing a young adult fantasy novel if he and I hadn't read and enjoyed so many together over the years. Noah also read a draft of this book, gave me some advice, and pronounced it awesome, adding that it was hard to believe his dad wrote it.

Quite a few other people also read early drafts or portions of this book and gave me encouragement and advice. Thank you to Christine Adamo, Susan Griepsma, Lisa LeFever, Margaret Mattson, Gerry Minerd, Tim Minerd, Christine Norris, Shannon Page, Alex Ruffino, Chuck Ruffino (who read two complete drafts!), Laura Ruffino, Stephen Ruffino, Bethany Slapinski, and Karen Due Theilade. Thanks also to my writing group: Amy Andrews, Bill Capossere, Geoff Graser, Jennifer Lloyd, and Gretchen Stahlman whose feedback was invaluable.

Thanks to Tim and Geraldine Minerd, my parents, for all their love and support. I couldn't have written this book without them, either.

And finally, a special thanks to Cliff Bowyer of Silver Leaf Books for giving this novel a home.

The Kingdom Of Spire

HIGHSPIRE MOUNTAINS

DRAGONBACK MOUNTAINS

PINEMONT→

GATMONT→

DRAGONS HEAD

SELEMONT→

SILKMONT→

OCEAN OF CLOUDS

FOOTMONT→

THE TWINS

The Sailweaver's Son

ONE

The day the giant airship exploded and sank beneath the clouds, Tak was one of the few people to see what happened. He was following the ship, one of the royal fleet's battleships, in his own small craft, the *Arrow*. He should not have been doing this. Tak had been told many times—by his parents, the Admiral of the royal fleet, even once by the King himself—not to slink along behind royal battleships.

Tak flew a half mile or so behind the ship, so it appeared no bigger in the sky than one of the models hanging from the ceiling of his bedroom. He would have liked to get closer, but the wind was tricky that day. The updrafts, downdrafts, and side currents kept shifting, which made it hard to keep the *Arrow* steady—she bobbed and lurched, her wing-like sail fluttering and snapping overhead. A close approach would be too dangerous.

So Tak sat in the stern of the *Arrow*, trying to keep her steady with one hand on the tiller and his feet on the wing flap pedals, and he spied on the battleship through his looking glass. He could tell by the shape of the hull, the number of guns, and the configuration of the masts and sails that this ship was the *Vigilance*, commanded by Captain Adamus Strake. Tak could identify most royal battleships by sight and tell you the names of their captains, if you cared to hear.

Like all airships of Etherium, the *Vigilance* looked something like an old-fashioned, wooden sailing ship—except that she was much, much wider and shallower in the hull, her keel plunged much deeper below her, and her huge triangular sails looked and worked more like wings, all the better to keep her upright and stable in the thick atmosphere. And while large battleships like the *Vigilance* often flew by sail alone, they were also equipped with powerful propellers in the stern, fueled by steam boilers built below their decks.

Tak was hopelessly in love with the big ships, as many fifteen-year-olds in the Kingdom of Spire were, which is why he stalked them. He watched the *Vigilance* for hours as she patrolled the sky, fascinated. Her polished wooden decks and rows of bronze cannons gleamed in the sun. Men in smart blue uniforms climbed the complicated rigging to trim the sails. The crew ran through a fire drill, hauling buckets of water up the masts and dousing the sails. The lookouts sat in their crow's nests, scanning the sky.

It was a gorgeous summer afternoon. The sky was rosily purple, and the cumulus clouds high up in the stratosphere were white and plump and peaceful as lambs. Even the thick gray clouds far below that always covered the surface of Etherium didn't look as sinister as they usually did. The sunlight had turned them into silver and gold. In the distance, Tak's home mountain range, the Highspire Mountains, rose above this blanket of surface clouds in vivid shades of pine-covered green. Flocks of birds and other flying creatures swirled in the open sky, their flapping wings or shimmering scales glinting and sparkling as they caught the sun.

Tak could never say what made him turn his spyglass down toward Etherium's blanket of clouds that day. Most sky riders prefer to avoid looking down at those surface clouds. It makes them uncomfortable. Sky riders know very little of the world beneath those clouds, but one thing they do know is that Gublins live there. They know this because Gublins have a tendency to climb up out of the clouds onto the mountainsides at night and snatch goats—or children, or anything warm and edible, but mostly goats—from the fields and pastures of the lower villages. Maybe Tak sensed movement or the glint of sunlight below him. In any case, his spyglass swung downward and Tak gasped as he saw something emerge from the cloud cover below.

He'd seen nothing like it in his life. No sky rider ever had. It was an enormous bubble. Twice the size of the battleship. As it rose into the sky, the bubble wobbled and shimmered, squished into lopsided potato-like shapes then snapped back to roughly round. It was more or less transparent, but its rippling surface glistened with a rainbow of colors where the sunlight played on it. The bubble rose with alarming speed, rolling this way and that with the wind. It was not on a collision course with the battleship—yet. It was some distance off the port bow.

The lookouts didn't see it until it was too late. As the giant bubble drew level with the battleship, Tak heard the faint ringing of alarm bells. The ship came to a full stop, propellers going still, sails slanting upward to create drag. Tak could imagine the startled looks on the faces of the men on deck. He was wearing such a look himself. Then the wind shifted and gusted again. The sky riders have an old saying: *Our lives rely upon the wind, and the wind is not reliable.* The saying proved true for the men on the battleship. The wind took hold of that bubble and hurled it directly at them.

Too late, the captain cried the order to turn hard to starboard, trying to veer away. Too late, the propellers leapt to life and the ship lurched, listing heavily with the effort of making the turn while men scrambled in the rigging to adjust the flapping sails. Large battleships like the *Vigilance* are known for their strength and forward speed, but they are not known for their maneuverability. The bubble hit the ship broadside and enveloped it entirely.

And then both ship and bubble exploded into a burst of fire that left a glowing yellow spot like the sun behind Tak's eyes, which had snapped shut. When he opened his eyes, blinking, the bubble was gone and the ship was engulfed in flames. The sails were ablaze. Horrified, Tak watched as burning men leapt from the deck like showers of sparks, their flaming parachutes useless.

As Tak sat stricken in the stern of the *Arrow*, gaping in shock and disbelief, he felt the first rumbles of the giant explosion in his chest. He felt hints of its heat on his face. And then he saw the shock wave expanding in all directions from the ruined ship.

Including his.

The atmosphere of Etherium is thick enough that under certain conditions it becomes visible to the naked eye. This was one of those conditions. The distant cumulus clouds in the stratosphere wavered and rippled as if they were reflections of clouds on the surface of a pond into which someone had dropped a large stone. Few of even the oldest and most experienced sky riders had ever faced such a wave. Tak had never seen anything like it. For a moment he froze. But then his training kicked in and he did his best to prepare himself. He made sure his lifeline was clipped securely to the belt on his waist and fastened tightly to the ship. He checked his parachute. No sky rider ever sets foot on an airship without making sure that he or she is wearing a well-functioning parachute. Tak would have liked to take his sail down but there was no time for that. The wave was almost upon him. He turned the *Arrow* to face it directly, angled the bow of his ship as high as he could, and held on tight.

The wave tossed his ship around like a leaf in a storm. The air became oven hot. The *Arrow* tumbled end over end. Tak was thrown from the deck. The lifeline yanked on the belt around his stomach so hard it squeezed the breath out of him. But it held. Eventually, Tak and his ship stopped tumbling. The air cooled. Tak ended up hanging by his lifeline below the completely capsized *Arrow*, nothing below his dangling feet but clouds.

One might think that hanging by a slender lifeline below his upside-down ship would be a frightening situation for a boy like Tak. In fact, he was used to it. Small airships regularly capsized, especially when raced and pushed to their extremes by reckless boys. And even if his lifeline had snapped, Tak still would have had his parachute. Sky rider parachutes are cunningly built. In the buoyant atmosphere of Etherium, they can keep a person aloft indefinitely, like an airship sail keeps a ship aloft. And they're equipped with toggles for steering. Many lost overboard airmen have caught lucky currents and steered themselves home by parachute, sometimes landing on the roofs of their own houses—tired, hungry, and cold, but otherwise not much the worse for wear.

Climbing up the lifeline hand over hand and righting the capsized craft was also a familiar task. Tak had done it countless times. Once he'd reached the overturned hull of the *Arrow* and planted his feet on it, he stepped out onto one of the short wings that extended from either side of the ship, got a good grip on the long keel, bent his knees and rocked and leaned until the craft righted itself. The sail—still in one piece—flapped and filled as it caught the wind. As the *Arrow* righted and began to rise on the wind, Tak flipped himself over the side and onto the deck in one deft movement.

Now all he wanted to do was go home. His heart pounded and his hands shook as he tightened his lines. The capsizing of his ship may not have frightened him, but a giant bubble causing the *Vigilance* to explode into flames certainly had. He knew he needed to tell the authorities what he had witnessed, as soon as possible.

He would get into trouble again—it would be pretty obvious that he'd been tailing the *Vigilance*. He shouldn't have been anywhere *near* it. His habit of stalking royal battleships had landed him in trouble before. Lookouts were trained to sound an alarm when unauthorized airships came too near, even small ones like the *Arrow*. More than once, Tak hadn't been able to resist stealing in for a closer look and had triggered a general alarm. A lot more than once. When this happened, he would tighten his sail, lean on his tiller, find a fast current and be away on the wind in a wink. The gleaming red *Arrow* making an escape was a familiar sight to lookouts in the royal fleet.

But Tak never managed to outrun trouble. His ship was too recognizable.

"I see you Taktinius Spinner!" ship captains would roar, leaning over command deck railings and bellowing into the wind. "You've been warned before! Your father will hear about this!"

What Tak wanted most at that moment was to sit down in his family's kitchen and have some of his mother's egg soup. Have her fuss over him. He was in shock, which made the things around him seem unreal. He couldn't take his eyes off the ruined, smoldering battleship. The initial force of the explosion had pushed him farther from the ship, but then the air had reversed direction, sucking in toward the ship to replace the oxygen that had been burned up. He'd ended up closer to the *Vigilance* than he'd been originally. It was badly scorched and burning in places, but it hadn't caught fully afire. Royal battleships are made from wood that is prepared to be fire resistant. There were holes in the deck and hull, rimmed by jagged planks blown outward, and smoke billowed from all the ship's open hatches—some or all of the powder kegs below must have ignited. The masts had all snapped and hung trailing over the sides, their stays burnt away. Tak shut his eyes. He couldn't get the image out of his head of those men leaping overboard all aflame.

The men! Could there be any left alive onboard? Maybe some who'd been in secure holds below decks when the bubble exploded? In his haste to head home, this thought hadn't occurred to Tak. He steadied the *Arrow*, took out his spyglass, and scanned the deck of the ship more closely. The cannons, snapped free of their breechings, were strewn about like so many broken toys. The ship's once neatly stored gear and tackle were also scattered about the deck. Most of the rail and deck wood had blackened. Here and there, stray flames or coals flickered redly. Tak held his breath against seeing bodies. But he let it out in relief when he spotted none. The deck appeared lifeless...

There! A man! A man struggled up out of a smoking hatch onto the deck. He crawled clear and fell onto his belly. His hand scrabbled weakly at the parachute pack on his back, trying to pull the cord. He tried. And tried again. If the chute would open, it would lift the man off deck.

"Come *on*," Tak muttered to himself, willing the parachute to work.

It didn't. The man either gave up or passed out. He lay face down on the deck. But his sides heaved with breath.

The man would need someone's help to get off board. Tak looked to the sky, hoping to see countless large airships already speeding to the rescue. The explosion must have been seen and heard for miles and miles around. Half the royal fleet should be there by now. Or at least several merchant or fishing vessels. But the sky was empty. Birds and other flying creatures had disappeared, frightened off by the explosion. The only sign of life was a few sailweaver spiders drifting nearby on the silken parachutes they'd woven, looking agitated and disoriented. The creatures were a common sight. There were no other ships coming to the rescue. Not even the glint of a sail in the distance. If that man were to get off the *Vigilance*, Tak was his only hope.

A large part of Tak urged him to just go home. No one would blame him for not trying to rescue the man. That kind of thing was not something a fifteen-year-old boy was meant to do. In fact, his mother and father would be *furious* with him if he tried. It would be dangerous. For one thing, a stray flame might ignite the *Arrow*, which was not especially fire resistant. For another thing, there was no telling if all the smoldering ship's powder kegs had ignited or if there were still some waiting to explode. And finally, without sails to help keep what was left of the *Vigilance* aloft, the ship was slowly starting to sink. The stern dipped toward the surface clouds first, as the stern was heaviest because of the steel boilers there. And little by little, the stern was dragging the rest of the ship down with it.

No one would even have to know about that man, a part of Tak whispered. *You wouldn't have to tell anyone about seeing him. By the time anyone else gets here, the Vigilance will be long gone beneath the clouds.*

It would be a secret.

TWO

With a guilty conscience, Tak pointed the bow of the *Arrow* toward home. He was already choosing his words for the authorities about how he'd scanned the deck of the *Vigilance* with his looking glass and found no survivors. As Tak angled his sail to get some lift, preparing to find his way out of the south-flowing current he found himself in, something soft, wiggly, and definitely *alive* came out of nowhere and smacked him in the face. It was one of the sailweaver spiders—black and glossy, about the size of a chicken egg—that had been drifting nearby. The spider landed on its back in Tak's lap, parachute deflated, legs kicking.

Tak yelped, jumped up, and swatted the creature to the deck. The idea of a spider crawling on him made him shudder. Tak raised a boot to squash the stunned spider under his heel, and hesitated. He brought his boot down, and took a deep breath. For almost any other boy in the kingdom, being afraid of spiders would've been okay. Not something you'd advertise, of course, but something you could get away with when no one was looking. But Tak had been born into the Spinner family. For generations, the Spinner family had farmed sailweaver spiders, harvested their superbly strong and water-resistant silk, and woven the material into sails.

Being part of the Spinner family meant you had to learn to care for sailweaver spiders, feed them, even milk them for silk—all without any yelping or squashing.

When Tak was little, his father had taught him to sing a children's song to help calm his fear of spiders. Letting the *Arrow* drift in the southerly current, Tak sang softly to himself.

Spider, spider it may be true
That I'm a hundred times bigger than you
But I'll not mash you, or smash you, or turn you into goo
So don't fear me, and I won't fear you

The old song always helped. Tak was in control of his fear, instead of letting it control him. He knelt on the deck and peered at the spider. It was no longer stunned, and it hadn't been injured. It busily wove a new silken chute, legs moving in a flurry of precise action like so many miniature knitting needles, strands of silk stretching from the glands on its abdomen and forming into a tiny, dome-like web on its back. Tak coaxed the spider into the palm of his hand. Its prickly touch wasn't so bad. When the parachute was finished and the spider ready, Tak stood and held out his hand, helped the spider on its way with a gentle breath. The creature floated off his palm, sailed south with the current, back toward the *Vigilance*.

Tak narrowed his eyes at the *Vigilance*. Took another deep breath. His fear about trying to rescue the man on the sinking battleship was still there. It sat in his chest like a lump of cold steel. But it, too, was no longer in control of him. Instead, it centered and steadied him, gave him weight. Tak knew what he had to do. He was sure that one day he would serve on a ship like the *Vigilance*. One day he would be a man like that man. And if he were trapped on that burning, sinking ship, he would want anyone at all to try to help him.

So Tak made himself do it. It was as if he were watching himself from outside. He pushed on the *Arrow's* tiller until the bow came around, pressed the foot pedals that worked the wing flaps—banking the ship into a sharp turn—and steered himself toward the *Vigilance*. He came as close to the battleship as he dared in the buffeting wind, then threw a grappling line. It caught, and he pulled himself closer, until the hulls almost touched. He unclipped his lifeline. Checked his parachute. Then he leapt across the small gap onto the deck of the battleship. It leaned at an alarming angle. He scrabbled across the deck to the man and rolled him over. Gasped.

The man was a fright to look at. His hair and eyebrows were gone, burnt away. His uniform was singed and blackened. The exposed skin of his hands and face blazed an angry bright red, bubbling with white blisters. The man opened his eyes. They widened when they saw a strange boy with brown eyes and shaggy brown hair leaning over him, a partly determined, partly disgusted expression on his hawklike face. The man's blistered lips worked, trying to form words. "Stupid boy," he managed to say, trying to push Tak away. "Leave me. Get off this ship."

Tak rolled the man back over onto his belly with an effort. He was a large man, much broader in the shoulders than the usual sky rider, who tended to have light builds. If Tak could just get the man's parachute to work, he would float off the deck. Tak could then retrieve him with the *Arrow*.

But the parachute pack was badly damaged. The cord had been burned down to a charred stub. The leather harness straps were cracked and blackened. And what was worse, there were holes burned through the sturdy canvass of the pack itself, suggesting the parachute inside would be full of holes as well. Even if Tak could get the chute open, it would no longer hold the man's weight.

"Get *off* this ship," the man wheezed. "It's going down."

Tak knew what the airman said was true. He couldn't see over the side of the ship, but he knew it was dropping steadily toward the surface clouds below. The increasing pressure on his eardrums told him so. Tak's eyes watered with the sting of wood smoke. Stray tatters of sail and snapped ropes flapped in the wind as if in alarm. The ship's wooden beams creaked and groaned as if gasping their last.

Tak's mind raced. If he were not going to abandon this man, there was only one option. He would give the man his chute. He would get him safely off the burning ship, then make it back to the *Arrow* and retrieve the man from the sky. Tak unbuckled the harness of his parachute without thinking about this plan of action further, because he knew if he stopped to think about it he would never do it. Sky riders don't like parting from their parachutes.

Sky riders are fearless when it comes to heights. They consider the sky a second home. They grow restless and impatient when confined to the ground for too long. However, sky riders do have the good sense to be afraid of falling. Objects fall slowly in the thick atmosphere of Etherium. Still, a drop from airship height would be fatal. So any sky rider would be uncomfortable—to say the least!—with the idea of taking off his chute for any period of time, even if he were standing on the deck of a sturdy ship in fair weather. To take off one's chute on the listing deck of a sinking ship and give it to another, with one's only chance of survival a leap across the gap to one's own nearby ship—that would be crazy.

Getting his chute onto the injured man was much harder than Tak thought. The buckles had fused on the man's harness so Tak had to cut it away with the knife he wore at his belt. Tak's own harness had been fitted to his tall, lean frame, so getting it around the man's thick shoulders and waist, adjusting the leather straps and tightening the buckles, was almost impossible with his shaking hands. On top of that, the man fought him, struggling weakly to push him away. When Tak knelt on his chest to hold him down, the man made awful sounds of pain. And he smelled of burnt hair. Tak's face screwed up tight as he struggled to complete the task. Tears of frustration and panic leaked from the corners of his eyes. The pressure bored into his eardrums and he was sure that any minute he and the battleship and the man would sink beneath the clouds. But his hands kept moving somehow, and finally he had the parachute harness more or less secured around the airman, who had largely given up the fight, his head lolling back onto the charred wooden planks.

Tak rolled the man over onto his front and pulled the

cord of the chute. The chute blossomed open and lifted the man off the deck, his arms and legs dangling limply. Tak scurried up the tilting deck to the rails where the *Arrow* sat just a few feet away. Tak climbed up onto the railing, then hesitated. Everything in his body told him not to jump. His back felt strangely naked without the familiar weight of the parachute pack. He looked down. The stern of the *Vigilance* was just starting to disappear into the top layer of surface clouds, which had become a sinister gray mist.

Tak jumped.

He landed chest-first squarely on the deck of the *Arrow* with his arms around the foremast. The ship lurched. *Don't think!* he told himself. *Just act. Move!* He picked himself up, grabbed his lifeline and clipped it to his belt. He didn't waste time trying to yank the grappling line free. He cut it with his knife. Then he climbed into the stern, took hold of the tiller, and urged the *Arrow* to climb as fast as possible.

When Tak looked down again, the *Vigilance* was nothing more than the gray ghost of a ship disappearing beneath the surface clouds.

Tak looked up. The man in the parachute drifted far above in a fast northeasterly current. For a skilled sky rider like Tak, it wasn't too difficult a matter to find that current, climb beneath the man, keep pace with him, then gently ease the *Arrow* upward until the man settled down onto the deck and his chute went limp. Tak cut away the chute so it wouldn't fill with wind again and drag the man off deck or tangle in his rigging. The man lay on his side, groaning. At least that meant he was alive. Tak clipped a lifeline to him.

The northeast current was a mercy. That was the direction Tak needed to take him back to Selemont, his home mountain and home to the kingdom's capital city, Selestria. Tak pointed his bow toward home. The *Arrow* flew.

* * *

As Tak approached Selemont with the half-conscious airman still sprawled and groaning on the deck of the *Arrow*, the sight of the green mountain comforted him. It was the mountain on which he'd been born and called home. The base of Selemont, as near to the surface clouds as the inhabitants dared, had been carved into terraced fields planted with potatoes, onions, cabbages, carrots, and other crops. There were also sloping pastures where herds of goats, pigs, and sheep grazed. Winding paths climbed up through the fields and pastures. Wide, paved roads wound in spiraling paths up the mountainside. At points along these roads, houses clustered into villages. About three-quarters of the way up the mountain sat the great wall of the city of Selestria. This wall stood thirty feet high and ran the entire circumference of the mountain. It had been built with carved blocks of mountain stone, and it was dotted with watchtowers at regular intervals that flew the flag of the Kingdom of Spire.

Inside the city wall, the fields and pastures were replaced with tightly packed stone houses and paved streets. The houses became larger and more ornate and the streets busier with traffic the closer you got to the top of the mountain until, near the very top, they butted up against a second wall, the wall of castle Selestria. The castle sat atop the peak of the mountain like a shining crown. It appeared as if the battlements and watchtowers had grown out of the mountain itself. And in a way they had. Like the city wall, castle Selestria had been built centuries ago from mountain stone, laboriously carved and carted up the mountainside from quarries below. The highest towers and spires of the castle were often lost in the clouds, and on cloudy days you could see nothing but mist and fog from their windows. On sunny days, you could see all of the Kingdom of Spire.

Tak headed straight for the castle's main dock. No sooner did he get within sight of the castle walls, however, than a four-man sentry ship intercepted him. It shot straight at him, forcing him to veer off course and slow down. Two sentries stood on the foredeck with nocked arrows, although their bows were not drawn. "Tak Spinner!" the sentry leader called, "By wind and weather you turn that ship around this instant! We'll have none of your blasted games today!"

Tak and the *Arrow* were as familiar to castle sentries as they were to lookouts of the royal fleet. On summer afternoons when there were no lessons, and he grew bored with the races and games the other boys were playing, and there weren't any girls to show off for, Tak enjoyed playing a little game he called "testing sentry responsiveness." This involved buzzing the castle walls and taunting the sentries into a chase. Sometimes they caught Tak. Mostly they didn't.

The sentries weren't nearly as fond of this game as Tak was.

Tak slowed his ship to a crawl, let it drift closer to the sentry ship. "Help!" he called. "The *Vigilance* has been destroyed! I have an injured man here!" Tak's voice had only recently deepened into that of a man's, and it cracked wildly in his excitement.

The sentry leader frowned. "What new game is this...?" he muttered. But he could see the crumpled form of a man in a blue airman's uniform on the deck of the *Arrow*. The sentry ship edged alongside the *Arrow*. The leader boarded Tak's ship, which rocked briefly with the extra weight. He knelt down next to the airman.

"What in the *heavens*?!" the leader exclaimed when he saw the state of the injured man. "What happened here?"

Tak tried to explain. But the words came out all in a jumble and refused to make sense. On top of that, his voice was still cracking and his body shook.

"Okay, take it easy boy," the sentry leader said, laying a hand on Tak's shoulder. "We'll get this sorted out." Another sentry ship had pulled up alongside the first, and the man shouted to it, "A surgeon! We need a surgeon on the double!" The men on that ship nodded in acknowledgement of the order. The ship made a graceful dip, turned, and glided away.

The man Tak had rescued started to stir. He gripped the arm of the sentry leader and pulled himself partly up. He struggled to speak. At this moment, both Tak and the sentry noticed something about the man they hadn't before. His shoulder epaulets, which bore his insignia of rank, had survived the fire more or less intact. The insignia was that of four golden feathers.

It was the insignia of a battleship captain. The man was Captain Adamus Strake.

"The King," he sputtered. "Take me to the King. Now."

THREE

As it turned out, Captain Strake did not get to see the King that day. The young surgeon who arrived on the scene took one look at him and ordered him taken directly to the infirmary—no ifs, ands, or buts. "If you want him to live, do as I say," the surgeon said. "And even so the chances are not good."

Captain Strake, who'd lapsed back into unconsciousness, didn't argue.

So it happened that Tak, after several hours of waiting in an antechamber to the throne room, was ushered into the presence of the King all by himself, unless you counted the armed guards.

The King's throne room sits atop the keep of castle Selestria. It's a vast, wide-open, circular space, with rows of tall windows set into the curving walls to let in air and sunlight. Its marble columns rise to such a height and are spaced to such a width that no matter where you stand, you can't take in the entire room with your eyes. It seems to go on forever. Birds and flying reptiles roost in the vaulted arches of the ceiling. No one has ever been able to roust them out, and everyone has long since quit trying. The floor is brightly gleaming polished marble, and a team of attendants have been assigned to keep it that way, mopping up the droppings as soon as they hit. Bird droppings are a fact of life for those living on Etherium.

The echoes of Tak and his armed escort's footsteps on the marble floor were quickly swallowed up by the sheer volume of the room. At the far end from the tree-tall double entrance doors, the King sat on a raised throne, on a circular dais approached by ten steps. Many of the King's advisors stood gathered together on the step below the throne, conversing with the King. Tak's father—Taktinius Spinner senior—was often in this group of advisors, which is the reason Tak tended to get off lightly when caught stalking battleships or buzzing the castle walls. But Tak's father wasn't in this group today. He was on Silkmont, several mountains away, tending to the spider farms and overseeing the care of this year's vlisken crop. Tak's father was Chief Sailspinner of the realm, as had been Tak's grandfather and great-grandfather. Tak didn't know it at the time, but a fast messenger ship had been dispatched to retrieve his father from Silkmont as quickly as possible.

As the guards brought Tak close to the dais, the conversation broke up among the King and his advisors. All eyes turned to Tak. He recognized many of the faces. There were friendly ones and not-so-friendly ones. Whenever people heard about the latest trouble Tak had gotten himself into, many would shake their heads and say he needed discipline. "That boy needs to have his wings clipped but good," the old baker who owned the pie shop around the corner from Tak's house would say to his customers. "He should have that little red ship taken away for a month or two. It would do a world of good for him."

None of the old baker's customers disagreed.

Among the friendly faces was Giraldus Wright, Chief Shipwright of the realm. Friendship between the Wright and Spinner families went back for generations. It made sense, people said, as a sail without a ship was as useless as a ship without a sail. The two middle brothers of the Wright family, Lucias and Marcus, were like brothers to Tak.

There was also the kind and wise face of Terentius Liberverm, Chief Scholar of the realm and head of the University. The Liberverm family were frequent dinner guests at the Spinner house. Tak's father loved to read old books of history and lore, and he and Terentius would often stay up late into the night, sipping wine and discussing the fine points of ancient texts as they lounged in comfortable chairs before the fireplace.

Less friendly faces included Gasparus Miner, a lean, tired -looking man whose job was to ensure the kingdom was supplied with enough coal, iron, sulfur, and other things obtained under the mountains to keep it going. His job had become difficult lately because the kingdom's supplies of coal were growing scarce. Coal was used not only in the kingdom's smithies and forges where weapons and farm implements were made, it was used to fuel the boilers that kept the immense propellers of the royal battleships spinning.

And speaking of battleships, Tak groaned inwardly to see Admiral Scud, head of the royal fleet, standing closest to the King and looking hardest in his direction. Admiral Scud and his father were definitely not friends. Everyone knew why. As young men, Scud and Tak's father had been in love with the same woman. Scud had been engaged to marry her. It's a story for another time, but the outcome was this: The woman married Tak's father instead.

Admiral Scud's eyes were the flickering gray of storm clouds. His short-cropped hair was bright white but showed no sign of thinning. Likewise, the Admiral stood tall and broad-shouldered and lean in a way that belied his fifty-odd years. The only outward sign of his age, other than the white hair, was his weather-beaten face. It was creased and tanned to a harsh brown from years of life on the deck of battle-ships. Admiral Scud had served as a young lad of eighteen in the Gublin War. Later, as a rising captain in the royal fleet, he'd led an expedition that circumnavigated the globe. The man had also tangled with his fair share of dragons. More than his fair share, his men often said, as he usually went out of his way to provoke them.

The most distinguishing feature of Admiral Scud's face was the thick white scar that ran from the base of his left ear to his chin, slicing across his cheek and twisting his lower lip into a permanent, scowling frown. He'd gotten that one in the Gublin War. But he bore other scars as well. Some on his body. Others in places more difficult to see.

"Here's the boy!" Scud growled. "Now we'll have some answers. Let me question him, Highness."

The King held up a hand for silence. Scud quieted. He had broken protocol by speaking before his majesty spoke.

The King was older than Scud. His gray beard was neatly trimmed, and his long gray hair was pulled back from his forehead and held in place by a golden crown whose points were worked into the shape of feathers. His face was softer than Scud's, and his blue eyes were kinder. The King was fond of the Spinner family, and of Tak in particular though he couldn't say he knew the boy well. The King had been a bit wild in his youth, so he empathized with Tak. When Scud or the captain of the castle watch complained to him about the boy, the King would wave a hand dismissively and tell them to try to remember when *they* were boys.

The King studied Tak's face shrewdly. You didn't get to be King without being a good judge of men. In fact, this particular King could usually tell what a man was about to say just by studying his face. And know the exact proportion of lie and truthfulness in it as well.

Tak lowered his eyes and bowed.

"How's your heading today Taktinius Spinner?" the King asked. This was the equivalent of "How are you?" Standard replies varied from "Fast and sure," if you were having a good day to "Foundering and lost," if you were having a bad day.

"Steady enough," Tak said, which was the middling reply. His legs were shaking from exhaustion and nervousness. He'd met the King before, but never had this kind of face-to-face audience with him. Tak usually enjoyed being the center of attention, but this was too much. Still, even though his voice rasped as he replied—his mouth was dry and he was terribly thirsty—Tak kept his words steady and he controlled his quivering legs. He stood with his head up and back straight. His father had told him never to show weakness at court. Tak wished his father were there with him now.

Tak didn't realize it, but his face and clothes were streaked with soot. The King ordered a chair be brought so that Tak could sit at the foot of the steps to the throne. And water, so that he could wet his lips. This indulgence would never have been offered to an adult member of court. Tak knew he should refuse—but he badly wanted to sit down and have a drink of water. And wouldn't it be rude to refuse the King's hospitality once offered? Again, Tak wished his father were there to guide him to the right decision. In the end, Tak accepted with a grateful nod and word of thanks. But he sat up straight in the chair, and he didn't gulp the water as he would have liked but sipped it casually, as if he were drinking it only to be polite.

"Now boy, tell us your story," the King said. "Start at the beginning, and end at the ending. And leave nothing out in between."

Tak tried his best. He did a better job than his wild jabbering to the castle sentries. He confessed to following the *Vigilance*. He tried to describe the bubble as best he could, and the explosion moments after it enveloped the battleship. The men leaping from the decks. The shock wave that capsized him and the devastation wrought on the battleship. Finally, his struggles with the burned captain and his efforts to get him off the ship and bring them both home. When Tak got to the part about giving Captain Strake his own parachute and leaping back unprotected to the deck of the *Arrow*, several eyes among the King's counselors widened in surprise and admiration. Others narrowed suspiciously.

Admiral Scud barely waited until Tak had finished his story before shouting, "Nonsense! Tales of giant exploding bubbles? Your majesty, this is nothing but the product of a child's imagination. The explosion described is consistent with the ship's store of powder kegs being ignited either by a dragon attack or...some *other* misfortune or accident. I have other, more reliable reports that are exactly consistent with that conclusion."

At this, Admiral Scud gestured to a group of merchant-men who stood off to one side. They moved forward and bowed to the King on one knee, but didn't speak.

"These men witnessed the same explosion as our boy Tak here, and they saw no fanciful bubble."

The merchantmen nodded in agreement. They had in fact seen the *Vigilance* explode, but from much farther off, more than two miles. And assuming the fire had been the work of an attacking dragon or dragons, they hadn't ventured closer to investigate. They'd turned their bows toward home and made for safety as fast as they could.

Once again, the King held up his hand to silence Admiral Scud. But his eyes never left Tak's face.

"So you say Admiral," the King said. "But if that were the case, why would the boy invent such a tale?"

The advisors murmured among themselves. Admiral Scud smiled with a grimly satisfied smile as if he had been waiting for just that question. He drew himself up to his full height and looked down upon Tak.

"That!" he said, voice booming, "is exactly what *I* would like to know. Tell us boy, why are you lying?"

As Tak gaped wide-eyed up at Scud, too shocked to speak, the room erupted into a confusion of shouting. Scud's accusation was a terrible insult to Tak and the Spinner family. Everyone was trying to speak to the King at once. Some to defend Tak and urge the King to reprimand the Admiral, others to agree with Scud and urge the King to demand an answer from Tak. And the Admiral's voice continued to boom above the general din.

"This boy has been spying on royal battleships and probing the castle's defenses for years. Why, I wonder? *Why?* And was it simply coincidence the boy was there at the time of the explosion..." and here Scud paused dramatically, "...or did he have some part to play in it?"

At that, the shouting in the room ceased for a moment so that everyone could gasp simultaneously in surprise. Even Scud's supporters were stunned. It was one thing to accuse Tak Spinner of exaggerating or lying about his role in rescuing Captain Strake, but what Scud had just suggested amounted to an accusation of sabotage and *treason*.

Then, with everyone's lungs renewed, the shouting erupted into a pitch that the throne room hadn't known in decades. The noise frightened the birds and flying reptiles above in their roosts, sent them fleeing and squawking out the open windows, their shed feathers and scales drifting down onto the crowd below.

Tak sat dumfounded. He knew there was no love lost between Scud and his father, and himself. But to accuse him of treason? To the King's face at open court?

Tak didn't know the animosity between his father and Scud had become part of a larger conflict deeply dividing the kingdom. Tak's father headed a group of advisors who believed it was time to leave their fast-disappearing supplies of coal behind and find new fuels. Admiral Scud led a group of advisors who believed the proposed new fuels were hogwash. Scud and his followers said the only real solution was to use intimidation—and outright war if necessary—to get the coal they needed from neighboring kingdoms. Scud talked often and loudly about making war on the Gublins, too, and taking their coal.

Tak couldn't know it, but Admiral Scud didn't actually believe his accusation. He was only trying to stir up the crowd, to discredit the Spinner family and, by connection, Tak Spinner senior's ideas for solving the kingdom's fuel problem. It was all politics.

Politics, however, has a way of getting people extremely worked up.

The shouting in the throne room continued to rise in pitch and volume. For the third time that hour, the King raised his hand for silence. But it did nothing to quell the chaos in the room. The volume of enraged voices continued to swell, and then shoving matches broke out between the Spinner family's supporters and detractors. It wasn't long before someone drew a sword. The King's advisors were among the few civilians allowed to carry weapons in his presence.

At that, the King gestured to his castle guards, four squadrons of which stood at the ready on either side of the dais. They charged into the fray and surrounded the King with a phalanx of drawn swords. Some disarmed the rash advisor who'd drawn his blade. Others shoved the rest of the shouting and fighting advisors down the steps and subdued them to silence with threatening looks and half-drawn swords. The King's own personal guard, all six of them, even managed to wrestle Admiral Scud down the steps and keep him more or less quiet. Though, as he struggled against their grip and cursed them, it was hard to say who was more afraid of whom.

Once silence had settled over the throne room, the King rose to speak. His eyes looked tired and sad. "*Gentlemen* of the court," he said, with an obvious ironic edge to the word. "This is a sad day, and it is symptom of a sad state of affairs in our kingdom." He drew a breath to continue, but never spoke the next words he meant to say...

At that moment, alarm bells rang from every castle wall and tower.

Everyone looked up. Through the open windows, the startled shouts and curses of soldiers could be heard. Sergeants were calling, "To the walls, men. To the walls!"

Of course, everyone's first thought was dragons. The King, whose hands had rested calmly on his hips until that moment, drew his sword and leapt into action. Echoing the cry, "To the walls!" he charged through the crowded chamber and was the first out the massive double doors. His guards rushed to fall in behind him. The recently subdued advisors picked themselves up and followed suit. After only a few moments' hesitation, so did the pages and assistants and more lowly members of the court.

Out on the walls of the castle keep, every eye looked skyward. The sun sat low on the horizon and the purple sky was just beginning to deepen toward black. Those newly arrived on the battlements had only to follow the pointing fingers of those already there to see what the alarm was about.

It was nothing any sky rider in the Kingdom of Spire had ever seen before. Except for Tak, who huddled at the rear of the crowd, still in various states of shock, and one badly burned battleship captain who lay in a bed at the castle infirmary.

It was an enormous glistening bubble. Rising in the dimming sky like a mockery of the moon, wobbling and shim-

mering, not a mile off from the city itself. All eyes watched
as it rose higher and higher. And then, when it was so high
it looked no bigger than a copper coin held at arm's length,
it burst into blue and yellow fire.

Everyone on the battlements ducked at the blast. As they
began to rise, they felt the rumble of the explosion through
the stone in the soles of their feet. The heat on their faces
made them squint as they looked up in awe at the shock
wave—the sky rippled like water outward in every direction
from the blast. When the shock wave hit them, it knocked
most of them flat. The walls shook. Sturdy soldiers who'd
manned the battlements for years shouted in surprise and
fear and dropped their weapons.

And then it was gone. The last few ripples faded, and the
sky resumed calmly changing to night. The first stars winked
on. People picked themselves up and dusted themselves off.

The King hadn't fallen or dropped his sword. Neither
had Admiral Scud, who'd found his way to the King's side.
They both stared up at the sky, faces stricken with identical
expressions of surprise and fear. And then, realizing that
other's eyes were on them, they composed their features into
the hard lines of command.

"This is the work of Gublins, no doubt," Scud said.
"Some new damned Gublin weapon turned upon us."

"The wizard," the King said. "You must talk to the wizard. He'll know what we're dealing with."

From the back of the crowd, Tak caught Admiral Scud's
eye. Lifting his chin defiantly, he gave the Admiral an *I told
you so* look.

Scud scowled back at him.

FOUR

The Spinner house, like most houses in the city of Selestria, was built directly into the steep side of the mountain. It's made of mountain stone, framed with pine beams, and roofed with pine shingles. It sits in the Northeastern quadrant of the city, just above the second turn of the Southern Spiral road. The house is accessible from the road, but most people don't reach the Spinner house—or any house in the city of Selestria—by foot. They arrive by air. For that purpose, an expansive pinewood deck juts out from the top story of the house. In terms of pure area, it's nearly as long and wide as the house itself, and it projects out over the road and city below. The structure serves as both deck and *dock*, allowing people to sit outside and enjoy the view while at the same time allowing airships to tie up at the wooden mooring posts along its edge. These airships tug gently at their mooring lines as they strive to rise upon the wind.

It was to this deck that a ship from the castle delivered Tak from his audience with the King, well after dark. His mother was waiting, hands folded in front of her, as the ship made fast to the deck and two guardsmen escorted Tak off. She wore a simple blue dress, and her brown hair, the same shade as Tak's, was gathered up in a neat bun fastened with several long pins. She had Tak's brown eyes too. She nodded to the men and held out a hand to Tak. She was familiar with this situation. So were the men. No one felt it necessary to exchange words. Tak took his mother's hand, eyes fixed down on his boots. The men nodded and boarded their ship again, set the sails and rudder, made a neat dip and turn, and took off.

That left Tak and his mother on the deck. She put her arms around him, and he rested his head on her shoulder. It had been the worst day of his life. The surprise and terror of the explosion and rescue, followed by the confusion and uproar and accusations at court. It was a lot for a boy to handle. So Tak let himself just rest for a moment like a child in his mother's arms. She stroked his hair and kissed his forehead. She smelled like home.

"You need a haircut," she said.

Tak shrugged. He didn't feel like talking.

"Well," she sighed. "Come in and have some soup before your father gets home."

Tak's mother's egg soup was made from an old recipe, handed down for generations. The key was to simmer the water slowly, to not quite let it reach a boil. That way the onions, herbs, and soup bones gave their flavor slowly and completely to the broth. Then, at exactly the right time, the eggs were eased into the water from their cracked shells. If the simmering broth was too hot, the eggs would cook too fast and become yolky blobs. But if the temperature was just right, and if you used the right kind of eggs and a few other secret ingredients, they would cook and dissipate slowly and completely, disappearing but giving their rich flavor and texture to the soup.

Tak's mother, whose given name was Marghorettia, was good at a lot of things—archery, fishing, gardening, and especially, arguing. But she excelled at making egg soup, a pot of which could almost always be found simmering on the hearth in the Spinner family kitchen.

She led Tak to the kitchen table and ladled him a bowl. She ladled a bowl for herself and sat beside him. She knew that now was not the time to talk or ask questions. She had heard the story from many people already. She had many things she wanted to ask, and she had many, many more things that she would be sure to say. She would do this in her own time. For now, she sipped the soup from her spoon silently and delicately as her son dug into his, slurping noisily and with great satisfaction.

* * *

If you knew where to look, there was a little hollow at Taktinius Spinner senior's throat, just above the collarbone on his right side. There was an artery there, and it throbbed when he was upset. It had been throbbing for quite a while by the time he was delivered all the way from Silkmont to the deck of his own house. He leapt from the ship onto the deck before the ship's crew had even secured a mooring line. Tak senior had learned his son had been in danger of dying that day, and that frightened him. It made his insides feel like ice, in fact, because he couldn't imagine life without his son. It made him so emotional he felt he might lose control and spill tears. But Tak senior wouldn't let anyone see him cry. So he shouted and pounded on things instead. It took his mind off of crying.

Tak senior burst into the kitchen where Tak and his mother were seated at the table in front of the hearth, and he pounded so hard on the pine plank table top that Tak junior's spoon jumped in his empty soup bowl.

"Did Scud really do it? *Did he?* I want to hear it from your own lips," Tak senior leaned his face in close to his son's. "Tell me he did *not* accuse you of treason at court."

"I'm afraid he did, father," Tak said reluctantly.

"*Damn* his old, scarred filthy hide!" Tak's father pounded the table again, this time so hard that Tak's spoon jumped completely out of his bowl and clattered to the stone-tiled floor. Tak senior paced back and forth in the kitchen, fingering the hilt of his sword. "I'm finally going to call that old, bitter goat out and challenge him to a duel. The Spinner family cannot tolerate this kind of insult." Tak senior's hair was darker than Tak's, almost black, but it had the same shagginess about it, always seeming to be in need of a trim. Tak and his father shared the same pointed chin and wide cheekbones, although Tak senior's chin and cheeks were covered with a close-clipped black beard streaked with white. Strands of silvery spider silk clung to his hair and beard, and his clothes. They fluttered in his wake as he paced.

Tak picked the spoon up off the floor and placed it back in the bowl. He didn't like to think about his father dueling with Admiral Scud. Both Tak and his father trained weekly in swordsmanship with an expert instructor. Despite an old wound that still sometimes pained and stiffened his right arm, Tak's father was a much better than average swordsman. But Admiral Scud was widely recognized as the best fighter in the kingdom, with any weapon you cared to name.

Tak and his mother exchanged glances. She was evidently having similar thoughts. She cleared her throat, and she employed an age-old tactic which, among both mothers and magicians, is known as distraction and redirection. "My dear," she said. "Aren't you even going to ask your son how he *is*?"

The tactic served its purpose. Tak senior whirled to face his son again, spider silk swirling around his head. "And *you*," he sputtered. "Tell me you did *not* jump aboard that burning battleship and did *not* remove your parachute to rescue the captain."

"He would have died," Tak said.

"*You* could have died. Did you ever think of that?"

"I was trying *not* to think about that," Tak said.

That left Tak senior at a loss for words.

Tak pressed his advantage. "In fact, father, I was thinking about what people would say about me and about the Spinner family if I'd just left him there to die. They'd call us cowards."

That left Tak senior at even more of a loss for words, because the first thing that popped into his head to say was *I could care less about family honor when your life is concerned! When you encounter dangerous situations, you just do the smart thing and keep yourself safe from now on! Hear me?* But of course Tak senior couldn't say that. It was exactly the opposite of what every boy and young man was taught about bravery and family honor. So Tak senior swallowed those words down with a little growl. Finally, it occurred to him to say, "You shouldn't even have *been* there in the first place. You were disobeying me. *Again!*"

"I know father. I'm sorry." Tak looked down into his empty bowl. He couldn't think of a single reason to justify why he'd disobeyed his father's orders. Other than that he just couldn't help himself. And that didn't seem like the right thing to say.

His mother interjected in a calm voice, "If Tak hadn't been there, no one would have known what truly happened. They would have all thought dragons destroyed the *Vigilance*. And captain Strake would be dead along with all his men." Tak's mother was no less frightened than his father by the thought of Tak risking his life. In fact, she was even more so, as only a mother can be. But women have stronger hearts than men, when they have to, and they can sometimes be more reasonable when it comes to this sort of thing.

Tak senior crossed his arms and faced his son. He was beginning to breathe more slowly. The artery in the hollow of this throat had ceased throbbing. "That was a brave thing you did today Tak. You did the kingdom credit and you should be honored for it." Tak senior laid a hand on his son's shoulder. "You have done our family proud, and I am most proud of you myself."

Tak smiled faintly, but he could tell by the tone of his father's voice that there was a "but..." coming. A big one. He waited for it.

"But you have also disobeyed me, time and again. You have embarrassed me in front of the King and the court. I'm going to have to ground you. No flying in the *Arrow*. And I mean it this time."

"For how long, father?" Tak asked in a small voice.

"Until I say otherwise," Tak senior said.

Tak hung his head. He knew he shouldn't try to argue against his punishment or negotiate a shorter sentence. He usually did, and he usually succeeded. His parents had exceptionally soft hearts where Tak was concerned. Tak's father and mother had very much wanted children and had tried to have a child for years after they were married. But it seemed they weren't able to. Then, late in their lives, long after they had quit hoping, Tak arrived. When Tak was born, his father threw a party for most of the city of Selestria that lasted three days. In the weeks that followed, Tak's father and mother could scarcely take their eyes off their newborn baby, and when they walked they felt their feet didn't quite touch the ground.

"As you wish father," Tak said. He was sick inside at the thought of not being able to fly in the *Arrow*. For one thing, if he wanted to go anywhere he would have to walk, and *nobody* walked in the city of Selestria if they could help it. Sky riders consider walking an extremely undignified and socially unacceptable mode of transportation. For another thing, losing your airship was like losing your mobility *and* your best friend at the same time. Tak felt so in tune with every nuance of the *Arrow* and the unerring way it responded to his handling that he sometimes found himself believing the ship was in some impossible way alive and able to understand him.

There was a long silence in the room. Tak senior continued to face his son with crossed arms. Strands of spider silk settled to the floor. Tak realized the conversation was not over. There was an "and" coming. Tak sensed that this "and" would be even bigger than the "but." His heart sank. He knew what his father was about say.

"And..." Tak senior said. "I've decided that you'll spend the rest of the summer with me on Silkmont, working the spider farms."

"*All* summer?" Tak couldn't control the outburst. "What about the academy trials...?"

Tak senior held up a hand for silence. "You can come back to Selemont for the trials. But the rest of the time you'll be on Silkmont, with me, and out of trouble."

Tak had applied for admission to the air fleet academy in the fall when he turned sixteen. Applicants were required to demonstrate flying and weapons skills during trials scheduled for late summer. Tak senior had hoped his son would choose the family trade, but he wasn't the type of man to force his son against his wishes. And, in his heart of hearts, he doubted whether his son would actually make a good Chief Sailspinner. The boy still tended to go pale and twitchy around spiders.

Spiders! Tak was thinking about them himself. This time, he not only hung his head, he cradled it in his hands. This would be the worst summer of his life! None of his friends would be on Silkmont. No girls. No races. No fishing or camping. No sneaking off on excursions to the Dragonback mountains. On Silkmont, there would be only two things for him: work and spiders. And plenty of both. Spider silk practically coated Silkmont. Hence the name. It floated in the air like stringy snow. Caught in his hair and eyelashes. Sometimes he breathed it in and it stuck in the back of this throat. And the creatures themselves! You couldn't fence in spiders. They went where they wanted to go, and they wanted to go everywhere. They even got into the bunkhouses and crawled into your bed at night!

Tak rubbed his face miserably. "As you wish, father," he said weakly through his hands.

A glimmer of pity shone in Tak senior's eyes. "I'll give you one last week here. Spend some time with your mother. Have some fun and say goodbye to your friends." Tak senior grunted and rubbed his hands together in a way that told everyone that this particular difficult conversation was over. "Now," he sighed, coming over to kiss his wife at the fireside, "is there any more of that soup left?" He breathed in deeply. "It smells *wonderful*."

FIVE

Tak broke his father's grounding after only three days.

Early on the morning of what would have been the fourth day, Tak got up while everyone else in the house was still asleep. The top of the sun was just beginning to break over the eastern horizon. Tak grabbed his pack, tiptoed to the kitchen, and stuffed it full of as much food and water as it would hold. Then he slipped out to the dock and climbed into the *Arrow*. He loosed the mooring lines and let the craft rise with as little flapping of sail and snapping of rope as possible. An hour later, Tak was flying miles southwest of Selemont. The Highspire Mountains rose behind him and to his left, their green flanks coated with silvery morning mist. They threw massive, miles-long shadows on the blanket of surface clouds below as the sun began to climb over them, its rays peeking through the lower valleys. Tak shivered and wrapped his cloak more tightly around him. His breath came out in cloudy puffs. Mornings were cold in the shadow of the mountains.

Tak was also disobeying another direct order from his father: he was following a battleship that morning. And not just any battleship, the fleet's flagship, the *Dragonbane*, captained by Admiral Scud himself. The massive battleship had cast off from castle Selestria's main dock at the crack of dawn. She headed southwest, out into the Ocean of Clouds, trailing a cloud of smoke behind her as her propellers churned. Tak trailed a mile behind, doing his best to keep the *Arrow* between the *Dragonbane* and the rising sun.

Tak knew that what he was doing would in some ways break his parents' hearts. Guilt twisted his gut. But this time, he told himself, he wasn't breaking the rules out of stubbornness or selfishness, at least not mostly. This time he was on a mission. He really *must* do it.

The *Dragonbane* was headed to the wizard's floating island. Scud had been ordered by the King to talk to the wizard, find out all the wizard knew or suspected about the mysterious exploding bubbles that had appeared in the sky, and report back. Tak felt he must follow Admiral Scud because he knew in his heart that Scud wouldn't do this job right. Tak wasn't alone in this belief. Many of the King's advisors felt the same way. But they were unable, or unwilling, to do anything about it.

The issue came up during Tak senior's noon audience with the King four days ago, the first day of Tak's grounding. It was originally intended to be a private audience with Tak senior and Tak. The King's original intention had been to congratulate Tak on his brave rescue, but also to lay down the law with the Spinner family, to threaten punishment if Tak senior could not rein in his son. But when Tak and his father arrived, the throne room was already crowded and buzzing with the talk of dozens of advisors, Scud among them. The topic was the exploding bubbles. Explosions in the sky had been observed near and far overnight.

And more bubbles had been reported that morning, some spinning and tumbling through the kingdom's crowded shipping lanes. Already another ship, a merchant vessel with a crew of fifty, had been hit and obliterated. There had been no attempted rescue, no survivors. And there'd been other close calls. Many shipping companies had grounded their fleets. And everyone was wanting to know what the King was going to do about it.

When Tak senior was presented to the King among the hubbub, Tak in tow, Tak senior bowed low, then said, "Your majesty, I most humbly apologize for the actions of my son, but I must also beg leave to address the accusation of treason that has been made against the Spinner family." Tak's father said this last with his hand on his sword hilt, eyes locked with Admiral Scud. Scud looked back and grinned a slow malicious grin.

The King waved a hand impatiently. "I have no time for family squabbles today, Sailspinner. We have much more important matters to address." Many advisors chimed in to agree with the King. Under ordinary circumstances, the treason accusation and impending duel between Spinner and Scud would have been a matter of intense delight and much wagering at court. But that day it was nothing more than a distraction.

Tak Spinner senior kept his face composed, although those nearest to him may have noticed a pulsing at the hollow of his throat. Tak certainly did. "I humbly beg your majesty's apology," he said. "I know there are larger matters at stake here. Yet as a matter of family honor I cannot simply ignore the accusation that has been made."

"Heavens!" the King gasped. "I'm sure that accusation was ill-considered and ill-conceived. It was made at a time of intense confusion and excitement." The King turned to Admiral Scud. "Is that not correct Admiral? Will you not withdraw that ill-advised accusation, in light of the new evidence that surrounds us, and offer your apology to the Spinner family?"

Scud's eyes had never left those of Tak Spinner senior's. Tak was silently praying to himself that Scud would do as the King asked. The thought that Scud and his father might begin to fight right there, right then, made Tak's heart pound and his stomach lurch. After a pause, Scud said, "I will your majesty. I withdraw my accusation with my most humble and heartfelt apologies to the Spinner family." But his eyes, locked with Tak Spinner senior's, said, *I will fight you another time, anytime.*

"Does that retraction satisfy you, Sailspinner?" the King asked.

"It does," Tak Spinner senior answered. But his eyes answered Admiral Scud's. *Soon*, they said.

"Good!" the King said. "Then let us deal with the matter at hand."

It was agreed that the wizard must be contacted as soon as possible.

The wizard possessed more knowledge than all the scholars at the University of Selestria put together. With certain exceptions, he shared his knowledge freely. You could ask him almost anything. The problem was understanding his answers. They tended to be as lengthy as they were unintelligible. When people asked the wizard why the sky changed from green to blue to purple during the course of the day, for example, he responded with a lecture about atmospherics and optics that made them regret ever wanting to know.

Another problem when it came to asking the wizard a question was locating him. The wizard lived on a floating island, and nobody knew where it was most of the time. The wizard could steer the island wherever he wished, and he had a fondness for exploring out-of-the-way places. A messenger bird hadn't been received from the wizard's island for many days. The King ordered a bird released from Selemont immediately, with a message relating news about the dangerous bubbles, requesting the island's position, and notifying the wizard that Admiral Scud would be visiting him as soon as possible.

"Admiral Scud," the King said. "You will have the *Dragonbane* ready to depart on a moment's notice, once we know where the wizard is."

Scud nodded.

Terentius Liberverm, head of the University of Selestria, cleared his throat. He stood with a group of the kingdom's scholars.

"What is it, Scholar?" the King asked.

"Your Highness," old Liberverm said. "We think that one of us should join the Admiral on this visit to the wizard." Many advisors nodded in agreement, including Giraldus Wright and Tak senior. Scud frowned, twisting the scar on this cheek, and crossed his arms.

"And why is that?" the King asked.

"You see your Highness, the Admiral has made it well known that he thinks these bubbles are weapons of Gublin origin. He is a fierce proponent of that theory. While my colleagues and I think that may be a possibility as well, we also believe it possible the bubbles are a natural phenomenon and have little or nothing to do with the Gublins at all."

"And so?" the King said.

"Don't you see, your Highness?" Liberverm said. "You are sending a man on a fact-finding mission who already believes he knows the facts. What use will that be? What we know of human psychology tells us the Admiral will tend to discard any information the wizard offers that does not fit with his theory that the bubbles are Gublin weapons. We believe you should also send one or more people who are more...open minded. That way the information that returns will be more complete and reliable."

The King considered this. He was an excellent judge of men's characters and their words. He was a wise man and always willing to listen to a well-made argument. If the King had one shortcoming, however, it was that in times of stress and danger he relied too heavily on his military advisors and tended to ignore the others.

Scud looked as if he would like to wrap his hands around the old scholar's neck. "There is no room for untrained civilians on my ship," he growled, looking Liberverm up and down. "Especially not doddering old scholars likely to tumble overboard at the first stiff wind. This won't be some sort of sight-seeing trip or pleasure cruise."

"Mind your manners!" Tak senior said to the Admiral, bristling at the insult to his old friend. "And anyway *I'll* go. I'm an experienced airman and I'll stay out of your crew's way."

"Sailspinner," the King said. "Have you not recently informed me that the lack of rain on Silkmont has forced you to undertake some rather extensive irrigation efforts?"

"Yes," Tak senior sighed. He knew what the King was getting at.

"Then you will be going nowhere but back to Silkmont to oversee those efforts personally. On the next available ship."

Tak senior nodded unhappily. However, many other advisers volunteered in a chorus to make the trip on the *Dragonbane*, including Giraldus Wright.

"Your Highness!" Scud shouted over their voices, "I can *not* have civilians hanging about on my ship!"

"Well..." Liberverm said. "It occurs to me there's no need for us to make the trip on the *Dragonbane*. Once we know the location of the island, we can visit it on our own ship." The scholars and others exclaimed in agreement to this new idea.

"Oh really?" Scud eyed the group of scholars contemptuously. "Have you forgotten that the wizard is almost certainly more than a day's journey away? Have you forgotten that the last time I traveled to the wizard's island, I had to cross the Ocean of Clouds, at *night*? Are any of you little bookworms up for that trip?"

The scholars and other advisors paled and suddenly looked much less enthusiastic about the thought of visiting the wizard. Some looked down at their feet. Only the most experienced—or foolhardy—of sky riders journeyed out into the Ocean of Clouds at night. It was an exceedingly beautiful place, but its beauty was exceeded by its danger.

In the end it was decided that Scud and his crew would

make the trip by themselves in the *Dragonbane*. Scud grinned smugly at the decision. Tak narrowed his eyes at the Admiral, and a smug smile spread across his face as well. Tak senior noticed his son smiling and Tak junior stopped, wiped his nose and pretended to cough. Tak senior frowned at his son. He knew the look on the boy's face meant that he was up to something.

Tak had made up his mind to follow Scud and to somehow listen in on his conversation with the wizard. For the good of the kingdom.

The fact the excursion would delay his sentence to Silkmont, well, that was just a bonus.

SIX

The *Dragonbane* used its steam-powered propellers, and it trailed a cloud of white smoke miles behind it. The smoke trail made it easy for Tak to follow the ship from a safe distance. It was a calm day. The morning sky was a pretty shade of pale green, with just a few wisps of cirrus clouds high up. A pale moon was out, near full, looking for all the world like the smudge of a thumbprint on the sky. A school of great, gaseous rays flew leisurely past the moon, their wings undulating and spiny tails swishing. Each of these big animals was about the size of the *Arrow*. Their bodies contained bladders of light gas that kept them aloft like balloons.

A group of small cumulus clouds passed nearby to the west. Looking at these more closely, Tak realized one of them wasn't a cloud at all. It was a giant jellyfish—one of Etherium's largest and most dangerous sky creatures. Their puffy, lumpy white bodies had evolved to resemble clouds. But Tak spotted the difference by the way the sunlight reflected off the jellyfish, suggesting a surface more solid than the clouds around it. And looking below the creature, Tak could just make out the shimmering of the nearly invisible, translucent, hundred-foot-long tentacles trailing there.

One of these tentacles had caught something. A ray by the look of it. The slow-moving, gentle, none-too-smart rays were common jellyfish prey. Entire schools of rays sometimes blundered into a forest of jellyfish tentacles, not a single animal realizing the danger until it was too late.

Tak took out his spyglass to watch more closely. It wasn't every day you saw a giant jellyfish catch and eat a ray. He felt sorry for the poor ray, but he would also enjoy recounting what he saw to his friends Lucias and Marcus Wright.

Except Tak's spyglass revealed the thing stuck to the jellyfish wasn't a ray at all.

It was a small airship like Tak's own! A human figure struggled onboard.

Tak scanned the sky, once again hoping someone else had noticed the ship in distress and was on his way. Tak really couldn't afford to take the time to help. He might lose the *Dragonbane*'s trail and not be able to find it again, and his mission would be over.

But the sky was empty of rescuing airships. With a heavy sigh, Tak pressed his feet to his wing flap pedals, leaned on his tiller, and turned the *Arrow* toward the giant jellyfish.

The snared ship was about the size of Tak's own, but that's where the resemblance ended. While the *Arrow* was sleek and smooth, designed by a master craftsman, painted a glossy red, this other ship looked as if it had been hastily hammered together out of roughly-shaped pine planks—by someone who wasn't all that clear on what he was making, exactly. As Tak moved closer, he saw the ship's troubles extended beyond its questionable design and construction. It had also taken a beating by something—something clearly other than the jellyfish. The ship's sail was in tatters. The pine planks of its hull were crisscrossed with deep scratches. And it looked as if small bites had been taken out of the wooden keel and rudder.

The figure on board was a boy about Tak's age, but of heavier build and with yellow-blond hair. He was dressed in rough wool clothing. This red-faced boy was hacking at the tentacle, which had wrapped itself in a loop around the stern of the ship, with a small woodsman's axe. The frantic boy was doing as much damage to his own craft as to the jellyfish.

"Ho there!" Tak cried, pitching his voice to carry through the thick air. "Do you require some assistance?"

The boy turned, startled. He was sweating. His eyes widened at Tak, then glared in annoyance. "Assistance?" he shouted, emphasizing the word with one more hard whack at the tentacle. The small axe bounced off the rubbery jellyfish skin. "Very clever of you to notice, city-boy! First I get attacked by grekks. Then I drift out into the ocean and hit this jellyfish. Now I've got a fancy pants off my bow asking if I *require* some *assistance*—as if I'm some doddering old Lord at court who can't wipe his own fat ass!"

Tak blinked, completely taken aback. "I'm only trying to help," he said.

"Then *help*. Do something!" the boy shouted.

"What?"

"Anything!"

"Well, I suggest you abandon that bunch of sticks before it falls apart and get yourself into my ship."

At that, the boy turned another look on him, and this

time his expression was not merely annoyed but furious. "Bunch of *sticks*...!" The boy shook the axe at Tak, and Tak thought the boy might actually hurl it at him. "I will not abandon this ship. It's *mine*." He turned his back on Tak and resumed his useless hacking at the tentacle. He said more quietly, almost to himself. "I *made* it."

Tak heard the tone of wounded pride in the boy's words. And he realized something that he should have before. This was no city-dwelling boy like the ones Tak flew with. Sons of diplomats and merchants. This was a boy from one of the more distant mountains, son of a farmer or goat herder. He didn't have a top-of-the-line ship handed down from father to son. He made what he could as best he could. And if there was one thing Tak understood, it was fierce pride in one's ship. Suddenly, Tak felt ashamed of himself. Realized how arrogant he must seem from the boy's perspective.

"I'm sorry," he said, edging the *Arrow* closer. "It's really not that bad of a ship. It's..."

"Awww, it's a piece of *junk*," the boy said. His shoulders slumped. He dropped the axe and sat on the gunwale. His hand patted the wooden planks, absently, fondly. "Always has been. Might as well let the damned jellyfish have it."

There was an awkward silence between the two boys. Tak squirmed anxiously. For one thing, he was losing precious time in his pursuit of the *Dragonbane*. For another, the boy and his ship were being slowly, inexorably drawn up to the mouth of the giant jellyfish above. Then Tak got an idea. He rummaged about in the gear he had stowed in the *Arrow* and found his sword. He drew it from its scabbard with a long, slow *shhhhhhink* and held it up for the boy to see. The blade was nearly three feet long, made of finely honed, razor -sharp steel that gleamed in the sunlight.

"If we're going to cut you and your ship free," Tak said. "This will probably work better than that little axe of yours."

The boy's eyes widened at the sight of the blade. His tone became several degrees more respectful. "All right," he said. "What do you have in mind?"

Tak had never severed a jellyfish tentacle before, but he'd heard stories about how it was done. He explained to the boy that it took two people: one to steer a craft as close to the tentacle as possible, the other to lean out as far as possible on one of the wings and cut the tentacle. A key part of this strategy was not to accidentally let the ship come into contact with the jellyfish. If that happened, the ship would most likely become securely stuck and as helpless as the one it was trying to rescue.

"You steer," Tak said. "I'll cut."

The boy nodded. He didn't look thrilled at the idea of having to steer an airship close to a jellyfish. But he un-clipped his lifeline and made the short hop into the *Arrow* as Tak brought it close to the bow of the snared ship, being careful to keep clear of the tentacle-bound stern. Tak saw the boy wore a sky rider pack on his back similar to his own. It had two main parts, a large top section that rode high on the shoulders and contained a parachute, and a smaller section below that functioned as a standard backpack. Tak gave the boy the tiller and let him fly the *Arrow* in a few circles, getting the feel of it.

"Wow," the boy said. "This is some ship. I've never flown anything like this."

"Thanks," Tak said. "You ready?"

"As I'll ever be."

The boy flew the *Arrow* a good distance away from the tentacle, keeping clear of others that dangled nearby. Tak had lengthened his lifeline and clipped it securely to the aft mast. He climbed out onto the starboard-side wing, sword in his right hand, his left gripping the lifeline. The tentacle was so thick that Tak doubted his arms could wrap all the way around it. It would take two or three cutting strokes with his sword to sever it completely, he judged. "Go," he said. The boy steered the *Arrow* back toward the tentacle in a wide arc, aiming at a point about ten yards above his own stuck ship. As they drew closer and closer to the jellyfish, Tak leaned out farther and farther on the wing, gripping the lifeline in his left hand to keep him steady. This caused the ship to list and start turning to starboard.

"Stop doing that!" the boy said. "You're making the ship turn."

"I have to do it!" Tak said. "Compensate with the wing flaps!"

"Do *what* with the wing flaps?"

Tak had taken his eye off the tentacle for a moment to shout his order at the boy. When he looked again, the tentacle was much, much closer. So close it looked like a solid, rubbery object now, and Tak could see the small, circular sucker-mouths that covered its surface.

It was also clear the wing Tak stood on was going to hit the tentacle.

"Turn away!" Tak shouted. "Turn away!"

In his fear and panic, the boy pushed the wrong way on

the tiller. Instead of veering clear of the tentacle, the *Arrow* swerved directly at it. There was no time for Tak to do anything but shut his eyes and utter a short shriek before the *Arrow* hit with a wet squishing sound. Tak was thrown forward by the force of the impact right into the tentacle. He barely had time to turn his face before he made full bodily contact.

The sensation was awful in a way Tak had never experienced before. Imagine dozens of cold, clammy sucking mouths, each one about the size of a quarter, fastening on to you. Tak was stuck to the jellyfish all along his right side, from his face to his arm all the way down to his knee. If it had been a stinging jellyfish, Tak would've been experiencing pain beyond his wildest imaginings. If it had been a venomous jellyfish, Tak would've been dead in seconds. Fortunately, it was neither. But that wasn't much comfort to Tak at the moment.

Tak knew the longer he stayed stuck to the jellyfish, the more tightly stuck he would become. "Get me off!" he screamed. "Get me off!" Although since he could only scream with the left side of his mouth, the right side being fastened shut by the sticky kiss of a jellyfish mouth, the words came out more like "Rrrr mrrr rrofff! Rrrr mrrr roffff!"

The boy understood. He was strong, and he acted swiftly. He climbed out onto the wing and gripped Tak tightly by his free left arm and by the collar at the back of his neck. The boy gave Tak a tremendous yank backward.

Tak came free with dozens of tiny wet popping sounds as the jellyfish mouths were forced to let go of him. He and the boy fell backward together into the *Arrow*. The ship lurched, then steadied.

"Are you all right?" the boy asked.

"I think I'm going to be sick," Tak said. "Can't you *steer*?"

"I'm sorry," the boy said. "I panicked. What do we do now?"

Tak shook his head to clear his mind and assessed the situation. The *Arrow* had hit the jellyfish edge on, right at the curving point where the starboard-side wing sprouted from the hull. It was a very narrow edge, as sky rider ships are wide and shallow, and the *Arrow* was an especially stream-lined ship. So there wasn't much there for the tentacle to grab. The jellyfish had only a weak grip on the ship with a few mouths, but the lower portion of the tentacle was al-ready curling upward, and more sucking mouths were begin-ning to attach to the underside of the wing.

"We've got to cut it away before it's too late!" Tak said. "My sword! Oh no, where's my sword?" Tak realized he'd dropped his sword, that it was probably already halfway to the surface clouds below, and the realization brought tears to his eyes. Not only did that mean they couldn't cut them-selves free, it meant that if they somehow did manage to es-cape, his father would be angry and disappointed beyond words. His father had that sword made especially for him. It wasn't fancy looking—it wasn't inlaid with gold or covered with gems—but it was extremely well-crafted. It had been a special gift from father to son, and his father had made him promise to take good care of it.

"There!" the boy pointed. "Your sword is there!"

There it was. Stuck securely to the tentacle by the blade, but the grip was free. Tak's heart leapt. "Get back on the tiller and keep her steady. *Steady* this time!" Tak checked his lifeline and leapt back onto the wing. He grabbed the sword by the grip with both hands and yanked. It came free. He planted his feet on the wing, leaned until his lifeline was taut, and struck the tentacle with a two-handed crosscut blow.

The sword slashed deep. The rubbery skin parted, revealing translucent, jelly-like flesh inside. The massive wound oozed clear, slimy liquid. Tak was about to strike again when the entire ship lifted upward, making his stomach climb into his chest and his legs fall out from under him.

"Keep her steady!" Tak shouted, regaining his footing.

"I am!" the boy said. "What's happening?"

Tak realized what was happening. He'd forgotten an important part of the stories about freeing oneself from a jellyfish. In response to an attack on one of its tentacles, the huge animal sometimes flailed and cracked the tentacle like a whip, attempting to fling away whatever was hurting it. The tentacle was rising swiftly in preparation for a whip-like crack. This might possibly dislodge the *Arrow*, but the massive force of the whipcrack would likely tear the ship apart.

There was little time. Tak's stomach tied itself in knots as the wind rushed past his face. He aimed carefully and struck again. His second blow severed two-thirds of the tentacle. The creature's colorless blood poured out, covering Tak's boots and the surface of the wing. The huge appendage began its undulating downward swing, causing Tak to lose his footing again and fall to his knees. But he kept his grip on his sword. "Hold on!" he called. On his knees, leaning as far out as he could, he struck a third time, a moment before the flinging force of the whipcrack travelling along the huge tentacle hit them.

Tak's last blow didn't quite sever the tentacle. But it was enough. Most of the whipcrack's force failed to reach them. The force that did hit them was just enough to tear the rest of the tentacle free. The severed end, with the *Arrow* and the boy's ship still attached, spun end over end, flung clear of the jellyfish. As Tak was thrown from the wing and the lifeline yanked hard around his stomach, he concentrated solely on keeping his grip on his sword. Well, not solely. A decent-sized portion of his brain devoted itself to screaming.

In the end they were all right. When a jellyfish tentacle is severed, it loses both the nerves and the hydraulic mechanism that make its sucker-mouths work. The *Arrow* and the boy's ship came free. The severed tentacle slowly slithered downward and disappeared beneath the surface clouds. Eventually the *Arrow* stopped spinning and tumbling. Once again Tak ended up hanging by his lifeline below his capsized ship, nothing below his dangling feet but clouds.

This time, however, Tak had company.

The boy dangled on his own lifeline just a few feet away. Once they'd stopped screaming and realized they weren't going to die, that they were in fact relatively safe and sound, they simply stared at each other, blinking. Neither knew what to say. It was a bit of an awkward moment.

Then the strangest thing happened.

The boys began to laugh. Just a few relieved snorts at first, but soon that grew into shaking, uncontrollable laughter. It was infectious. The more the boy laughed, the more Tak laughed. And the more Tak laughed, the more the boy laughed. Soon they were laughing so hard they could barely breathe. Their faces turned red and tears streamed down their cheeks.

"I thought we were going to *die*," the boy said.

"I thought we *were* dead," Tak said.

After what seemed like forever, but was really only a few minutes, the laughing fit subsided. Tak wiped his eyes, transferred his sword to his left hand, and held out his right to the boy. "I'm Tak," he said. "Taktinius Spinner of Selemont."

The boy grinned and grasped Tak's right hand in his own. "I'm Lufftik Herder of Gatmont," he said. "But my friends call me Luff."

Tak grinned back. "Well Luff, shall we get my ship righted, then go find yours?"

"Why not?" Luff said, rocking on his lifeline as if he were a kid on a swing and letting out one last little chuckle. "I don't have any other plans."

* * *

Once they'd located and attached a tow line to Luff's ship, called the *Ram*, the first order of business was to patch up its tattered sail. Luff had some rough thread made with vlisken fibers for this purpose. He inexpertly tried to thread a needle with the stuff while Tak looked on disapprovingly. After three failed attempts, Tak took the needle from his hand.

"Let me," he said.

Tak could tell the quality of a sail just by hearing it flap in the wind. He didn't need to run his hand over the rough weave of Luff's sail to know it wasn't a good one, that it was made mostly of vlisken fiber with precious little spider silk holding it together. It was certainly made by some third-rate sail weaver on one of the distant mountains. Even so, Tak knew the sail was probably the most expensive thing the boy owned. Even cheap ones didn't come cheap.

Tak had several spools of spider silk of various thicknesses aboard the *Arrow*. He chose one and threaded the needle without even looking at it, his hands working while he squinted up at the *Ram's* sail, gauging how to best repair the damage. Tak also had a harness that allowed him to scuttle up the Ram's fore mast and attach himself there so he could work with both hands free. With the spool of thread clipped to this harness, he sewed up the slashed sail in short order, his nimble, precise fingers making neat stitches.

"Nice work," Luff said. "You're like a big old spider up there."

Tak grinned as he slid down the *Ram's* mast and landed on its deck. "You can't be the Chief Sailspinner's son without learning a thing or two I guess."

"Chief Sailspinner's son!" Luff tried not to sound *too* impressed. "I guess my luck's changing today. Tell me, if you try really hard, can you make spider silk come out of your ass? Or just gold?"

Tak laughed. "Don't know," he said. "Never tried. So a flock of grekks tore up your sail, huh?"

Luff nodded and told the story. He'd been traveling

north, heading back to Gatmont from Selemont, after delivering a pair of breeding goats to a family there. About halfway back, he ran into the grekks. Grekks were flying lizards, a foot or two in length, with leathery wings spread between their fore and hind legs. As the nasty creatures often did, they mistook Luff's ship for a flying ray, one of their favorite foods, and they attacked with their sharp teeth and talons. Luff had no choice but to duck, cover himself, and wait. He knew that trying to fight off a frenzy of hungry grekks often proved fatal, and that it wouldn't take long for the animals to realize the ship wasn't edible and move on.

"They say on Selemont you're not a true airman until you get hit by a frenzy of grekks," Tak said.

"They say that on Gatmont, too," Luff said. "I guess that makes me a true airman. How about you?"

"No," Tak said. "I've never had the pleasure. But last year my first cousin on my father's side, he... uh, he..." Tak's voice trailed off as he realized Luff was looking at him with a peculiar expression.

"What?" Tak asked. "Why are you looking at me like that?"

"Holy crap," Luff exclaimed. "Do those hurt?"

"Does what hurt?"

"Do you have a mirror?" Luff asked.

"No, I don't have a mirror. Why?"

"You should see your face," Luff said.

"Why? What about my face?"

Luff removed his pack and dug through it. He'd recently started shaving, and he had a shaving kit with a small mirror in it. He held the mirror out to Tak. "Look," he said.

Tak looked. The skin on the right side of his face was covered with pink rings, each exactly the size of a jellyfish sucker mouth. Tak looked down at his right arm. Pink rings were beginning to emerge there, too.

Luff stifled a laugh. "If being hit by a frenzy of grekks makes you an ordinary airman, I wonder what being stuck face-first to a jellyfish makes you? I'd say a captain at least."

"Don't joke," Tak said, frowning at his face in the mirror. "It's not funny."

"Looks pretty funny from here, captain." Luff said.

Tak and Luff made sure the tow line to the *Ram* was secure. Luff's ship would have to be towed because its steering was damaged beyond any repairs the boys could make themselves. They made sure Luff had everything off his ship he needed. Tak sat in the stern of the *Arrow* and put his hand on the tiller, trying to decide what course to steer for. Luff sat on the gunwale nearby, his face turned expectantly toward the Highspire Mountains. They were still visible low on the northeastern horizon. Tak took out his spyglass and gazed southwest. A faint trail of smoke from the *Dragonbane* was still discernible against purple sky. It was only a few hours past noon. It would still be possible to catch up.

"Ummm," Tak said. "Would it inconvenience you terribly much if we took a slight detour before I returned you to Gatmont?"

The tone of Tak's voice made Luff squint suspiciously. "What kind of detour?" he asked.

Tak explained that he was following the *Dragonbane* to the wizard's floating island. And he explained why, as quickly as he could. He mentioned the destruction of the *Vigilance* and the arguments at court about the exploding bubbles and people's misgivings about Admiral Scud's ability to objectively complete his fact-finding mission. Tak also mentioned the fact they would have to cross the Ocean of Clouds at night.

Luff's face flitted through a series of emotions. Surprise, disbelief, confusion, fear. "Are you filling my hat with goat crap?" he asked.

"I'm not sure what that means exactly," Tak said. "But I don't think so. I'm serious."

"Are you sure that you're all right in the head?"

"Pretty sure," Tak said.

"How do you think you're going to cross the ocean at night?"

"Once it's dark, we can stick close to the *Dragonbane*. We should be safe that way."

"You keep saying 'we,' as if I've agreed to come along."

"Please," Tak said. "If I take you back to Gatmont now, I'll have to go home and face my punishment with nothing to show for it. And if you won't do it for me, do it for the good of the kingdom."

Luff was torn. He had no desire to anger the Admiral of the royal fleet or get himself killed crossing the ocean at night. He felt that he'd already experienced more than his share of close calls that day. On the other hand, he didn't want to let down his new friend. And Tak's self-imposed mission did seem like it could be an important service to the kingdom.

"Well," Luff said. "I guess I do owe you one..."

That was all Tak needed to hear. He leaned on the tiller and pointed the bow of the *Arrow* southwest.

SEVEN

The *Arrow* flew more slowly than Tak had hoped with the *Ram* in tow. They caught up to the *Dragonbane* barely a half-hour before sunset. It was a good thing, too, because once both the Highspire and Dragonback mountains had disappeared over the northern horizon behind them, and there was nothing but clouds no matter which direction they looked, the mood on the *Arrow* had grown tense and glum. Earlier that day, the boys had shared a meal from the food in their packs. Tak had several loaves of bread his mother had baked, a sausage, and some dried pears and apples. Luff had strips of salted goat meat, a sharp but flavorful goat cheese, and brown rye bread. They ate and talked in high spirits. But when the sun sank low and they still hadn't reached the *Dragonbane*, neither felt like dinner, even though they should have been hungry.

The boys knew that while the Ocean of Clouds is not especially safe to travel by day, it becomes much more dangerous at night. It's home to a variety of nocturnal predators. And the predator that weighs most heavily on the mind of a sky rider traveling the ocean at night is the Nagmor. In the old language, the name translates literally into "night death." Sky riders know little about the Nagmor because the creatures are only active at night, far out in the deep ocean, and because few humans who've encountered them have lived to report back. Survivors' stories have been wild, garbled, and sometimes contradictory. Two consistent pieces of information have emerged, however. First, the giant animals are capable of crushing a battleship to pieces. Second, they smell worse than anything on Etherium.

The lower the sun sank toward the horizon, the closer Tak edged the *Arrow* toward the *Dragonbane*. He approached the battleship from the west, keeping the *Arrow* low and hidden as best he could in the setting sun. When the sun had nearly set and the stars began to come out, the *Dragonbane* lit its lanterns. Its propellers slowed to a crawl, letting the slow southern current they traveled in do most of the work of carrying the ship. Evidently Admiral Scud considered it prudent to travel the ocean slowly at night. Tak was thankful for this. It made it easier for him to fly the *Arrow* in close under the cover of darkness. Tak flew in well below the battleship—out of sight of the lookouts—then rose as close as he dared toward the massive keel and hull above, keeping pace with the ship. Towing the *Ram* made the *Arrow* handle awkwardly, but Tak managed.

Luff held his breath while Tak executed these maneuvers. He let it out when he realized they actually had succeeded in sneaking in below the battleship without being seen—so close they could hear the creaking of the ship's wooden beams and the occasional commands called on deck. On the one hand, it was frightening to realize they were playing a game of cat-and-mouse with the most powerful ship in the royal fleet. They'd be in unimaginable amounts of trouble if caught. On the other hand, it was comforting to be so close to the powerful ship, with its complement of fighting men and cannons, as they traveled the Ocean of Clouds at night.

Tak too let out a sigh of relief.

"Nice flying," Luff said. "What do we do now?"

"Now we stay our course and wait," Tak said. "And keep quiet. Hungry?"

Luff found that he was. The boys lit a small lantern—there was no chance of the light being seen by anyone on the ship above—then broke out their provisions and began a late dinner. They laid into the food with gusto. But soon they found themselves distracted, then totally absorbed, by the sights of the Ocean of Clouds at night. Lights started to appear all around them, tiny flashes of blue and green and pink luminescence, as if the stars had decided to come down for a visit and go for a swim in Etherium's atmosphere. The lights were mesmerizing as they swirled and drifted this way and that, and the boys simply stared, forgetting to chew their food.

"What *are* they?" Luff whispered with his mouth full.

"I'm not sure," Tak answered. But he'd heard stories about creatures in the deep ocean, strange creatures that glowed with their own internal light.

And then one of them appeared, directly in front of the boys' tiny lantern, which hung from a hook on the foremast. It looked like a cross between a shrimp and a dragonfly. The boys had never seen anything like it. Is spindly crustacean legs wiggled, its two pairs of wings buzzed, and its tail flashed a bright pink. It darted this way and that about the lantern, its tail flashing, as if it were trying to send some kind of signal to this strange, new light that had arrived in its domain. Soon the creature was joined by another of its kind, then another and another, until a swarm of them danced about the lantern, buzzing and flickering in an increasing frenzy. Some of them actually smacked into the lantern. Tak, worried the creatures might somehow call attention to the *Arrow*, waved a hand at them to shoo them away. They scattered, disappearing. But the swarm was back again in minutes.

"Maybe we should douse the lantern," Luff said.

Tak agreed. He blew out the light. Soon, the pink glowing creatures dispersed.

No sooner had the creatures disappeared however, than the boys found themselves surrounded by a school of blue glowing jellyfish. Each was about the size of a hand, and they stretched as far as the eye could see in every direction. They undulated gently as they swam, the outlines of their bodies and tendrils limned in blue light. They made enough light that the boys could see each other clearly in the dark, each looking like a blue ghost to the other. The boys sucked in their breath with wonder, then let it out with a sigh. It was one of the most strange and beautiful sights they'd ever seen. Some of the glowing jellyfish became trapped under the *Arrow's* sail, filling the sail with their eerie radiance. One of the creatures passed within an arm's length of Luff. Instinctively, he reached out for it.

"Don't!" Tak said, "It might—"

But the creature settled comfortably in Luff's palm. It didn't sting. It just sat there, its body pulsing, as if content to keep Luff company for a while. After a few moments, Luff lifted his hand to his mouth, blew gently, and the creature floated off like so much dandelion fluff. Tak, now confident the creatures posed no threat, cleared the trapped ones out from under the sail, scooping them gently up in his hand and releasing them.

"Well," Luff said, "I never—"

And then every single jellyfish extinguished itself like a candle being blown out. The boys were back in complete darkness.

"Why did they do that, I wonder?" Tak said.

Luff's nose wrinkled. "Do you smell something?" he asked.

Tak did. There was a faint smell like rotting fish on the night breeze. The smell made him tighten his grip on the tiller and peer anxiously out into the dark.

The odor grew stronger. Evidently the crew of the *Dragonbane* smelled it too, because there was a sudden flurry of orders being shouted and activity on the ship above. Tak caught the words "Full stop!" and "Douse the lights!" and "Silence, men, total silence." The battleship's propellers went still. The glimmer of its lanterns went out. The battleship drifted slowly and silently on the current. Tak kept pace. His palm grew damp against the polished wood of the tiller.

Tak caught one more word whispered harshly from above. "Nagmor!"

The odor grew to a stink that made Tak and Luff's eyes water. They breathed as little as possible. Then they saw the creature, far above them and a little to the east, but heading in their general direction. Its body blotted out the moon and many of the stars. Heavens, it was huge! They couldn't make out much of it in the dark, just a suggestion of its outline against the background stars. Its body appeared to be cone-shaped. There was a roundish head at the wide end of the cone, and from this head long, snakelike tentacles streamed, seeming to slither on the wind.

As the Nagmor passed overhead, its stench became something almost solid. It was like having one's face shoved into a mountain of rotting fish. Scholars believe the animals have a primitive digestive system, a central chamber in which everything they eat simply sits and rots, with vents for expelling the awful gas. The reek clogged the boys' nostrils and stuck in the back of their throats. All of a sudden and in unison, they leaned their heads over the side of the *Arrow* and threw up their dinner.

Judging by the half-stifled retching sounds coming to them from above, it seemed that many men on the *Dragonbane* were doing the same.

The Nagmor passed them and continued moving northward. Whether it had not noticed the *Dragonbane*, or was just not hungry, or had business elsewhere, they would never know. The silhouette of the titanic animal grew smaller and smaller against the stars. Soon its stench faded and the boys could breathe again.

The *Dragonbane* didn't fire up its propellers or light its lanterns again, even after the Nagmor had been out of sight for hours. The royal battleship and its tiny unseen companion ship drifted on the current for the rest of the night in total dark and silence. Tak and Luff took turns at the tiller that night, letting the other sleep for a few hours. But their sleep was fitful and troubled, their dreams full of giant dark shapes half-seen in the night and cold, grasping tentacles.

*　*　*

When the first glimmer of sunrise appeared in the east, Tak stealthily reversed the maneuvers that had brought him close in under the *Dragonbane*. By the time the sun was fully up, the *Arrow* cruised more than a mile behind and to the east of the battleship, this time hiding in the glare of the rising sun. The battleship had fired up its propellers again and its smoke trail made it easy to track. The green peak of Lonemont was now visible to the southwest. The sight of a mountain lifting up above the endless clouds raised the boys' spirits.

They reached the wizard's floating island a little before noon. Both boys drew in their breath as they approached the island. They'd never seen it this close before, and it's quite a sight to see.

About a half-mile wide at its widest point and several hundred feet thick, the island seen from a distance looked to Tak like a piece of a shattered dinner plate. It hung impossibly in the sky. Drawing closer, the boys saw its bottom and its edges were naked stone. And a very strange stone it was: pitted and honeycombed with huge holes and pockets. It was a type of extremely light volcanic stone similar to pumice, the only stone that actually floats in water because it's filled with so many air bubbles. The island was a shard of Etherium's surface, kicked up into the dense atmosphere by an ancient meteorite impact, that was too light to sink back down again.

The island's top surface was green, covered with mosses and grasses. It was dotted with small sparkling ponds of water. There were herds of goats and goat herders that attended them, part of the wizard's small island community. There were even trees! Not tall trees but hardy dwarf pines and some other exotic trees that Tak didn't recognize. It looked to be a habitable and comfortable place.

The wizard had built a house on the island, a rambling, three-story structure made mostly of aged pinewood, plaster, and cut blocks of stone shipped to the island from mountain quarries. Unlike most of the houses Tak had seen, however, the wizard's house had no dock out front. Instead, the wizard had a wide, green front lawn that stretched all the way to the closest edge of the island. At this edge, a large dock projected out over the side of the island.

Through his spyglass, Tak saw the *Dragonbane* hovering near this dock. The huge battleship was much too large and heavy to tie up to that type of dock. Instead, a jolly boat had been launched from the *Dragonbane* and was making its way to the dock. Admiral Scud and several of his senior officers were aboard.

Tak chewed at a thumbnail, frowning. Of course, he hadn't clearly thought out a plan of action for when he reached the island. As he'd been told many times by his parents and teachers, he tended to act first and think later. But it was clear to him that he couldn't just go barging in on the wizard and his guests. Scud would probably have him arrested on the spot. After a brief discussion, the boys agreed they should find a hidden place to moor their airships, then do their best to sneak near the house and eavesdrop on the conversation.

After nosing around for a while, they discovered a small wooden dock jutting from the island's edge at a secluded spot not far from the house. It was a sturdy little dock of the type often built at the rear of houses for delivery ships—a kind of back entrance. Except for a grove of pines and a few large stones nearby, it appeared to be deserted. "Perfect," Tak said, and urged the *Arrow* toward this dock. If Tak had more experience with wizards, he would have been more cautious. You don't gain access to the floating island so easily.

When he got about thirty feet from the dock, he was startled by the whizzing sound of an arrow. The shot glanced off his sail with a *pop*! Fortunately the arrowhead couldn't punch through the tough spider silk. Both boys instinctively ducked, and Tak, realizing they were being fired upon, tilted the prow of his ship up sharply, to nearly forty-five degrees, in order to put the hull protectively between himself and Luff and whomever was shooting at them. He angled the sail sharply downward to keep them in that position.

"Hold!" cried a voice from the island. It was a high-pitched voice, but carried authority. "This is a private island, and no one sets foot on it without permission." The speaker emphasized this point with another arrow shot that slammed, quivering, into the ship's hull.

In hindsight, Tak realized he should have been more polite to whomever was addressing them. But few things made his blood boil more than someone intentionally damaging his ship. He'd jerked at the sound of that arrow striking the hull as if it had hit his own body.

"You put another arrow into this ship, and I'll put one between your eyes!" Tak shouted back.

This was largely an empty threat. Shooting accurately—or shooting at all, for that matter—from the deck of a ship that is tilting up to nearly forty-five degrees is pretty much impossible. For one thing, there's no place to firmly plant your feet. For another thing, you can't use your hands—because they are already being used to hang on tight to whatever stay or rope is nearest in order to keep you from falling out. For yet another thing, the ship tends to bounce up and down and back and forth on the wind.

But Tak did his best to make good on the threat. Grabbing up his bow and quiver, he had Luff take the tiller and pedals in the stern and keep the prow of the ship tilted upward. Tak climbed onto the base of the foremast, which was now somewhat perpendicular to the ground far below, and with his feet balanced on that he got his bow out and nocked an arrow. He had to curl one arm through the rigging to steady himself and hold himself in a position where he could see over the prow, and that severely reduced his ability to draw and aim. Still, he had the semblance of an arrow pointed back at their attacker, and that is what he wanted.

A thin, spindly figure dressed all in black stood on the dock. It hadn't been there moments before. Although it was hard to tell because of the distance, the island's guardian appeared to have another arrow nocked and pointed at Tak, with the bowstring at full draw. The high-pitched voice laughed. "I could have put one easily between *your* eyes, intruder. You're lucky I didn't. State your business or be gone from here."

"And who are you to make such demands of me?" Tak spat back, his feet wobbling for purchase on the foremast.

"I'm the one who has an arrow pointed steadily and directly at your nose. You, on the other hand, are the one whose arrow tip is bouncing around so much I doubt you could even hit the island from there."

Something about the calm, playful, mocking tone of the island's guardian made Tak lose his cool. "Oh yeah?" he said, and let his arrow fly, intending for it to hit near the figure in black and scare it.

The figure didn't duck. Or even flinch. The island's guardian had been wrong, however. Tak's arrow *did* hit the island—it bounced off the naked stone of the island's clifflike edge twenty or thirty yards below and to the right of where the taunting figure stood.

"Well," the guardian said. "I must admit I was wrong. But you'll pardon me if I fail to be impressed."

At this point Luff broke into the conversation. He wasn't used to handling the *Arrow* and was struggling desperately to hold the prow of the ship up. The *Ram* bouncing around and yanking on the tow line behind them wasn't helping. Luff's face was red and sweating. "*Tak!*" he shouted. "Take it easy. Put that bow away! Be a little more polite for heaven's sake."

At hearing Luff speak, the thin figure in black lowered its bow slightly. "Tak? Is that your name?" the guardian asked. It was not a common name among sky riders, except for in the Spinner family.

"Yes, Taktinius is my given name," Tak said. "Why

should you care?"

"Taktinius Spinner? The boy from Selemont who rescued captain Strake from the *Vigilance*?" The bow lowered further, and the guardian seemed to relax the draw. Tak sensed things might be turning his way.

"Yes, that's me," he said gruffly. "How did you hear about that?"

"We have our ways," the figure said. "Come closer."

"Not with an arrow pointed at us."

"If you are who you say you are, I won't shoot. I promise."

Tak exchanged glances with Luff. The boys shrugged. Luff lowered the prow of the *Arrow* and headed the ship toward the dock. "Put that damn bow *away*," he hissed. Tak stowed the bow and quiver. Luff struggled with the *Arrow's* tiller and sail. He was not the most skilled or lucky of sky riders, and he had no experience handling a ship as swift and responsive as Tak's. He should have angled the sail upward to create drag and slow them to a stall; instead he pulled the ropes that angled the sail downward, giving the *Arrow* lift and speed. He was coming in much too fast toward the dock.

Tak, who had unclipped his lifeline and stood on the prow with a hand on the foremast, ready to jump aboard the dock and make the ship fast with a mooring line, realized this. "Slow down! *Slow!*" he shouted. But it was too late. Instead of gently grazing the dock, allowing Tak to step lightly off, the ship more or less crashed into it, throwing Tak onto the wooden planks in an undignified heap at the black-clad guardian's feet.

"Sorry!" Luff called.

With a curse, Tak stood up, brushed himself off, and faced the island's guardian.

It was a girl.

And not just a girl—the most unusual girl Tak had ever seen. She was pretty in a way Tak hadn't known was possible. Her hair was straight and black and gathered in a long, weighted braid that hung halfway down her back. She stood a half-head taller than Tak, though she couldn't have been much older than he was, and her eyes looked down into his. They were black and almond-shaped, set above high cheekbones, and they glinted with humor. A smile played about her lips. Her skin was the golden color of the freshly baked loaves of bread in his mother's kitchen.

The most unusual thing about the girl was what she wore. It was a close-fitting, one-piece suit that looked like it had been made for flying; there were plenty of pockets and clips and a belt for storing and attaching gear. But the sleeves were extremely, impractically long and flowing. As the girl replaced her arrow in its quiver, slung her bow, then folded her hands into a formal pose in front of her, the long trailing sleeves made it look as if she were wearing some kind of black robe.

"You *are* Tak Spinner," she said. "You and your ship fit the description. And you wear the Spinner family ring." The ring she spoke of was a simple silver ring on Tak's left hand that contained no stone. Instead, its flat head was engraved with a curved triangle representing a sail full of wind.

"I am," Tak mumbled. His face felt hot and suddenly his tongue didn't want to work right. His blinking eyes struggled to hold the girl's gaze. Tak wasn't usually shy around girls. He tended to like the ones who were good flyers, and his usual approach was to challenge them to an airship race—with the condition that he'd claim a kiss, or sometimes more, as his prize if he won. Of course, a girl wasn't going to accept a challenge like that if she didn't want to be kissed. Sometimes they lost to him on purpose. Other times they won, and offered the kiss, and sometimes more, as a consolation. But something about this girl—about those deep, dark eyes—made all of Tak's usual confidence vanish.

"That was a brave piece of work with the *Vigilance*, the way I've heard it told," the girl said.

Tak couldn't think of a single thing to say. His face was blazing and his tongue had turned to stone. He dropped his eyes, and an uncomfortable silence hung between him and the girl.

She peered at his face more closely, noticing the pink rings there. They had faded overnight, but their color became more intense as Tak blushed. "Have you been trying to kiss a jellyfish?" she asked, dark eyes narrowed as if puzzled, but still with a glimmer of humor in them.

At this point, Luff broke in and rescued Tak. Having made their ships secure to the dock, he bounded up to the girl and extended his hand. "More like the jellyfish was trying to kiss *him*," Luff said. "My ship got stuck, and Tak here cut me free. The name's Lufftik Herder, of Gatmont."

The girl turned her smile on Luff. She took his hand and squeezed it firmly. "Pleased to meet you, Lufftik of Gatmont," she said. "My name is Brieze. Daughter to wizard Radolphus of Sky Island."

Brieze held out her hand to Tak. "Two rescues in one week," she said. "Much more impressive than your shooting."

Tak swallowed, managed to grasp the girl's hand, look her in the eye again, and even give her something of a smile. "My shooting gets better on solid ground," he said.

"I can only hope that is the case," Brieze answered. "Now, if it wouldn't inconvenience you both too much, could you please tell me why you are trying to sneak onto my father's island?"

EIGHT

The sheer surprise that the wizard had a daughter jarred Tak out of his nervous stupor. The wizard was famous throughout the Kingdom of Spire, but Tak had never heard of his daughter before. Questions leapt to Tak's mind. Did she have brothers and sisters? Was there a Mrs. Wizard? But time was of the essence, and Tak knew that this was not the time to ask such questions. However, his tongue did loosen a little, and with help from Luff he managed to explain to the girl why they had followed the *Dragonbane* to the island. He recounted the argument at court between Scud and Liberverm and the other scholars. The girl listened intently, her lips pursed. She chewed on her lower lip a moment, thinking things over.

"I think you're right," Brieze said. "From what I've heard of Admiral Scud, I wouldn't trust him on this kind of assignment either. I think we should make sure the King has all the facts. I'll help you. Follow me."

With that, she turned and walked briskly down the path of white gravel stones leading away from the dock. Her limbs were long, and Tak couldn't help notice her stride was a bit awkward. She seemed to be all knees and elbows, reminding Tak of friends he'd known who had experienced a rapid spurt of growth and hadn't yet adjusted to their new bodies.

Tak and Luff exchanged glances, then followed her.

The path led to the rear of the wizard's house. Tak and Luff gaped up at the house, having never seen another like it. Once you got close to it, it was difficult for the eyes to grasp. There were walls, windows, cornices, cupolas, towers, balconies—but all seemingly thrown together at random, in a way that made no sense. It seemed like the house should either fall apart or collapse under its own weight. But it didn't. It sat there as impossibly as the wizard's island sat in the sky.

"No time for staring," Brieze said. "Get inside."

She led them up a short flight of porch steps, across the back porch, and through the back door. The inside of the house was no less confusing than the outside. The boys were confronted with a maze of hallways and doorways. Brieze turned right down one hallway, then left, and left again, and the boys struggled to keep up. People bustled through the house, sometimes jostling the boys as they passed. The wizard had brought his entourage with him to settle the island. There were certain types of people the wizard gravitated toward, and who gravitated toward him. They were usually labelled as misfits and oddballs in their original communities, but they had special abilities.

Tak frowned, noticing that everyone in the wizard's house wore a type of mask—a bandana of white linen that covered their noses and mouths. Brieze led the boys to the house's front parlor, a vast room filled with shelves of books, paintings, sculptures, intricately woven carpets, exotic plants, and an assortment of musical instruments both ancient and modern. The room had a set of large bay windows that looked out onto the front lawn. Brieze led the boys to these windows. She motioned for them to stay low. They crouched among the potted plants there.

"Why the masks?" Tak whispered, sensing that whispering was necessary.

"Germs," Brieze whispered back, her eyes looking intently through the glass. "This is the season when we're most likely to contract certain respiratory infections from outsiders. Father is trying to protect his people."

Tak and Luff exchanged puzzled glances, then looked at Brieze as if she'd started speaking another, totally foreign language.

"What are...*germs*?" Luff asked. Tak's eyes echoed the question.

Brieze let out an impatient huff. "Listen you two, if you don't know what *germs* are then I've no time to explain them to you now. Let's concentrate on the matter at hand."

"Fine," Tak said. "What's going on out there?"

They peered through the windows as they hunkered among the ferns and palm fronds. The wizard had decided to entertain his guests on the front lawn that day. The wizard's house had a spacious dining room in addition to a spacious parlor, either of which would have been more than enough to accommodate Admiral Scud and his attachment of a half-dozen senior officers. But it was a beautiful day and the wizard had taken it into his fancy to have a picnic on the front lawn. Accordingly, he'd arranged for a large blanket to be set out on the grass, and for tea and tidbits be served to him and his guests. No chairs were brought out. The wizard sat cross-legged on the blanket. Tak suppressed a laugh to see Admiral Scud and his officers sitting likewise cross-legged on the blanket in their fancy uniforms and polished boots, sipping from cups of tea held in their laps, looking extremely undignified and uncomfortable. If any nobleman of Selemont had dared to receive the Admiral in such a fashion, Tak was sure that Scud would've had him thrown into the castle dungeon for insolence.

"I can't hear what they're saying," Tak said. "Can we get closer?"

Just as Tak spoke, a boy entered the parlor at a fast walk, headed for the front door. He also wore a white mask, and he struggled with carrying a large tray balanced on one shoulder.

"Hey there, Lothran!" Brieze called to the boy. "Where are you going?"

The boy paused, groaning under his tray. "I've got seconds of tea and cakes," he said. "To be served right away on the lawn."

"Please pause a moment. Set your tray down," Brieze said. The boy was only too happy to do so. He set the tray down on a side table in the parlor with a sigh of relief. A mischievous light sparkled in Brieze's black eyes. "You want to get closer?" she said to Tak. "I have an idea..."

When she'd explained the idea, Tak protested. "Are you crazy?" he said. "I'll be spotted for sure!"

"All you have to do is set down the tray," Brieze said. "Pour tea for anyone who wants it, then kneel beside my father and be ready to serve as necessary."

"Look at me!" Tak gestured to himself, his buckle- and clip-spangled flying clothes, his shock of wild hair, the pink rings on his face. "I'll be *recognized*."

"Not if you and Lothran switch clothes, and the mask. He's about your size," Brieze said. "If you're unobtrusive, the Selemonts won't notice you."

"Hey, I know a lot of fancy city language," Luff broke in. "But not *unobtrusive*. What's that?"

"It means to try my best not to be skewered by Scud or his officers," Tak said, already unbuttoning his shirt. To Brieze he said, "But surely your father won't be fooled?"

Brieze shook her head. "If he's deep in thought or conversation, as he's likely to be," she said, "he wouldn't notice if a flock of grekks bit him on the butt." She paused as Luff snickered. "If he does notice, I doubt he'll say anything. He'll know I have a hand in it, and he'll know there's a reason for it."

"That's comforting," Tak said. "Turn your back."

Brieze turned her back. Tak and Lothran completed their exchange of clothes. Lothran tied the white mask about Tak's face. It smelled of some unpleasantly medicinal substance. Tak hoisted the tray of tea and edibles onto his shoulder and made ready to exit the front door masquerading as a member of the wizard's island people. Brieze licked her hands and did her best to smooth down Tak's wild hair. Ordinarily Tak would not have put up with anyone running their—ugh!— licked hands through his hair. But in this case he found he didn't mind so much.

"One more thing," Brieze said, laying a hand on Tak's. "Your ring. That certainly will get you spotted."

Tak looked down at his left hand. "You want me to give you my family ring?" he asked. Removing and handing over one's family ring was a symbol of surrender. There were stories of men in the Kingdom of Spire who had preferred having their hand cut off—or being put to death—rather than hand over their ring.

"Just for now," Brieze said. "I'll give it back. I wouldn't want it to give you away."

Tak patted at his new clothes with his free hand, looking for a pocket into which he could stow the ring. But Lothran's simple clothes had no pockets. Tak suspected that Brieze knew this.

"The tea is getting cold," Brieze said. She drew herself up to her full height and looked down at him with a deep, dark-eyed gaze that Tak, without meaning to, felt like a warm glow in the center of his chest. His hand tingled pleasantly where her fingers rested upon it. Goosebumps blossomed along his forearm.

He gave her the ring.

* * *

Outside, Tak positioned himself to the wizard's left, knelt, and set the tray on the blanket. The wizard wore a black robe-like garment similar to Brieze's. Tak studied the wizard's face as best he could out of the corner of his eye, but he could see no family resemblance to Brieze. The wizard was fair-skinned, and his eyes were blue. However, they did hold that same deep, calm look overlaid with a sparkle of humor that Tak had seen in Brieze's eyes. The wizard's face was old, with deep lines framing his eyes and furrowing his cheeks and forehead. His hair was pulled straight back, and he wore it in a long braid similar to Breize's, although his hair was silver-white instead of black.

Fortunately, Tak had often helped serve at dinner parties that his parents gave for friends or heads of guilds. So he had some idea of how to serve at a function like this. "More tea anyone?" he asked quietly, his eyes downcast. Admiral Scud sat immediately to Tak's left. So close Tak could have elbowed him in the ribs. Tak's heart began to pound, and a sheen of sweat broke out on his forehead.

The men were deep in conversation. A few—including Admiral Scud—stuck their empty teacups out for refilling without even looking at Tak. That was good. He managed to refill the cups without spilling any tea. And if anyone noticed the teapot was shaking slightly, they didn't comment on it.

The wizard was lecturing. "Giant deposits of flammable gas like the ones you describe occur naturally beneath our world's surface," he was saying. "They are the by-product of the decomposition of organic matter that has been buried for millions of years. In essence, the energy that was once stored in this organic matter still remains in the form of volatile hydrocarbon molecules."

Scud and his officers nodded at this blankly, as one often nods at the wizard's talk. It was clear they didn't understand a thing. Tak, however, was surprised to find he could follow the general gist of the wizard's words. You didn't have Terentius Liberverm as a frequent dinner guest in your house without learning a thing or two. The old scholar often talked about the theoretical possibility that there were vast stores of alternative fuels to be had underground, and that these were somehow created from the remains of plants and other living things that had been buried for millions of years.

The wizard sighed at the men's blank nodding. "Let me put it this way, you're familiar with coal, yes?"

The men nodded vigorously. Coal they understood. If not how it came to be, at least where it could be found and what it could do.

"These bubbles are a similar thing. But instead of being solid they are gaseous in nature. Does that make sense?"

The men nodded once more. Understanding dawned on some of their faces, including the Admiral's face. Tak found himself nodding as well. He felt as if those particular words had special significance. They seemed to flip a lever in his brain that started the gears of his mind turning. He sensed his brain was working on an idea.

Admiral Scud grunted his approval at the explanation, set aside his teacup, folded one hand into a fist and laid the other on top of it. "But you said you believe the Gublins are involved in the release of this gas into our sky," Scud said. "Do you think they have learned how to weaponize this substance?"

The wizard smiled. "I do not," he said. "I know a bit about Gublins, and if they wanted to cause trouble for you, they could do much better than releasing giant bubbles of gas into the sky, hoping to hit your ships."

"But two of our airships were struck and destroyed by these bubbles," objected one of the officers. "They *explode*!"

Scud silenced the man's outburst with a look.

The wizard didn't appear to take offense. "I believe the destruction of your ships was an unfortunate coincidence. Those poor souls were simply in the wrong place at the wrong time. Once that flammable gas came into contact with the fire heating the boilers of your ships, an explosion was inevitable."

"I see," Scud said. "But we saw many other bubbles explode, high up in the atmosphere, without having hit a ship or anything else. Why would that be?"

"Ahhh yes," the wizard said. He held out his cup for more tea. There was an uncomfortable silence while Tak filled the cup. The silence was most uncomfortable for Tak. Definite beads of sweat had formed on his forehead, despite the cool breeze wafting over the island. He hoped that if anyone noticed they would put it down to a boy's nervousness at serving such important guests. The wizard met Tak's eyes for a moment as Tak finished filling the cup. The wizard's eyes flickered with surprise. One eyebrow went up and he fixed Tak with an amused expression. Then he turned back to the conversation as if nothing had happened. "It seems likely to me those other explosions were caused by sparks of electrical discharge. As the bubbles rose higher and higher into the atmosphere, the continual friction of the bubble surface against the air rubbed large numbers of electrons off the bubble, giving it an overall positive electrical charge."

Scud and his men were nodding blankly again.

"It's the same as when you shuffle your shoes against a carpet during the dry season and then touch a doorknob" the wizard said. "A spark of electrical discharge is generated as new electrons rush to take the place of the ones you've rubbed off your feet."

The men nodded somewhat less blankly. They were familiar with the doorknob spark phenomenon, at least.

"But of course the sparks that likely ignited those gas bubbles probably came from nearby clouds and were of a much larger scale," the wizard concluded.

"Of course," Scud echoed. "A much larger scale. But then how are the Gublins involved?"

"Well, we know how much Gublins love their mining," the wizard said.

The men nodded. Gublins loved iron and copper, were greedy for precious metals like gold and silver, and delighted in sparkling gems. But even if none of these could be found underground, it's likely that Gublins would continue their mining projects for the sheer love of nosing about in the dank bowels of the earth.

"I suspect one or more of their mining operations have released these pockets of gas," the wizard said. "The Gublins have likely considered them a nuisance and have thought no more about them once they've disappeared above the surface clouds."

Scud cleared his throat several times and rubbed pensively at the spot where his scar split the corner of his lower lip. He seemed at a loss for what to ask next. It was clear he didn't like this explanation of natural gas deposits released accidentally by the Gublins. This information wouldn't support his position that Spire should go to war against the Gublins. Tak saw wheels of thought turning behind the Admiral's gray eyes. He saw the glimmers of plans playing out there. Nasty plans.

"How can we be sure?" the Admiral asked. "How can we know if this possible explanation you've offered is the right one?"

"I can think of one way," the wizard said. "Go ask the Gublins."

At that, Scud and his officer's eyes boggled as if the wizard had suggested they set up a manicure parlor that tailored exclusively to dragons. All the men began speaking at once...

"Talk? To the Gublins? They'd just as soon spit and roast us as talk to us I'm sure," one said.

"They eat *children,* for heaven's sake!" another said.

The wizard waved his hand dismissively. "Oh, I'm sure those rare child-eating incidents were honest mistakes," he said. "A young unwashed mountain child probably looks and smells very much like a goat to them. Their vision is different from ours, you know. I've actually known some very nice Gublins in my time."

"How could we meet and talk with the Gublins even if we wanted to?" Scud asked. "Our ships can't travel beneath the surface clouds."

"Oh, well, you'd have to walk down the mountains to meet with them, of course," the wizard said.

At that the men burst into laughter as if the wizard had suggested they all rocket themselves to the moon by eating huge bowls of beans and then lighting their own farts. Scud quieted his men with a curt gesture, but even his eyes shone with a hint of a laughter. Sky riders have an extremely low opinion of walking as a form of transportation. They have several disparaging sayings about walking. One is that *two feet will only get you one foot off the ground*, meaning that a foot is about as high in the air as a person can jump. Another saying, which is usually shouted from airships at someone walking below on the ground, is *don't walk too far, friend, or you'll end up where you started!* This is in many ways true about walking around on a mountaintop: after reaching the peak there is nowhere to go but back down again. Or, if you are walking around the circumference of the mountain, you eventually circle back to your starting place.

The wizard didn't take offense. "I am not kidding, gentlemen. There is a path at the base of Selemont that will lead you to the nearest Gublin realm," he said. "It's on the lower east side, not far from an apple orchard, marked by a small wrought-iron gate."

"I've heard of this path," Scud shrugged, "maybe we'll try that." But it was clear he had no intention of doing so. Then he added, "So you have known Gublins? Do you have contacts among them?"

"I do," the wizard said. "In fact I know of a Gublin wizard named Deelok who lives not far from the base of Selemont. He's a decent fellow."

The men shuddered to think that Gublins lived so close to their own mountain.

"Could you ask him about these gas bubbles?" Scud asked.

"I could," the wizard said. "But unfortunately I cannot travel at the moment. I'm right in the middle of finalizing the fireworks display for the summer solstice festival. The solstice is less than two weeks away. If I spare time for anything else, the fireworks won't be ready."

The men nodded in understanding. The wizard was renowned for his fireworks, and the King commissioned him each year to create a display for the summer solstice festival. So at festival time, the wizard steered his island to Selemont. When nighttime came, he positioned the island directly above the city of Selestria. Then the fireworks began. It was as if the wizard were an artist painting in fire and light and all the night sky was his canvas. Rockets whistled up into the dark, trailing sparks, and then with booms and bangs the night sky became alive with blooming flowers, with flocks of iridescent birds, even with shimmering airships that dove and swooped over the treetops before dissolving into puffs of smoke.

But the most spectacular part of the wizard's fireworks display was the finale. For the finale, the wizard used stunning raw power rather than artistry. The finale was a bewildering series of colored explosions—red, orange, yellow, green, blue, purple—each one brighter than the sun and loud enough to shake the castle walls. It could be seen from every part of the kingdom. When it was over, the echoes boomed between the mountains and the atmosphere rippled so that the stars bobbed up and down and sideways, appearing to have been knocked loose and barely hanging on to the realm above. The people gaped upward in silent awe—and then let loose with roars of delight and approval.

As much as the men understood the wizard couldn't abandon his preparation of fireworks, they were obviously disappointed that he wouldn't be speaking with the Gublins on their behalf. It was not something any of them were eager to try themselves.

"However," the wizard said, sensing their disappointment, "I might be able to send someone to talk to Deelok in my place. Would that suit you?"

"Indeed it would," Admiral Scud gave the wizard what he hoped was his most grateful and charming smile. But Scud was not a talented smiler, and there was very little charm in it. "We would be much in your debt if you could arrange for some sort of communication."

"Consider it done then," the wizard said.

The men made as if to rise and say their goodbyes, but the wizard gestured for them to remain seated. There was now a most definite sparkle of humor—and mischief—in his eyes. He held out his teacup to Tak for another refill. "Before you take your leave, gentlemen, I would like to hear a little more about the unfortunate destruction of your ship the *Vigilance*. I heard there was a witness who observed the disaster at close range...?"

From the tone of the wizard's voice, Tak knew the wizard had guessed exactly who his new tea server was and was playing some sort of game. Tak had started to relax when the men began to take their leave, but his heart pounded again as he refilled the wizard's cup.

Scud waved his hand. "Not a reliable witness. Just a boy," he said.

Tak's temper rose at hearing Scud describe him like that.

"Still," the wizard said, eyes all aglitter, "the story goes that this boy actually boarded the burning ship and saved Captain Strake's life. Sounds like a brave lad to me. Someone who could be trusted...?"

Scud shook his head. "I would trust Taktinius Spinner

about as much as a hungry eel. He's the most reckless and bothersome boy in the kingdom. I have no doubt he's somehow exaggerated his part in the rescue of Captain Strake. Most likely the captain already got off the ship with his own parachute, and Tak recovered him from the sky. Then, hoping to avoid punishment for once again following too closely to one of our battleships, the boy did away with the captain's chute, put his own chute on him, then made up his improbable story. Once the captain comes to, I will—"

"I did *not*!" Tak leapt to his feet, whipped off his mask, and faced Admiral Scud with his hands on his hips. "I am no liar!"

Tak instantly regretted this course of action.

For one thing, Admiral Scud—quick as a snake striking—jumped up and grabbed him by the shirt collar. Scud's voice sputtered with surprise and anger as he shook Tak by the collar. "Tak Spinner! By all heavens...spying again are we? How on Etherium did you get here? What are you doing here?"

For another thing, the wizard was looking at him, and all traces of humor were gone from the wizard's eyes. They flashed darkly under bushy white brows. "I would like to know the same thing, Admiral. So tell me Tak, why did my daughter allow you on the island, and what is your purpose here?"

But both the Admiral's and the wizard's jaw dropped as they realized that they were suddenly speaking to an empty shirt, still gripped tightly at the collar by Scud.

And that Tak was bolting shirtless across the lawn toward the house.

The wizard let out a little chuckle at that. "That *is* one reckless boy," he said. "And *fast*, too."

"Stop him!" shouted Scud, rising to his feet. His senior officers, none of them young men any longer, struggled up from their stiff cross-legged sitting positions with involuntary groans and many poppings of knees and the clatter of hastily discarded teacups. By the time they took up the chase, some of them rubbing their stiff backs as they ran, Tak had already disappeared inside the house. The men would not dare barge into the wizard's house without permission, so they bunched up uncertainly on the front porch, looking over their shoulder for guidance from the Admiral or the wizard.

"He'll be making for the dock out back, I suspect," the wizard said. "Probably fastest to run around the house. If you're not familiar with the inside, you could be wandering around in there for days."

The men ran around the house.

By this time, Tak was already halfway down the gravel path to the dock, Luff and Brieze sprinting beside him.

"You're not terribly smart, are you?" Brieze huffed as she ran. She moved fast on her long legs, but her running stride was no less awkward than her walking stride.

"He said I lied!" Tak spat breathlessly.

Brieze rolled her eyes.

The boys leapt from the dock onto the *Arrow*. Brieze undid the mooring lines and tossed them to Tak. "Head west, into the sun, and stay low," she said. "Stay below the island and try to keep it between you and the battleship. With any luck they won't spot you. I'll try to slow them down."

They heard shouts and booted feet crunching the gravel

on the path behind them. Tak nodded to Brieze, then he and Luff raised and angled the *Arrow's* sail. It bellied full with wind. Tak leaned on the tiller and the *Arrow* was off. Not as fast as it should be towing the *Ram*, but still fast enough. When Tak dared to look over his shoulder, the island looked again like a huge cliff looming in the distance. He could just make out the wooden dock, and a crowd of figures on it. But he couldn't make out what they were doing. Then he remembered Brieze's instruction to stay below the island. He pressed the *Arrow's* wing flap pedals and the craft descended. The island loomed above them.

Tak and Luff scanned the sky, but they didn't see any pursuing ships.

"That was *fun*," Luff said, grinning. "Boy will I have a story to tell back home. Visited the wizard's island *and* got chased by the Admiral of the royal fleet. Who will believe me?"

Tak grinned back. Then he shivered with cold. His hands reached down to button up his shirt and encountered bare skin. Tak stared down at his bare chest and the thin pair of breeches he wore. He groaned.

"Don't worry," Luff said. "I'm sure a rich city boy like you has a whole closet full of warm, fancy clothes at home. And I've got a spare shirt and cloak in my pack that you can borrow to keep off the chill."

"It's not that," Tak said. "My ring. She still has my ring."

"Oh no," Luff groaned and put his head in his hands.

"We have to go back," Tak said.

NINE

They sailed away from the island until it again resembled a giant fragment of a broken dinner plate floating in the sky. Then they waited, letting the *Arrow* drift. The sun dipped down toward the horizon, and the sky turned the deep plum color of evening. They watched the smoke trail of the *Dragonbane* heading northwest, back toward Selemont, and finally disappearing in that direction. They didn't see any other ships in the sky.

"Probably didn't bother to send any ships after me," Tak said, munching on a dried apple. "They know they couldn't catch me."

"Oh ho, it sounds like my new friend is a bit of a boaster," Luff said, rummaging through his pack for something to eat. "He thinks he can outrun the royal fleet."

"I'm not boasting," Tak said, swallowing noisily. "Just stating facts."

"You mean they've *tried* to catch you before?" Luff sat straight up, eyes wide.

"Many times. They rarely do."

"But *why*?"

Tak explained his habit of tailing battleships and buzzing castle Selestria's walls.

Luff was silent, clearly mulling this new information over. He broke off a piece of brown bread from the loaf in his pack and chewed it thoughtfully.

"What?" Tak said. "What are you thinking?"

Luff leaned back against a gunwale and crossed his arms with a sigh. "Well, if you want to know the truth, I was thinking that if I'd just let myself stay stuck to that jellyfish a bit longer, someone a whole lot less *crazy* might have come along to rescue me."

"Thanks a lot," Tak said.

"I was also thinking that the Admiral knows he can pick you up easily enough in Selestria sooner or later. Unless you're planning to never go home?"

"I know. I *know*," Tak groaned. "Can we just get my ring back and we'll figure out the rest later?"

"Fine by me."

They set the sail and slipped as quietly as possible back toward the island. Normally, they would have lit lanterns at the prow and the stern so other vessels could see them in the sky and avoid colliding with them. But it seemed more prudent not to, in case Scud had left a ship or contingent of men waiting for them on or near the island.

Tak steered the *Arrow* until the island once again loomed like a giant cliff in front of them. He made for the spot where he thought the dock was, but it was hard to see in the growing dark. As they drew closer, Tak grimaced at every snap of sail and slap of rope against the masts and yards. He wished they could be perfectly quiet. It felt like they were making an awful lot of racket in the dusk. Easy enough to hear for anyone who was listening for them.

Tak had Luff take the tiller. He lit a lantern and stood in the prow of the boat, holding the lantern aloft. He had to risk some light to find their way back to the dock.

"Do you see it?" he whispered loudly to Luff.

"No. I can hardly see anything in this dark," Luff whispered loudly back.

They heard something strange. A sound like fabric rustling or flapping, vaguely winglike, above them. They both looked up into the dark. They saw nothing. But they felt the unmistakable lurch of something large landing *on the ship*! Luff and Tak yelped in surprise. Tak dropped his lantern overboard. They were in complete darkness now. Tak's ears could hear something breathing heavily in the dark. Something that wasn't himself or Luff.

"What *is* it?" Luff squeaked in a horrified whisper.

"Shhhhh! I don't know," Tak slipped the knife from his belt. Held it ready. "Light another lantern."

Luff fumbled in the dark. "Whatever it is, it's *big*," he said. There was the sound of flint striking steel. Then the ship was bathed in lantern light.

Brieze stood just in front of the ship's foremast, smiling at Tak with her almond-shaped eyes. She was so close she could have reached out and touched him. Her face was flushed and her hair windblown. She wore the same robe-like garment she'd been wearing that afternoon.

"Hello," she said. "Did you miss me?"

"Are you *crazy*?" Tak cried when he could get his voice back. "Sneaking up on us like that! I could have stabbed you right in the heart!"

"Oh of course," Brieze's smile changed to a smirk. "I

should've been more careful." It was clear she didn't consider Tak or his knife a threat.

"How did you get here?" Luff asked.

Brieze turned to him, her smirk changing to a mysterious smile. "Now now," she said, raising an eyebrow. "A wizard's daughter must keep her secrets."

"Well, what are you doing here?" Tak demanded. "You scared us half to death." The pounding of his heart was beginning to slow.

She looked a little hurt. "I really did expect a warmer welcome from you boys. Especially since I came to return your ring."

She held it out to Tak. He put his knife back in its sheath. Took the ring from her and put it back on his finger.

"Thanks," he mumbled.

"Also, I need transportation," Brieze said. "And I thought that since you boys are heading where I'm heading...?"

"You're going to Selemont?" Tak said. "Why?"

"My father wants me to visit the Gublin wizard Deelok and see what he knows about these gas bubbles."

Tak and Luff exchanged speechless glances. A girl? Going below the surface clouds to visit the Gublins? Something Admiral Scud and his men wouldn't even dare to do? It made no sense to them. Seemed utterly impossible. Seemed like suicide.

"I'll take your silence as an agreement to give me a lift," Brieze said, seating herself primly on the *Arrow's* thwart bench and folding her long legs underneath. She had a black pack on her back, and she removed this and stowed it under the bench as well, along with her bow and quiver of arrows. Neither of the boys noticed that she didn't appear to be wearing a parachute pack. "And now, if you two would like to stop gaping at me like a pair of gaffed eels, maybe we could turn about and get underway? I'd like to get there by morning."

Tak and Luff looked at each other again. An extremely important reason why they should definitely *not* get underway had just occurred to them.

Luff gave voice to the thought. "Ummm," he said. "Am I the only one who thinks we shouldn't travel back across the Ocean of Clouds tonight by ourselves?"

"No," Tak said. "I agree. We should wait until morning."

"Why?" Brieze asked. "Certainly you traveled the ocean last night to get here?"

Tak explained that they had stuck close to the *Dragonbane* last night for protection. Of course, that was impossible now. The *Dragonbane* was far away, and surely flying without lights. It would be impossible to find or catch up to the battleship in the dark. Tak also mentioned their close encounter with the Nagmor last night.

"Oh, that was lucky!" Brieze exclaimed. "My father has told me about the Nagmor. I'd give anything to see one of those creatures."

"No you wouldn't," Luff said.

Brieze frowned and chewed her lower lip. "All right," she said. "I understand you boys are scared. Let me propose a safer plan. We're not *that* far out into the ocean. Instead of heading north-northeast back to Selemont the way you came, why don't we head east-northeast and make for Foot-mont—my original home, by the way—at the southernmost end of the Highspire Mountains? That should take five or six hours at the most, not all night. We'll cross a much shorter stretch of ocean and minimize the danger. Once we reach Footmont, we can follow close to the Highspire Mountains all the way north to Selemont. Would that be agreeable to you?"

The boys looked at each other once more, then muttered in agreement. They didn't like the plan, but they were too proud—too ashamed—to object. They had bristled when Brieze used the word *scared*. Here was a girl, no older than they were, intending to undertake the unthinkable task of walking beneath the clouds to the Gublin realms. All she wanted of them was a lift. They just couldn't admit to being too afraid to offer her that service. So they toughened their hearts and made ready to get underway.

In a few minutes, they were fully underway, heading on an east-northeast course to Footmont, steering by the stars. The *Arrow* was big enough to carry three people, though the space was a little tight. Tak sat in the stern with his hand on the tiller. Luff sat forward on the gunwale, keeping an eye on the *Arrow's* sail and glancing back now and then at the *Ram*, still on its tow line behind them, visible in the moonlight.

Brieze moved forward and sat next to Luff on the gunwale. She cleared her throat, fixed her eyes on him, and made sure that she had his full attention. As their eyes locked, all traces of humor vanished from Brieze's face. "And just for your information, Lufftik of Gatmont," she said. "I'm *not* that *big*."

* * *

On the course Brieze had proposed, it took them about six hours to reach Footmont. The plan had been for each of them to take shifts at the tiller, as a group of sky riders will often do when flying through the night. But Tak and Luff couldn't sleep. They spent those hours peering every which way into the darkness, their noses raised and sniffing the wind for any hint of Nagmor. Brieze, on the other hand, had curled herself up and fallen into a deep slumber. The boys saw no point in waking her.

The boys couldn't see much of the mountains in the dark. But they sensed them nonetheless. They smelled pine, earth, and wood smoke. And the *Arrow* responded to the mountain updrafts, her hull rising and sail rippling cheerfully as if she knew she were near home. Tak turned her on a northerly course that would lead them to Selemont. But he had no doubt that even if he hadn't done so, even if he had somehow fallen asleep at the tiller, the *Arrow* would have taken him there anyway.

When the stars began to fade and the first flush of green crept into the sky, signaling the sunrise, Tak could just make out the shadow of Selemont far to the north, tallest among the other distant mountains. Luff had fallen asleep in the bow and Brieze was just stirring from where she slept on a bench. As the sun broke over the horizon, its rays first hit the castle of Selestria, the highest point in the Kingdom of Spire. At that distance, the castle gleamed like a tiny jewel of fire crowning the mountain.

The sight made goose bumps prickle Tak's arms. He hadn't realized he was staring at the mountain until he noticed Brieze had sat up and was watching him thoughtfully.

"You love that place, don't you?" she asked, her voice rough with sleep. Luff continued to snore in the bow.

Tak felt suddenly shy, as if he'd been caught doing something secret. "I guess I do," he said.

"It must be nice," she said, "to *be* from someplace."

Tak frowned. He didn't understand. Everyone was *from* somewhere. Then he thought maybe he understood. He tied the tiller to fix them on their northern course, then took a seat on the bench next to Brieze. "You mean living on the floating island, it's like you never get to settle anywhere?"

"Yes," she said. "And no. It's more than that." They were sitting so close that their knees touched, and Tak was acutely aware of this fact. Brieze chewed her lower lip the way she had when she was trying to make up her mind to help Tak spy on Admiral Scud or not. It seemed like she wanted to say more, but didn't know how, or wasn't sure if she should.

"What?" without realizing it, Tak put a hand on her knee. "Tell me."

So she told him a little bit about her life. She'd been born on Footmont, the least of the southernmost Highspire Mountains. The place was given the disparaging name of Footmont because many considered it to be no more than a foothill to the actual mountains and because the people who lived there usually traveled by foot, not having the means to travel by airship whenever they chose. Brieze had lived with her mother on Footmont until she was thirteen years old.

Her father had been a merchantman from one of the far-away Eastern Kingdoms, where people had honey-colored skin, straight black hair, and black almond-shaped eyes. Her father's ship had stopped at Footmont for a few days to take on water and provisions for the home journey. During that short time, her father and mother had fallen in love. Her father had promised to return after he'd brought his merchant ship safely home and to claim her mother as his bride. But her father never did. Her mother never saw or heard from him again.

Life was tough for a different-looking, fatherless kid on a backwater mountain. Brieze had no friends growing up, no brothers or sisters for company. She didn't feel like she belonged there. It didn't help that the other kids called her *slant eyes*. She kept to herself most of the time, and she read a lot. She'd read every book on her mountain, in fact, by the time she turned ten. There weren't many of them. Her mother, eager to nurture her daughter's happiness in any way she could, spent what little extra money she had to buy whatever books she could from passing ships. So Brieze had read a lot about a lot of different things. Farming. Well digging. Metallurgy. Medicine.

It wasn't long before she tried to put some of the things she read into practice. Once, when the mountain's goats were falling ill with a pox disease described in one of her books, Brieze tried the recommended cure, shavings from the bark of the *Vitrellia* tree stewed with garlic and onions, on her grandfather's herd. It was the only herd that survived that season intact. Another time she located and tapped an underground freshwater spring, higher up on the mountain than anyone believed possible, that allowed her village's famers to double their crop.

Word of her abilities spread through the villages of Footmont. And then to other mountains. When Brieze was thirteen, the wizard arrived. His arrival threw her village—the entire mountain in fact—into an uproar. The wizard had never seen fit to visit Footmont before. But he was extremely polite. He stayed for three days, and spent nearly the entire time with Brieze. He asked her countless questions. He showed her how to add, subtract, divide, and multiply numbers with special notations on a sheet of paper. She learned quickly. He gave her books and asked her to read passages from them, then he asked her questions about what she had read.

At the end of the third day, the wizard asked if she would like to become his apprentice and live with him and his community on the floating island. Her mother would be allowed to come too. Brieze couldn't believe her luck. Finally, she was able to get off that pissant mountain and be part of a community of people who read books, did experiments, and thought about more than goats and crops. The wizard adopted her formally as his daughter, although he did not marry her mother of course. That's how it goes with wizards. They don't have time for marriage or families. But when wizards choose an apprentice they legally adopt him or her to ensure the apprentice inherits all of their books, equipment, and scholarly work.

The floating island was better than Footmont. But still, it was small. Although Brieze did get to travel to exciting places, there weren't many children her age on the island. And those that did live there kept their distance from her.

She was regarded with equal parts awe, respect, and fear. The kids never asked her to join their airship races or games of tag. She didn't have any close friends. It was as if everything had changed, and nothing had changed.

"Well, I guess I'm just going to have to come visit you every now and then," Tak said. "To make sure you don't get too lonely out there." They had edged closer together as they talked and now their legs and shoulders touched.

Brieze had been staring out at the sky with a wistful half-smile on her face as she told Tak her story. Strands of her loose hair had blown across her face, and one had caught in the corner of her mouth. She looked into Tak's eyes, and her smile brightened. "I think I might like that," she said.

"And when we get to Selestria, I'll give you a personal tour of the city," Tak said. "I'll show you the castle, the libraries, the parks, you'll love it. And you'll always be welcome there."

A little glimmer of that usual humor came back into Brieze' black eyes. She squeezed his hand. "Thank you, Tak," she said. "That sounds wonderful."

* * *

The only other notable incident during their journey happened later that morning, once the sun was fully up. Tak was at the tiller and Luff stood amidships adjusting the sail when a large flock of birds passed overhead, throwing flapping shadows onto the deck. Luff looked up, startled, his eyes and mouth wide open. He can be forgiven for this mistake because he was recently attacked by a flock of grekks, so of course any flying creatures passing close overhead would startle him. But every experienced sky rider knows the last thing you want to do when a flock of birds or anything else passes directly overhead is to look up. Especially with your mouth open. This is because, as was mentioned before, bird droppings are a fact of life on Etherium.

Tak and Brieze kept their faces lowered, so they didn't suffer Luff's fate. A smattering of thick white drops hit the deck. One landed near the toe of Tak's boot. Another hit Brieze on the shoulder. And a third landed directly into Luff's open mouth. Luff made a retching, gurgling sound and staggered backward, tripping over the thwart bench and cracking his head on the gunwale as he went down. The *Arrow* rocked violently.

Tak steadied the *Arrow* with the tiller and wing flap pedals. Brieze knelt at Luff's side, feeling at the back of his head.

"Is he all right?" Tak asked.

Luff lay sprawled on his back and semi-conscious, making weak gagging noises. Brieze cradled his head in her lap and wiped his mouth with the sleeve of her robe. She raised his fluttering eyelids with her thumb and examined his pupils.

"He'll be fine," she said.

"You know," Tak said thoughtfully, "I get the feeling that our friend Luff here is not the luckiest boy in the sky."

"Mmmmmgh-ack," Luff moaned.

Brieze patted Luff's head soothingly. "I think you may be right," she said.

TEN

Trying to fly as inconspicuously as possible, Tak guided the *Arrow* to the base of Selemont. They flew close over the fields and orchards, at treetop level, trying to spot the place that marked the path that led down to the Gublins. The farmers and herders out working in the afternoon sun barely spared them an upward glance. Both Tak and Luff surveyed the surrounding sky with their spyglasses, but no battleships or royal craft of any kind were visible.

"There," Brieze said. She pointed toward an orchard of old, twisted apple trees. The orchard sat barely a stone's throw from the mist that marked the beginning of the surface clouds. No one was working in this orchard. In fact, no house or farmer's hut was visible from it. Tak brought the *Arrow*, and the *Ram* in tow, down at the edge of the orchard. He and Luff lowered their sails, anchored their craft with rope and wooden stakes pounded into the ground, and for good measure tied them to two of the nearest apple trees.

It was mid-summer, and the blossoms had fallen from the trees. The white petals of apple flowers lay curling and browning on the ground. Small green bulbs of fruit struggled for life on the gray branches of the trees, but many of them were already worm-eaten. It seemed this orchard hadn't been tended in a long while. The trees hadn't been pruned and their branches were full of old, dead limbs. Last year's harvest of apples lay brown and rotten to mush on the ground under each tree.

"Lovely place for a picnic," Luff said as they surveyed the place. He'd fully recovered from his incident with the bird droppings.

"Shush," said Brieze, and pointed again. "There."

At the farthest end of the orchard, right at the edge of the mist, a little wrought-iron gate stood, similar to any gate that might be built into a wall or fence. Except that there was no wall or fence. Just two old rusting iron posts with the gate hanging between them. As they came closer, they saw a jumble of old, mossy stones stretching out in either direction from the gate that might once have been a wall. Two little wrought-iron figures topped the gate, built into its intricate design. They looked like two human figures standing and clasping hands. On the other side of the gate, the mountain-side dropped steeply and was mostly naked rock with little vegetation. A path had been carved, or perhaps worn by the feet of many travelers, into this gray rock. The path was only wide enough to travel single file, and it disappeared into the mist below.

Although she could have clambered over the old stones, Brieze pushed on the gate instead. It swung open with a long, loud creak of rusted iron.

She hesitated to walk through the gate and step onto the path. She ran her hands through her hair, and she adjusted the straps of her pack, pulling them tight. She made sure her bow and quiver of arrows were slung securely over her shoulder. She turned to Tak and Luff.

"Well, thank you for the lift, Lufftik Herder of Gatmont and Taktinius Spinner of Selemont," she said. Her voice lacked its usual confidence. It was higher-pitched than normal and seemed to quaver a little. She took each of their hands and squeezed them between her own as she'd done when they first met. "I am in your debt."

Her hands were trembling.

She appeared to be waiting for them to say something. Or do something. There was a hopeful expression on her face.

"Umm, good luck?" Tak said.

"Yes, uh, good luck," Luff echoed. "I hope all goes well down there."

With that, Brieze's eyes narrowed at them both with a look of utter contempt. Clearly, they hadn't said or done what she'd wanted. She squared her shoulders, turned her back on them with a toss of her head that sent her long braid whipping about, and stepped through the gate onto the path. She walked with determined, if awkward, steps and soon her thin black form disappeared into the mist.

Tak gazed after her and wondered what he'd done to deserve that look. Hadn't he given her transportation to this spot just as they had agreed to, even braving the Ocean of Clouds at night to do so? His head was filled with thoughts of getting back to his home and into a decent pair of clothes and having some of his mother's egg soup. He was certainly glad *he* wasn't the one who had to walk the path beneath the clouds and face the Gublins all by himself. That would be... that would be, um...

Oh crap.

All of a sudden and all too late, as happens with boys and men of every type in every world, Tak understood. With a muffled curse, he turned and ran back to where the *Arrow* and *Ram* were anchored. When he returned moments later his pack, his bow, and his quiver were slung over his back. He carried Luff's pack, bow, and quiver in his arms. He tossed them to his friend.

"What?" Luff said, catching the pack but dropping the bow and quiver. "What are you doing? What are *we* doing?"

"We're going with her," Tak said.

"Why on Etherium would we do *that*?" Luff asked, visibly horrified by the idea.

"She's afraid to go by herself. She wants us to come with her," Tak said.

"And how could you possibly know that?" Luff asked. "Did she *say* so?"

"No of course not. Girls don't *say* things like that. You have to read the signs."

"Well that doesn't seem fair," Luff observed.

"Even so," Tak said, "she's afraid and wants our help. And she's undertaking this journey for the sake of the kingdom. Are we really the kind of boys who are going to let a girl walk beneath the clouds and face the Gublins all by herself when we could do something to help her?"

"I think we could be..." Luff said hopefully. "Couldn't we? *I* definitely could be."

"No we couldn't. Come on." Tak hurried through the gate and down the path at a brisk pace, almost jogging.

Luff gathered up his spilled arrows and placed them back in his quiver. He slung the quiver, bow, and pack over his shoulders. Then he gathered up his courage and followed after Tak. "I really, *really* should have let myself stay stuck to that jellyfish," he muttered under his breath.

* * *

When Tak and Luff caught up with Brieze a minute or two later, the relief was obvious on her face. It seemed as if she were about to grab and hug the two boys. But then she did her best to hide her feelings. She smothered her smile. She stiffened and crossed her arms. "What are you two doing here?" she asked.

"We're coming with you," Tak said.

"Why?" Brieze demanded.

Tak was at a loss for words. The first thing that popped into his head to say was *because you're afraid and you want us to*. But he knew instinctively that wouldn't be the right thing to say. Brieze wouldn't admit to being afraid.

"Umm," Tak said, "We just thought you could use some company."

"Yes," Luff chimed in. "Some company."

"And I've never seen the underworld before," Tak said. "I'm curious."

"Oh yes," Luff said. "We're both definitely most curious about that."

Brieze regarded the two boys doubtfully with her black eyes. "All right," she finally said. "I suppose you can come if you want to. I suppose it wouldn't hurt." She unslung her pack and rummaged through it.

Tak and Luff exchanged a quick glance, and smiled at each other knowingly.

Brieze fished two pieces of pine resin gum out of her pack, flavored with mint. "Chew these," she said. "It will help with the popping of your ears."

So they chewed the gum and began their descent down the path. In places where the incline was especially steep, steps had been carved into the rock. These were damp and slippery. Soon, the sky was no longer its afternoon lavender color but became a gray mist, like the mist all about them, and the sun turned fuzzy and dim. The fog was so thick they could see maybe thirty yards ahead of them. The mountainside was bare except for the occasional boulder or old dead tree. These would loom darkly out of the fog as they drew close, then recede into invisibility as they passed. Occasionally, a fist-sized black spider would scuttle across their path.

The first spider startled Tak so badly he yelped and slipped. He would've fallen if Luff and Brieze hadn't each caught him by an arm.

"Did that spider scare you?" Luff asked.

"Not at all," Tak said, heart thumping as he recovered his footing. "I just slipped on this blasted wet rock."

Brieze looked at him intently, frowning. "Umm hmm," she said.

"Let's keep moving," Tak said.

They'd gone only a dozen steps when Luff asked, "What are you muttering to yourself? Are you singing under your breath?"

"Nope," Tak said. And from then on he sang the spider

song silently in his head.

Spider, spider it may be true
That I'm a hundred times bigger than you
But I'll not mash you, or smash you, or turn you into goo
So don't fear me, and I won't fear you

Tak's ears popped painfully, but the gum helped. They walked down the mountain for what seemed like hours. The sun became just a pale ghost of the sun far above them, and the mist closed in tight all around. They could barely see ten yards ahead of them. Surprisingly, the temperature was rising instead of falling. In fact, it was becoming uncomfortably warm. And everything was damp—their skin, their clothes, their hair. Some sort of whitish-gray algae or lichen grew on the rock all around them, and it was squishy and slippery under their boots. This didn't seem like a place where people should be. It was completely unnatural, and uncomfortable, and menacing.

"I don't like this at all," Luff whispered.

"Shush," Brieze said. "We should be quiet."

"Why? What's out there to hear us?"

"Just be *quiet*," Brieze hissed.

"I can't see," Luff complained. "Let's light a torch. I've got some in my pack."

Brieze shook her head and unslung her pack, rummaging around in it. "Torches won't burn down here," she whispered. "Too damp. Father gave me these instead." She produced a glass rod about a foot long, filled with clear liquid. She shook the rod vigorously and the liquid inside glowed with a clear blue light. Her features suddenly flared up out of the dimness. Her face was covered with beads of perspiration, and loose strands of her hair were plastered to her wet forehead.

Tak and Luff let out low whistles of surprise. "What kind of magic is this?" Tak asked.

"They're called light sticks," Brieze said. "My father invented them." She handed one each to Tak and Luff.

Talk turned his over in his hands. "How do they work?" he asked.

"I don't have time to give you a crash course in chemistry," Brieze said. "You shake them and they make light. That's all you need to know. You can hold them out in front of you like a torch or you can stick them through your belt if you want your hands free. Now let's go."

Tak and Luff shook their light sticks, and their eyes widened as the rods blazed with bluish light. Tak was surprised that the glass itself remained cool. They hurried after Brieze. The boys thought they would feel better once they had some light. But they didn't. For one thing, the glow of the light sticks was strange and unnatural. It wasn't familiar or comforting like sunlight or the blaze of a good pine torch. For another thing, the light didn't penetrate all that well into the fog that continued to close in around them. It helped them see maybe a few feet farther, but then it bounced back off the fog, creating an eerie blue-white curtain all around them. The twisted black shapes of dead trees loomed even more scarily and ghostlike out of the blue mist.

And that was before they noticed that something—some *things*, actually—were following them.

It started with a stray pebble skittering here and there, knocked downhill by something unseen. Then they heard breathing like a heavy panting. They caught whiffs of an unpleasant odor like wet dog hair.

Eyes appeared in the mist. Flashes of luminescent green reflecting the glow from their light sticks, just at the edge of where they could see, low to the ground and set close together. Behind the eyes, there was a sense of hulking gray, animal-like shapes. The eyes flashed ahead of them, and behind them, and to either side—never in one place at one time—just darting in and out of their field of vision.

Tak, Luff, and Brieze bunched up and moved more slowly. They stuck their light sticks in their belts, unslung their bows, and nocked arrows with none-too-steady hands.

"What are they?" Tak whispered.

And, as if in answer, a long piercing howl sounded behind them. More howls answered from ahead, and to either side.

"Wolves!" Brieze hissed.

"Wolves?" Tak exclaimed. He knew that wolves ranged in the lower reaches of many of the kingdom's mountains, but he'd never heard of wolves hunting below the clouds. "What do we do?" he asked.

"Don't show fear," Brieze said.

"Too late for that," Tak said. "What else?"

Luff was the one among them who had dealt with wolves before. Gatmont was the mountain richest in sheep and goats, and wolves ranged thickest around its base, always looking for an opportunity to attack a stray from the herd. The Herders of Gatmont had plenty of experience fighting wolves. Instead of striking fear into their hearts, the howl of wolves made their blood itch for a fight.

"Kill the leader of the pack," Luff said, stepping forward with his bow at full draw and aiming at the nearest pair of eyes. His face was flushed and his eyes fierce. "Then kill as many others as you can."

He let his arrow fly—it *thunked* into flesh and a wolf howled in pain. That set the other wolves howling and growling even more fiercely. One leapt out of the mist straight for Tak's throat. He shot it down. It landed twitching at his feet, smelling of rank wet hair and foul animal breath. More wolves leapt at them all at once. Luff shot the wolf lunging at him, and Brieze got the one springing toward her, but Tak wasn't able to nock and draw another arrow before a big wolf hit him, sinking its teeth into his shoulder and knocking him down. Tak screamed. He couldn't reach the knife at his belt. He punched the animal with his bare fists and struggled to push it off him. Luff reacted in an instant, drawing his knife and sinking it into the wolf's neck. But even as he did, another wolf lunged out of the mist and clamped its jaws onto his calf. Brieze was the only one able to nock, draw, and aim fast enough to keep the wolves off her. She got the one at Luff's calf but Tak had dropped his bow and Luff was struggling to nock another arrow with shaking hands and Brieze couldn't cover all three of them at once.

Things would have gone very badly had not two human figures appeared in the mist. They carried long, curved swords in each hand and they set upon the wolves from behind. They made terrifying hissing noises and their swords flew faster than seemed humanly possible, the blades flashing and darting. Wolves yelped and screamed in pain and fear. In a few moments, it was over. The wolves fled, their glowing eyes disappearing into the dimness, leaving many dead and dying animals behind them.

Tak, Luff, and Brieze were too surprised and dazed from the fight to properly realize what had happened. Brieze helped Tak to his feet. He clutched at his bitten shoulder. Luff stood unsteadily on his wounded leg. The three breathed heavily, their hearts racing.

One of the human figures in the mist turned toward them and came closer. Its swords were sheathed, but it strode toward them swiftly, purposefully. It emerged from the mist and looked them full in the face—thrust its face toward theirs in fact and sniffed inquisitively.

It was a Gublin.

Most humans, on seeing a Gublin for the first time, don't react well. Brieze, who'd been prepared for the encounter by her father, took a startled step backward. She gasped and covered her mouth with a hand. But she strove to remain standing and to meet the Gublin's eyes.

Tak and Luff, however, didn't do as well. Not even nearly as well.

They screamed like little girls and fainted dead away.

Screaming like a little girl and fainting is not an especially unusual reaction for a human who meets a Gublin face-to-face for the first time. That response has been fairly common, according to historical accounts, even for grown men who are used to facing danger.

ELEVEN

When Tak came to, he was lying on the floor of a Gublin cave with his pack placed underneath his head as a pillow. His shoulder had been bandaged and it stung and burned as if some sort of antiseptic had been applied to it. Luff lay next to him, still unconscious, with his pack under his head and his leg bandaged. Tak sat up and looked around. The cave was lit mostly by a small fire in a stone fireplace at one end. But there were also a few dim candles set in elaborately wrought metal sconces mounted on the bare rock walls. Once Tak's eyes adjusted to the dimness, he was surprised to see the cave was lined with shelves of books and scrolls. He had never thought of Gublins as reading books. The center of the cave was dominated by a large workbench upon which sat glass tubes and bottles and beakers, filled with different colored liquids. The bench was also scattered with nuts and bolts and screws and springs and pretty much every kind of tool that a human could think of—and many more that they hadn't.

There was a smaller table, more like a kitchen table, positioned in front of the fireplace. The most surprising thing Tak saw in that cave was Brieze sitting at this table, across from a Gublin, both of them sipping mugs of what appeared to be hot tea and chatting as if they were neighbors and Brieze had just dropped by to say hello.

Luff stirred and sat up next to him. "Ungh," he said, shaking and trying to clear his head. "Where are we?"

"Don't panic," Tak said. "But I think we're in a Gublin cave."

That startled Luff into full consciousness and made his eyes open wide.

Brieze noticed the boys stirring. Before Luff could say or do anything she was kneeling beside them, calming and re-assuring them. "It's all right," she said. "We're safe. How are you feeling?"

The boys admitted they were feeling all right. They stole wary glances over Brieze's shoulder at the Gublin at the table.

"I need you both to be calm," Brieze said. "And *polite*."

The boys nodded.

"All right," she said. "Come meet Deelok. He's the Gublin wizard my father sent me to talk to."

The boys got to their feet uncertainly. For Tak, the fact that he was about to be introduced to a Gublin made him feel as if he were choking on his own heart, which had crawled up into his throat. Luff looked more than a little pale and sickly. Brieze led them to the Gublin's table. He rose politely as they approached.

"Deelok," Brieze said. "These are my friends, Taktinius Spinner of Selemont and Lufftik Herder of Gatmont."

"Pleased to make your acquaintance," the Gublin smiled and held out his hand to them. He was as white as a corpse, but his voice was surprisingly deep and rich. Tak had never been smiled at by a Gublin before. The sight of all those glittering sharp teeth up close was unsettling. And those black eyes! Big and bulbous like a bug's eyes, and spaced too far apart. Tak would have rather stuck his hand into a grekk's nest than shake the Gublin's dead-white and oddly shaped hand, but he knew to refuse would be incredibly rude. He clasped hands with the Gublin. The Gublin's grip felt odd but firm, and Tak was surprised that the flesh was warm, just like a human hand. He'd expected it to be cold and clammy.

"Pleased to meet you," Tak said.

Luff, who is a brave boy with a good heart, also shook hands and mumbled a greeting.

"Please sit," the Gublin Deelok said. "Can I offer you some hot tea?"

The boys looked at Brieze. "Yes," she said. "We would all like some more tea." As the boys took a seat at the table, Brieze said to them, "It's tree root tea." She fixed her eyes on them and added in a pointed tone, "It's *good*."

The Gublin bustled about with startling speed. In the blink of an eye he had set two more clay mugs on the table, grabbed up the kettle from where it hung on a hook over the fire, and poured out more steaming tea for everyone. It was fascinating to watch his hands, because they moved so completely independently of each other. As he poured the tea with one hand, for example, the other reached out with a large spoon to stir a pot of something simmering over the fire. And looking more closely, Tak realized the Gublin didn't have just one thumb per hand, but two! Where his pinkie should have been, there was another thumb, opposable to his three long dexterous middle fingers and his other thumb. That's why his handshake felt funny.

The boys sniffed suspiciously at the tea. It gave off a faint rotten-egg aroma of sulfur. Slowly, they lifted the mugs to their lips. The Gublin smiled again at them as they sipped, and Tak realized it was the smile of an anxious host, hoping to please his guests.

The tea tasted like dirt.

"Mmm!" Tak said in what he hoped was a convincing tone, forcing himself to smile rather than wince. "Good!" Luff followed suit.

The Gublin appeared to be pleased. He drummed his long middle fingers on the table top. "How are you both feeling? Healing nicely, I hope?"

Tak had forgotten that he had a nasty wolf bite on his shoulder. It throbbed under the bandages. He rubbed it. "My shoulder feels all right," he said, surprised.

"So does my leg," Luff said.

"I applied a salve to prevent infection and promote healing," the Gublin said. "It's one of my own inventions."

"Thank you," Tak said. He noticed two crossed swords mounted above the fireplace, and something occurred to him. "I suppose I should also thank you for saving our lives back there. That was you, wasn't it?"

The Gublin Deelok waved a hand dismissively. "Yes, yes," he said. "Me and my assistant Deegor. But it was nothing. We heard the wolves howling outside and went out to investigate. They can be quite the nuisance, can't they?"

"Yes," Tak said, and forced himself to take another sip of tea. "Quite the nuisance." Something else occurred to him.

"You speak our language. How is that?"

Deelok smiled. "I speak many languages. Linguistics is one of my specialties." He gestured to Brieze. "This young human's father has been very helpful in my efforts to learn. He has worked with me quite a bit on my pronunciation."

Although Gublins have a few ancient words similar to human language, they mostly communicate through a series of variously pitched hisses. These hisses are punctuated by elaborate tongue clicks and sounds made deep in the throat that humans make only when violently nauseated. So mastering the human tongue, as Deelok had, was a difficult feat. In fact, he was the only living Gublin fluent in the human language. Some of the other more learned Gublins knew a few words here and there. Mostly monosyllabic words like "rock," "meat," and "kill." And even so they mangled the pronunciation badly.

"Now," Deelok said. "Before you meet the King, would you like a real meal? You'll probably need something to keep your strength up."

Tak didn't hear anything Deelok said after *meet the King...*

"Meet the Gublin King?" Luff said. "But won't...won't he roast and eat us?"

Brieze kicked Luff's shin under the table. Hard.

But Deelok didn't appear to be offended. In fact, he chuckled, which for a Gublin sounds like a human trying to clear his throat—of a pinecone lodged there.

"No, no," he said. "I seriously doubt that. For one thing, you are official emissaries from Spire, are you not?"

The boys looked at Brieze, who nodded, then at each

other. It was true, they realized. Admiral Scud had been acting on the King's behalf when he asked the wizard to speak to the Gublins. The wizard had delegated that authority to Brieze. So she was an official emissary from the Kingdom of Spire. And if they served as her escort by her choice then they were considered official as well. Admiral Scud would have an attack of apoplexy that would likely result in an exploding head if he knew it, but it was all very much according to the rules.

"And for another thing, the King won't harm you because he doesn't want war with you humans," Deelok said. "Although unfortunately most Gublins do."

"Why?" Tak asked. "Why would they want that?"

"Well, as I've just been explaining to this young female human here, it's because of the sneak attacks you humans have been conducting through the old forbidden mines."

"*What*?" Tak and Luff exclaimed together.

"What forbidden mines?" Tak asked.

Brieze huffed in surprise. "The old mines leading down to the Gublin realm?" she said, as if this was something everybody knew. "The ones that started the Gublin War in the first place? Didn't you two study history?"

Tak and Luff shrugged.

"I know the war started because the Gublins invaded our mines," Tak said. "And we drove them out."

"Not exactly," Brieze said. "Nobody invaded anybody. The war started because human and Gublin mines started running into each other. You can imagine what it was like—a tunnel suddenly collapsing into another tunnel, rocks falling, screaming and frightened humans and Gublins suddenly thrown together. They fought instinctively. Each side thought the other was attacking."

"How can a collapsing mine tunnel start a war?" Luff asked.

"Not just one," Brieze said. "It happened several times. And we assumed they were invading, or at least trying to steal our resources. They assumed the same about us."

"Terribly sorry about that," Deelok said. "We presumed the worst about you."

"It sounds like we returned the favor," Tak said.

"Neither side could talk to the other," Brieze said. "So there was no chance to sort things out. The random skirmishes turned into a full-blown underground war."

"Which we won," Luff said.

Brieze huffed condescendingly. She had an amazing talent for conveying a wide range of feelings with that simple sharp exhalation of breath. "Nobody *won*," she said. "In fact you could say both sides lost. Mining operations ground to a halt. Thousands of humans and Gublins were killed. The war was costing both sides too much. So finally they figured out how to talk to each other and negotiated."

"My late father, the wizard Deevok, helped negotiate that treaty," Deelok put in. "As part of the agreement, all the mining tunnels connecting human and Gublin realms were sealed off with stone and rubble."

Deelok finished the story. Several days ago, humans had gone down into those old mines, burrowed through the blocking stones, and attacked unarmed Gublin miners. The attacks had been quick and cowardly. The humans snuck up behind the Gublins in the dark, then lit torches and charged, killing as many of the surprised and frightened miners as they could before fleeing. Sometimes the humans simply rolled a barrel of gunpowder with a lit fuse attached toward the unsuspecting Gublins and fled before it exploded. The ambushes killed dozens of Gublins, and they had stirred up a frenzy of anger in the underworld.

"Blast it!" Tak said, turning to Brieze. "Do you think the King authorized these attacks?"

"I doubt it," Brieze said. "It's my understanding that he was waiting for Admiral Scud to return with information from my father before he took any action."

"Scud!" Tak spat the name. "I'd bet anything this is *his* doing. It would be just like him to try to start a war behind the King's back."

"I was thinking the same thing," Brieze said.

Tak turned to Deelok. "The humans that attacked you. What did they look like? Were they heavily armored, carrying broadswords?" This would have been typical of a ground soldier of Spire.

"The survivors told stories of men in blue uniforms," Deelok said, "very lightly armored, using thin swords."

That sounded exactly like airmen from the royal fleet.

Talking further, the group determined that the attacks had started six days ago—the very day after the destruction of the *Vigilance*. But no attacks had occurred in the past two days—which coincided with the time Scud and his men had been away visiting the wizard.

"But Scud is surely back at Selemont now," Tak said. "If he and his men are behind these attacks, they could start up again any time."

"That would be extremely bad for relations between our realms," Deelok said.

Brieze looked earnestly across the table at Deelok. She laid a hand on top of his. "Deelok," she said, "please know that this is a mistake. I am certain our King did not authorize these attacks and knows nothing about them. We have a fleet Admiral who is a bit…crazy and hateful when it comes to Gublins. He believes the exploding bubbles are some kind of weapon you are using against us. He wants war. But the rest of us do not."

"I believe you," Deelok said. "But it's not me you have to convince. It's my King."

Brieze, Tak, and Luff stared glumly down into their cups of tree root tea. How in the world were they supposed to do *that*?

"No use worrying, young ones," Deelok said. "Now, how about a meal to fortify you before you meet the King? I find that everything seems more possible with a full belly."

Luff's stomach rumbled in agreement. "Sounds like a fair idea to me," he said.

"Well you're in luck, young one," Deelok said. "I've got a very nice centipede stew simmering on the fire. It's perfectly done. The segments of the centipedes have just separated and they're still a bit crunchy."

The boys looked at Brieze again. Their looks said that they could drink dirt tea to be polite, but eating centipede stew was out of the question.

"I'm sorry," Brieze said to Deelok. "But we don't eat centipedes. We can't, um, digest them properly."

"That's a pity," Deelok said. "Well no problem. I've got

plenty of beetles. Do you like dried or would you prefer fresh?" He gestured to two large glass bottles. They sat on a nearby shelf carved into the rock that served as a pantry. In one bottle, the tightly packed beetles lay still. In the other, their legs squirmed feebly.

"Umm, well, actually, the same goes for beetles," Brieze said. "It's the exoskeletons you know. We're just not equipped to digest them."

"Oh of course," Deelok said. "No exoskeletons. It's vertebrates you like. Bats then?" he pointed up toward the roof of his cave. "Yes, let's roast a few of them. I'll get my assistant Deegor to gather some. They're quite plump and juicy this time of year." The three official emissaries from the Kingdom of Spire looked up and noticed countless bats roosting in the darkness of the cave's ceiling.

"You know," Brieze said tactfully. "We brought our own food in our packs. We really should eat what we brought, otherwise it might spoil and go to waste."

The boys brightened instantly at this idea.

Deelok looked disappointed. "I suppose you are right," he said. "Suit yourselves. You don't mind if I have some stew, do you?"

"Of course not," Brieze said.

The boys quickly brought their packs to the table and spread out the food contents. There was a loaf of bread, several dried apples, fresh carrots, goat cheese, and many strips of dried, salted goat meat.

Deelok's nostril slits twitched, and he inhaled deeply. "Is that…goat?" he asked, licking his lips.

If there's anything Gublins love more than silver, gold, or

gems, it's goat meat. They're crazy for it. This is because most of the creepy crawly things they're forced to eat in the underworld just don't taste good, even though they would never admit this. Also, even though Gublins evolved long ago to live underground, there is still a part of their hearts, buried deep, that longs for sunlight, fresh air, and green grass. When they taste goat, they can sense all these things in its flesh. They experience the warmth of the sun and a fresh breeze rippling the grass of a pasture, and it satisfies that ancient longing in them like nothing else can. That's why so many of them venture aboveground at night to snatch goats from the mountainside pastures. They can't help themselves.

"Yes, it's goat," Brieze said. "Would you like some?"

"Well...I really shouldn't..." Deelok said. But a greedy, ravenous light shone in his eyes.

At this point, they were all distracted by a loud sniffing noise. They turned to find another Gublin standing at one of the several dark entrances to the cave that led off into different passages. This Gublin's nostril slits also twitched, and the same greedy, ravenous light shone in his eyes.

"Goat?" this new Gublin said, though the word came out more like *goagh*.

"Allow me to introduce my cousin and assistant, Deegor," said Deelok. "Deegor is the one who, uh, startled you so badly earlier today. I apologize for that. He can be quite forward."

"Goat good," Deegor said. "Give goat?" Deegor was the Gublin second most fluent in human language. He attempted a friendly smile, baring his teeth, which was truly startling.

"See what I mean?" Deelok said. "I apologize for his rudeness." Deelok and Deegor conversed animatedly for a few moments in Gublin language, which sounded to the sky riders like two giant snakes hissing, gagging, and clucking their tongues. Even so, it was clear that they were arguing, and that the argument was growing heated.

Brieze decided to intervene. "Please, please friends," she said. "There's no need to argue. We would be honored if you would join us in sharing this goat meat. It is the least we can offer you after you saved our lives today."

The Gublins stopped arguing. "Well, when you put it like that..." Deelok said.

"Please," Tak said. "Help yourselves."

The Gublins needed no further encouragement. Deegor sat next to Deelok at the table. Tak pushed the pile of salted goat strips across the table in their direction. Gublins move fast under ordinary circumstances, but they move especially fast when attacking a pile of goat meat. Their fingers flew and their lips smacked as they ate. They grunted deeply with delight, and their pointed black tongues snaked out to lick their colorless lips and white fingers. It was not the most appetizing of sights, and it put the sky riders off their food. They managed to chew and swallow a few bites of bread and apples, keeping their eyes lowered. But they weren't really hungry anymore.

When the meat was gone Deelok sat back with his hands folded on his belly. "Thank you," he said. "Thank you so, so much. That was just...exquisite."

Deegor burped and said, "Thank!"

And then there was the sound of a flat, webbed foot slapping stone at one of the cave's entrances. This was the Gublin equivalent of a knock at the door. Deelok called, "*Come in!*" in Gublin language and six armored and armed Gublins entered the cave. They bore on their breastplates the insignia of two curved, crossed swords. This identified them as the King's personal guard.

"Well," Deelok said. "Time to meet the King."

TWELVE

The official emissaries rose from the table, hearts pounding. The Gublin guards conducted a search of their persons and their packs. After a brief discussion with Deelok, whom the guards treated with obvious respect, it was decided that the emissaries could bring their packs if they wanted, but their weapons would stay behind. Tak and Luff removed the knives from their belts and set them next to their quivers and bows, which leaned against a wall along with Brieze's bow and quiver. Then the emissaries followed the Gublin guards down one of the dark passages that led from the cave. The passageway was wide enough for three to walk abreast. Three Gublin guards led, followed by Tak, Luff, and Brieze, then Deelok and Deegor. The remaining three guards brought up the rear.

The passageway was pitch black. The sky riders couldn't even see the three Gublins ahead of them. As the passage twisted and turned, the three humans were guided with gentle words and nudges from Deelok so they didn't stumble or run blindly into a wall. The Gublins made several turns—a left, another left, then a right, then bearing left at a Y-shaped intersection—until Tak had completely lost his sense of direction. The only sounds were the slap of Gublin feet against stone and the occasional clank of their weapons or armor.

Tak's mouth grew dry as he realized that, should things turn ugly for any reason, he would never be able to find his way out of there by himself. He and his friends were now completely at the Gublins' mercy.

Luff and Brieze were evidently having the same uneasy thoughts, judging by how the three of them unconsciously moved closer together and took hold of each other's hands. Luff's hand was large and sweaty in Tak's left, and Brieze's hand was delicate and cool in his right, but gripped his tightly. Tak swallowed and strove to keep up with their Gublin leaders. The strain of not being able to *see* was driving him crazy.

Luff let go of Tak's hand and made a sudden movement, reaching over his shoulder to pull something from his pack. Tak wasn't sure what Luff was up to until he sensed him vigorously shaking something and the passageway blazed with blue-white light. The smooth stone walls and the Gublins ahead of them became visible. Tak squinted against the sudden glare of light after being in the dark so long. But he felt a sense of relief at being able to see and was about to turn to Luff and say "good idea" when the Gublins started squealing. The group stumbled to a halt as the Gublins shielded their eyes with their hands, exclaiming with angry hisses.

"Put it out! Put it out!" Brieze said. "You're hurting their eyes."

"Yes, please!" Deelok said. "It is very painful."

"Sorry!" Luff said, and stuffed the light stick back into his pack. The passageway went dark again.

Deelok and the Gublin guards conversed in angry tones for a while. But Deelok calmed the guards down. The group formed up again and they set off.

"I explained to them that you meant no harm," Deelok whispered. "But do not do that again."

"I won't," Luff said.

"Also, I want to study one of those later," Deelok added.

Gradually, Tak became aware of a dim glow ahead. The golden glow brightened as they approached it, but not so bright as to hurt the Gublin's eyes. The glow came from an immense stone archway, at least twenty feet high, that led into the Gublins' main hall—the throne room of the Gublin King. And then they passed through the archway and entered the cave.

The three emissaries gasped as one. Tak had been in caves before. With his father and friends, he had explored some of the caves that wound through the mountains of his kingdom. But to call what lay before him now a *cave* would be like calling all of Selemont a *rock.*

It was immense beyond his imagining. Though it was dimly lit with oil lamps, Tak could not see the ceiling. Nor could he see the walls on either side of him. The cave stretched away in all directions into the dimness beyond his sight. Giant natural pillars, made of millions-of-years-old stalactites meeting stalagmites, rose from the floor of the cave and disappeared into the darkness above. They were thicker around than the thickest, oldest pine trees Tak had ever seen. The chamber glittered with crystals of every color. They grew from the pillars and from the floor of the cave in fantastic formations. Some resembled bushes or trees with intricate branches. Others mimicked flowing water, rippling down the pillars or across the floor in hues of purple, blue, and milky white.

But the most startling thing about the cave was that it was filled with Gublins.

Thousands of them. Tens of thousands. Most dressed in glittering armor with swords at their hips. Tak had never imagined there could be so *many* of them. That vast sea of white Gublin faces turned to stare at him and his companions. Every black Gublin eye was fixed on them. The sibilant hissing of their whispers—some in obviously angry tones—echoed through the cavern like an eerie wind. Tak's legs started to shake, and he thought that given the choice to be where he was now or back outside facing those wolves again, he might prefer to take his chances with the wolves.

The Gublin guards ushered them forward. There was a paved path that led more or less straight through the center of the cave, twisting or turning here or there to go around one of the natural pillars. It was paved with granite tiles polished as smooth as glass and fitted seamlessly together. As they walked along it, between the ranks of Gublins on either side, Tak realized this path led to the far end of the cave, which he could see now in the distance. There, upon a raised dais carved out of the living rock, sat the Gublin King upon his throne.

The throne had been carved from one huge, milky white crystal, shot through with purple veins and more than ten feet tall. It had been carved into the shape of a Gublin hand, so cleverly that it resembled a living thing more than stone. The palm of the hand, upon which the King sat, was level with the floor. The three long middle fingers curved upward from the palm to form the back of the throne. And the thumbs hooked inward to form armrests on either side. It seemed to grow out of the rock floor and looked so lifelike

Tak imaged that the giant hand might move.

The Gublin King's crown was wrought from silver, in an intricate pattern of interlocked hands and crossed curved swords. It sparkled with diamonds, sapphires, and emeralds, as did the lengthy and elaborate necklace he wore. The necklace hung in multiple coils of silver and gold chain around his neck, and the gems in it had been cut and shaped into miniature versions of animals the Gublins knew: tiny glittering bats, spiders, crabs, fish, and a variety of bugs Tak couldn't identify. The King himself was plainly old. Tak had never imagined an old Gublin before. His face was lined and his hands were bony and wrinkled. His teeth were dull and yellow.

Tak's eyes widened at a fat brown spider squatting in the King's lap, large and furry as a housecat. It seemed to tense up as the emissaries approached, its fur bristling and its multiple black eyes fixing on them. Tak dragged his feet and edged himself ever-so-slightly behind Brieze, rather than staying at her side. The King scratched the spider's back reassuringly. Gublins have a fondness for spiders. They admire the elegant structure and symmetry of their bodies. Spiders are common house pets in the Gublin realm. Gublins also model many of their ingenious machines for digging and mining on the spider's body. The Gublin word for spider, *araken*, is one of the few ancient Gublin words similar to human words.

The guards and official emissaries from Spire stopped at the foot of the dais. Brieze bowed low before the King, and she signaled for Tak and Luff to do the same. They held their bows until the King cleared his throat and beckoned them forward with a bony finger. They approached until they were within easy speaking distance of the King as he sat on his throne. Deelok accompanied them as interpreter, naturally. The guards joined the other squadron of Gublin guards standing on either side of the throne, keeping a close watch on the humans with their hands on their sword hilts. The old King's black eyes studied the humans shrewdly as he stroked his spider's fur. Tak sensed a deep intelligence in those eyes, and a sadness, that reminded him of his own King.

The whispering of the Gublin crowd stilled until it was so quiet you could have heard a bat squeak.

The Gublin King hissed and clucked something that sounded like a question, and Deelok translated. "Our King asks if it is usual for humans to send their children on diplomatic missions, or if this is some sort of insult?"

Brieze, her back and shoulders straight, calmly explained the circumstances that led to her and Tak and Luff visiting the Gublin kingdom. Tak looked at her with wonder out of the corner of his eye. If he were the one who had to address the Gublin King, he doubted that he'd be able to summon up more than a dry-mouthed wheeze of terror.

At hearing Brieze was the wizard's daughter, a glimmer of respect shone in the King's eyes. The wizard and his power were well known even in the underworld. The King nodded and seemed satisfied with Brieze's explanation. He hissed another question, and this one was voiced much louder, meant to be heard by the crowd.

"Well, what do you humans have to say for yourselves?" Deelok translated. "Why are humans murdering innocent Gublins in cowardly attacks?"

At that, the Gublin masses erupted into a pandemonium

of shrieks, hisses, and guttural exclamations. Gublins shook their fists in the air, and many drew their swords—one in each hand—and clashed them noisily together above their heads. The King's pet spider jumped up in alarm and scuttled off the throne into the darkness. The King rose from his throne and held up a hand for silence, but it was a full minute before the crowd quieted.

Brieze swallowed. Tak could tell she would very much have liked a drink of water. But she bowed her head and strove to explain. She apologized profusely for the Gublin deaths. She said that she believed the attacks had been ordered by the royal fleet's Admiral without approval from the King. She said that she would make sure they stopped. She explained that the Admiral had jumped to the conclusion that the gas bubbles the Gublins had released from their mines were weapons because two airships had so far been destroyed by them, one of the ships a royal battleship. Hundreds of humans had been killed. She said that even if the bubbles were natural phenomenon and not weapons, they exploded in the atmosphere and were dangerous to the humans, and that many humans were angry at the Gublins for setting these bubbles loose on them, regardless of the Gublin's intent.

At that, the King looked at her with unmistakable surprise. He hadn't known about the destruction of the airships or the human deaths. But then he composed his features and, still standing, made a pronouncement:

"I find your human explanation weak and unconvincing," the King said, his voice pitched loudly to travel through the cave. "This senseless aggression against the Gublins must cease immediately, otherwise we will rise up and visit ruin upon the humans!"

At that, the chamber erupted into Gublin pandemonium again. The King didn't even try to quiet the crowd this time. He lowered himself tiredly back onto this throne. He crooked a finger at the humans and Deelok, beckoning them closer. He leaned forward as they approached, and they realized he wanted to say something to them privately. Something no one else would hear above the shouting and sword clashing in the cave.

He leaned close as they gathered around him. His black eyes looked weary, and anxious, and sad.

"You must help me," he whispered to the humans via Deelok. "I do not want war with the humans. But if these attacks do not stop I will not be able to hold my people back. I can not appear to be weak."

"I will do my best, your Highness," Brieze said.

"Most of my men are too young to remember the last war with you humans," the King said. "They are naïve and full of spirit and want to test their swords against yours. But I remember that war. We lost much. It is not something I would choose to lead my people into again."

"These gas bubbles," Brieze said. "We have your word that they are natural phenomenon and their release was not intended to harm humans?"

The King nodded. "They have been a nuisance to us, but nothing more. I apologize for the death of your men. It did not occur to any of us that the gas would harm you."

Tak surprised himself by voicing part of a thought that his brain had been working on ever since he'd visited the wizard's island and listened to his theories about the gas bubbles. "Excuse me, your Highness, but can this gas be...

contained somehow? I don't know...bottled up or stored in some way so it can't reach us?"

The King pondered that. He consulted Deelok, and the two had a brief whispered conversation in Gublin. Deelok was one of the most knowledgeable Gublins about natural phenomenon, as well as mining and engineering.

"We think it can be done," the King said. "For now, we will halt any mining operations that might release more of this dangerous gas. And our engineers will begin to work on a way to contain it."

"Our most sincere thanks, your highness," Brieze said. "I will convey that to our King."

"Stop your aggressive Admiral at all costs," the Gublin King said. "Otherwise I fear disaster for both our peoples."

Brieze nodded her understanding. The crowd had quieted and it was no longer possible to speak with the King without being overheard. He raised his voice and addressed the crowd one last time, gesturing at Brieze theatrically. "You are dismissed from my presence and from the Gublin realm!" His voice boomed through the cave. "Take my message to your King and let him know we Gublins are sharpening our swords in preparation for vengeance!"

The Gublin masses roared with approval. At a gesture from the King, both squads of Gublin guards on the dais descended and ushered the humans out of the cave. The King's guards made sure to surround the humans completely on their way out, as they passed through ranks of angry Gublins who shouted and shook their swords at them. Tak didn't like to think what might have happened had the guards not been there to protect them.

THIRTEEN

Back in Deelok's cave, the Gublin wizard served more tea while they all sat around the table by the fireplace. Deelok checked the timepiece on the mantle. It would be several hours still until the sun set in the world above. Then Deelok and Deegor would escort the young sky riders to the surface and back up the mountainside. Until then, they had time to kill.

Tak, Luff, and Brieze fidgeted and sipped their tea distractedly. They were all shaken from their encounter with the Gublin King, and they were anxious to get back to the world above. Deelok asked them to tell him stories about themselves. "Such a rare treat," he said, "to have three young human subjects to converse with. So much to learn. What an opportunity!" He was also hoping to distract them from their fears and worries.

Brieze began. She told Deelok about growing up on Footmont and about how she became the wizard's apprentice and daughter. Tak told the story about the destruction of the *Vigilance* and his rescue of captain Strake. Deelok asked for many details about the *Arrow* and about how human airships worked. Luff was shy and had to be prodded by Brieze, but he told a story about last winter, when he'd helped fend off a particularly large, nasty, and hungry pack of wolves. It was an exciting story and everyone enjoyed it. Deegor in particular. The assistant was especially fond of action stories. He clapped and grinned at the part where the leader of the wolf pack had leapt at and knocked down Luff's father—only to find himself howling and retreating with the rest of the pack with Luff's arrow in his rump.

Luff was so encouraged that he launched into another story, this time a more humorous one. His family's prize she-goat had disappeared. She was about to bear a litter of kids and everyone was worried about her, not only because the kids she would bear would be valuable but because Luff's family all had grown fond of the she-goat, who had an unpredictable but affectionate personality. The family combed the mountainside all day, finally returning to their house after dark, tired and discouraged—to find the prize goat curled up and sleeping underneath their kitchen table. The last place anyone would have thought to look! She had borne her kids and they were curled up sleeping against her belly. And of course the goats had left their droppings all over the kitchen floor.

Deelok laughed softly at that, a high-pitched hiss broken up into little staccato bits. *Sss-ss-ss-ss-ss-ss-ss*! "That reminds me of a funny story," he said. "It's an old one but a good one. Did you young humans see the long necklace wound about the King?"

They nodded.

"That piece of jewelry is called the *Fayex*," Deelok continued. "It is worn by the King and no other. It is extremely old, so old in fact that that no one knows who made it or how it was made. But we do have a story about it. It's what you would call a folk tale, I believe. Would you like to hear it?"

They nodded again.

Deelok began. Once upon a time, so long ago that no one remembers exactly when, there was a crazy old Gublin King. This King loved gold, silver, and precious gems so much that he decided they must be the perfect food. So he stopped eating the usual Gublin fare. No more centipedes, bats, or beetles for him. For breakfast, lunch, and dinner, he ordered that a plate of gold and silver nuggets should be served to him, the freshest to be had from the mines. After these, for dessert, he ate a bowl of uncut gems—rubies, sapphires, emeralds, opals, and diamonds. He swallowed them whole and smacked his lips.

Needless to say, after a few days the King wasn't feeling well. His stomach ached terribly. His advisors begged him to stop his new diet and return to eating real food. But the King was stubborn. He refused. He ate nothing but gold, silver, and gems for another three days. On the morning of the seventh day, the King was so ill he could not rise from bed. The best Gublin physicians, surgeons, and wizards were summoned to his bedside, but they could do nothing for the old crazy King. He dismissed them all.

Then the King was seized with a strong urge to use the chamber pot. With great difficulty and in great pain, he crawled out of bed and squatted over the pot. He groaned miserably. And then, directly into the pot, he squeezed out the longest, most intricate, most beautiful necklace that had ever been made. No one was more surprised or delighted by this than the King himself. He scooped it out of the pot and—after cleaning it thoroughly—put it on. He wore it proudly to the end of his days, although he went back to eating real food and forbade anyone else to eat precious metal and gems.

Tak, Brieze, and Luff couldn't help but laugh. A Gublin folk tale with a crude chamber pot joke at the end! Who could have imagined it? The humans, smiling, all lifted their mugs for another sip of tea and were surprised to find that the mugs were nearly empty. Just then, the timepiece on the mantle chimed.

Deelok sighed. "It is time," he said. "But before we go, I have a few gifts for you."

As much as Gublins love to make things, they also love to delight other Gublins by making gifts of their creations. Gift-giving is an ancient and popular tradition among them. Every Gublin loves to see another's eyes light up with surprise and pleasure at being presented some new invention— a more accurate timepiece, a stronger blade, a clever tool or toy. Every holiday or special occasion is an excuse for gift-giving among the Gublins. The arrival of ambassadors from other realms—including human realms—was such an occasion. And it was traditional for a Gublin host to present his guests with gifts upon their departure.

Deelok reached into the folds of his robe and produced what looked to Tak like three silver brooches or medals. "These are from the King," he said, pinning one on each of their chests. With his Gublin hands, he was able to fasten one to Tak's chest and Luff's chest at the same time, using only one hand for each, his nimble fingers neatly working the pins and clasps. And he used only one hand to secure the final one on Brieze's chest. "Given the current state of diplomatic relations, he didn't want his subjects to know he was giving you these. But he asked me to bestow them on you privately."

The silver medals were worked into the shape of a Gublin hand giving the universal sign of peace—palm up and empty. Deelok explained that the medals would signal to any Gublin in the kingdom that the bearer was under the King's personal protection. While wearing them, Tak, Luff, and Brieze could wander through any cave or tunnel in the Gublin realm in perfect safety, if they cared to. "Though given the current feelings most Gublins have about humans, I wouldn't advise this just now," Deelok added.

"Don't worry," Luff spoke up quickly. "We won't."

"You must thank your King for us," Brieze said. "We are honored by his gift."

"I will," Deelok said. "And now, since I have been your host, I will present you with my own gifts." He fixed his eyes upon Brieze and considered her carefully. "Yes...yes," he murmured. "I have just the thing." He moved about the cave, searching the stacks and rows of stone shelves carved into its walls. To the humans' surprise, he did so while seated in his chair. They hadn't noticed before, but small wheels had been ingeniously fastened to the legs of Deelok's chair, so that the Gublin was able to scoot himself around the cave while sitting in the chair simply by using his legs. Tak and Brieze exchanged glances. A chair with wheels! They had never imagined such a thing. Finally, Deelok located a shiny cube made from finely beaten bronze, edged and inlaid with gold. A winding key protruded from one side. He placed the cube in Brieze's hands. "Go ahead," he said. "Wind the key."

She wound the key and let it go. Strange music emerged from the box, sounding as if it were played on tiny bells. It was an eerie, haunting piece of music, in a key none of them had ever heard before. It started with one melody line, then another joined in, then another and another. Some of the notes sounded right to their ears, while others sounded too sharp or flat, but as the notes mixed and joined and wound about each other, the result made the hair on their arms and necks rise with a shiver of delight.

When the tune was over, the music had cast such a spell over them that no one wanted to break the silence. Finally Brieze said, "It's absolutely beautiful." Her black eyes shone. "What is the name of that tune?"

"Ahh, I hoped you would ask," Deelok said. "It's what made me think of this gift for you. That song was written by one of our most famous composers. The name of the song roughly translates as *A Lullaby for My Lovely Daughter*."

"Thank you," Brieze said in a hushed voice, wiping a tear from her cheek.

Deelok turned to Luff. "Now for you, young one," he said. After more scooting and searching, Deelok located a gift for Luff on one of his shelves. "Hold out your hand," he said to the boy.

Luff did so, much more eagerly than he would have thought possible just a few hours before.

Into his palm Deelok placed a mechanical bat. Though made of metal, it was life-sized and lifelike in every way, from the fine webbing of its folded wings to the delicate curves of its tiny pointed ears. "Hold your hand out straight and still, and keep it there," Deelok said. As Luff did so, Deelok gently pressed upon the bat's left ear. The ear moved slightly backward, and there was a faint click. Then the bat's wings unfurled. It leapt off Luff's palm and flew about the cave, its flittering wings looking for all the world like real bat's wings. It darted up high, then dove low, then circled Luff's head a few times while the boy looked up at it, mouth agape, trying to remember to keep his hand held out. Finally, the bat landed directly onto Luff's open palm—making Luff emit a little yelp of delight. The bat folded its wings and went still.

"Do you like it?" Deelok asked.

"Do I!" Luff said, grinning.

"In addition to a source of power that will last for years, that particular *animatron* contains a system of gyroscopes and magnets that keep it internally oriented to our world's gravitational and magnetic fields," Deelok said. "It always knows where it is. It knows where it started from, and it is designed to always return to the same spot."

If Luff didn't understand the part about gyroscopes and gravitational fields, he understood the part about the tiny mechanical creature always returning to its starting point. "Wait till the boys on Gatmont see this," he said. "Thank you!"

"Finally, you," Deelok scooted himself close to Tak and looked intently into his eyes. Tak squirmed but met the Gublin's gaze. Deelok's big black eyes seemed infinitely deep, like the nighttime sky, and Tak had the feeling that the wizard could see directly into his mind.

"Yes...something *else* for you I think," Deelok murmured. "Tell me young one, you have a tendency to get into trouble, don't you?"

Tak nodded. Luff and Brieze also nodded unconsciously in agreement.

"And you have a habit of being in the wrong place at the wrong time, or am I mistaken?" Deelok asked.

Tak nodded again.

"I think I have just the thing," Deelok said. He scooted over to a far corner of the cave and brought back a dressing dummy, the kind tailors use to make clothes with. This dummy was on a stand also outfitted with wheels. Deelok scooted it to Tak's side. The dressing dummy was not hung with fancy clothes. Upon it hung a shirt of chain mail, made of interlocking rings so small that a single one would fit comfortably on the tip of a pinky finger. "I was making this for a young cousin of mine, on my mother's side," Deelok said. "But I have a feeling you will find it more useful. Do you mind if I take a few measurements?" Deelok produced from his robe a length of measuring tape. "Hold out your arms."

Tak obeyed. In the space of a few heartbeats, Deelok used the tape to take Tak's neck, chest, and arm length measurements. The measuring tape disappeared back into the folds of Deelok's robe, and the wizard wheeled the chain mail shirt on its dressing dummy over to his worktable. Then his hands flew, almost too fast for Tak to follow. The Gublin used a bewildering variety of tools. Tak was aware that the Gublin was clipping rings away from the shirt. They dropped onto the floor with little *pings* and rolled away into the dark corners of the cave. Deelok was also adding rings here and there, using other tools to fasten and weld them in place.

"There," Deelok said, pulling the chain mail shirt off the dressing dummy and rolling it up into his hands in preparation for putting it over Tak's head. "Take off your shirt and let's see how this fits."

Tak again obeyed. Deelok pushed the chain mail shirt over Tak's head and pushed and pulled his arms through the sleeves, for all the world like his mother making him try on a new wool sweater she'd knitted him for winter. The metal rings were cold against Tak's bare skin, making him shiver.

Deelok scooted back and appraised his work. "Not bad," he said. "How does it feel?"

Tak swung his arms experimentally. He'd worn chain mail before, during his exercises with his father and the swordmaster. Those mail shirts were heavy and cumbersome, and they pinched his chest and armpits when he moved. This shirt felt as light and comfortable as any summertime shirt he'd ever worn. It didn't pinch at all. But it did hurt where the rings grazed over his wounded shoulder. Tak winced and rubbed his wolf bite.

Deelok smiled. "The fit is good," he said. "If a wolf tries to bite you in that, he'll break his teeth. There hasn't been a blade forged yet that will pierce those rings. They're fashioned from a special alloy of my own devising."

"I don't know how to thank you," Tak said.

Deelok tossed Tak his shirt. "You can thank me by wearing it," he said. "Keep it on under your clothes. Sleep in it. At least for the next week or so. You'll find it's quite comfortable."

Tak pulled on his fabric shirt over the chain mail. Already the metal rings had warmed with the heat of his body and no longer felt uncomfortable against his skin.

"I hope you won't need it," Deelok sighed.

* * *

With Deegor leading and Deelok guiding them from behind with nudges and whispers, Tak, Luff, and Brieze made their way upward from Deelok's cave through a few dark twists and turns of tunnel. They emerged to the world above through an exit that was nothing more than a large crack in a low, rocky hill. Deelok called it his side door.

It was scarcely any lighter outside the Gublin caves and tunnels than it had been inside. The damp, humid cloud mist closed in all around them. The sun had set. They couldn't see any stars through the mist, of course, but there was a dim, fuzzy patch of light low in the sky that must have been the moon. The Gublins had no problem locating the path in the dark, and soon they were all ascending the mountainside. Tak, Luff, and Brieze unslung their bows and nocked arrows, keeping their ears and eyes open for any sign of wolves. The Gublins kept their hands close to their sword hilts.

Tak was distracted, however, by an idea that kept nagging at him. His mouth squinched up the way it did when he was thinking hard. The wizard's words kept replaying in his mind. *"You are familiar with coal, yes? These bubbles are a very similar thing. But instead of being solid they are gaseous in nature.*

Does that make sense?"

"Deelok," Tak said. "When you and the King agreed the gas bubbles could be contained, how do you plan to do that?" he asked.

"We will pump the gas into large storage tanks, probably made from glass, or possibly aluminum. Maybe aluminum lined with glass," Deelok scratched thoughtfully at his chin. "We haven't worked out the details yet."

"This gas. Is there any way to make it...burn slowly instead of exploding all at once? You know, the way coal burns?"

"Probably," Deelok said. "You'd need some mechanism for slowly releasing the gas from its storage tank. Some kind of valve, and metal piping of course."

"What are you getting at?" Brieze asked.

And then Tak had it. The exploding gas bubbles were a problem, yes, but also a potential solution! "The kingdom is running short of coal," Tak said. "And your father said this gas was like coal, but different. The Gublins say it can be stored and burned safely. Why couldn't we use this gas as fuel to make up for the coal shortage?"

At that, both Brieze and Deelok went "Hmm!"

The group walked in silence for a while with Tak, Brieze, and Deelok deep in thought. Luff and Deegor exchanged puzzled glances and shrugged. Brieze chewed her lower lip pensively, her brow furrowed. "You know," she said to no one in particular. "*I* really should have thought of that first."

When they reached an altitude where the cloud mist had thinned enough for them to see by moonlight, Deelok halted. "Deegor and I dare go no further," he said. "Your

King has likely placed scouts on the lower reaches of the mountains to keep an eye on our movements."

Tak frowned. Humans scouting below the clouds? He'd never heard of such a thing. It would have to be brave men undertaking such a mission. But the Gublin wizard probably knew what he was talking about. He seemed to know things about the brewing state of war that he wasn't sharing with them.

"You'll reach the gate in about a mile," Deelok said. "We'll stay here and listen close, but I doubt you'll be in any danger. I don't smell any wolves on the wind tonight."

"Well," Brieze said. "I guess this is goodbye."

The humans and Gublins shook hands solemnly. "I wish you the best of luck on your diplomatic mission," Deelok said. "And it is my dearest wish that you three should come back and visit me again one day."

"I'd like that," Tak said, and he was surprised to realize he meant it.

FOURTEEN

They didn't run into any human scouts on the way back up to the little wrought iron gate. Rather than trying to find their way over the old rocks on either side in the dark, they went through the gate. Its old, rusted iron creaked loudly in the night.

At the sound, several torches blazed up to reveal a squad of humans who had been waiting for them in the darkness at the edge of the apple orchard. They wore the blue uniforms of airmen with the *Dragonbane's* insignia on their shoulders. They were Admiral Scud's men. A small transport ship was anchored to the ground nearby with several heavy ropes and stakes. It hovered high above the apple trees, straining against the ropes, its hull faintly visible in the torchlight.

"So here you are," a lieutenant said. "Back from a little visit with the Gublin's, eh? You really should have taken the trouble to hide your ships better if you didn't want to be found. They were visible from the air."

The men started to surround them, but didn't draw their weapons. As the men moved in, Tak looked instinctively behind him and saw more men approaching from the rear. Tak and his companions were caught in a pre-planned trap.

"We weren't trying to hide," Brieze said, her arms folded

across her chest, not the least bit intimidated. "We are on the King's business, as Admiral Scud should know." Brieze explained that her father had sent her to speak with the Gublins in his place, and that Tak and Luff had joined her as her escort.

"So you say," the lieutenant replied. "I hope you don't mind if we search you…?"

"Fine," Brieze said. "But my father will know of this."

The men searched their persons and their packs, but they did so gently and respectfully, especially for Brieze. No one had a wish to upset the wizard by mistreating his daughter. The men noted the Gublin pins the three young sky riders wore on their chests. They found Deelok's mechanical gifts in Luff's and Brieze's packs. They also found Tak's obviously Gublin-made chain mail shirt beneath his clothes.

"I need to see the King immediately," Brieze said. "I have important information for him. I would be pleased if you would take me to him."

"Hold on there, miss," the lieutenant said. "These two boys escaped from Admiral Scud after spying on his meeting with the wiz…uh, your father. And you admit to visiting and talking with the Gublins. You emerge from the dark wearing some kind of Gublin emblem and bearing Gublin armor and other devices…"

"Mere toys!" Tak exclaimed.

"That mail shirt is no toy," the lieutenant said. "How can we be sure that…that…?" He sighed, hesitating to say what he meant. It would amount to accusing the wizard's daughter of treason.

Brieze finished the thought for him. "How can you be

sure we aren't *spies*?" she said. "Is that what Admiral Scud thinks? If so, he's a royal fool!"

The lieutenant's face reddened in the torchlight. But he maintained a respectful tone. "My orders, miss, are to bring you to Admiral Scud. I think you should tell him your tale, and then he can decide whether or not you should see the King."

"Admiral Scud will decide no such thing," Brieze said. "But if you want to bring us to him first that's fine. I want a word with him anyway."

* * *

There was no point in trying to return to the *Dragonbane* at night. The lieutenant only said that the ship was "away to the southeast" investigating the latest appearance of giant gas bubbles, and that it wasn't running any lights and would be impossible to find in the dark. Running without lights at night, Tak knew, was standard for ships of the royal fleet during times of war. He didn't like the sound of that, but when he asked the lieutenant why the *Dragonbane* was doing so, he got a look that said it was none of his business.

So they made camp with tents and bedrolls from their respective ships. The men cooked a pot of wildfowl stew over the fire, with onions, carrots, and herbs, and they la-dled out some for their "guests" in wooden bowls. As they ate around the fire, nobody talked. But some of the men stole looks in Tak's direction that made him think they *did* suspect he was a spy for the Gublins. Or perhaps they were just amazed that he and his friends had journeyed below the clouds to see the Gublins and had returned to tell the tale. Tak could hardly believe it himself. Either way, sentries were posted outside their tents all night.

In the morning, they packed up their gear. Scud's men launched the *Arrow* and *Ram* off the mountainside and got them airborne. Tak watched anxiously, biting a thumbnail, as the small craft were secured to the transport ship with tow lines. But the *Dragonbane's* crew were expert airmen. The *Arrow* didn't suffer the tiniest nick or scratch. A rope ladder lowered over the side of the transport ship. Some men scurried up the ladder while others made ready to pull up the anchoring stakes. These men would have the job of climbing up the dangling ropes once the ship was airborne and hauling the ropes in after them.

Before they ascended the ladder and made sail, however, the lieutenant ordered the three young sky riders to remove their weapons and their parachute packs and hand them over. This was standard procedure with prisoners. It was too easy for a prisoner wearing a parachute to simply jump overboard at the first opportunity and steer himself to safety. Tak and Luff hesitated. They were extremely uncomfortable with the idea of taking off their chutes. But they were surrounded by Scud's men. There was nothing to do but unbuckle their packs and hand them over. The boys felt naked and vulnerable without the familiar weight of the packs on their backs.

Brieze leveled her black gaze at the lieutenant. "You are making a big mistake," she said, "to make prisoners of us."

"My sincere apologies miss," the lieutenant said. "But I have my orders. I'll need your parachute."

"As it happens," Brieze said, "I'm not wearing one."

The lieutenant's eyes widened in amazement, then narrowed suspiciously. "Hand over your pack, miss," he said.

Brieze shrugged, then unbuckled her pack and tossed it at the lieutenant, with more force than was strictly necessary. He caught it with a grunt, then examined it. Sure enough, there was no parachute compartment to it. It was just an ordinary backpack.

"Why do you fly without a chute?" he asked, astonished.

Brieze folded her arms across her chest. The loose sleeves of her robe rippled in the wind. "There's much you don't know about the ways of wizards," she said. "But I'm sure my father will be happy to explain to you...when you meet."

Brieze's implied threat unsettled the lieutenant, who was already a little unsettled by this mysterious girl. He didn't want to think about meeting the wizard and having to explain making a prisoner of his daughter. The lieutenant hastily tossed the pack to one of his men. "Stow this with the others," he growled. "And keep a close eye on these three. Now let's get underway men, without any more delay!"

*　*　*

When the transport ship caught up with the *Dragonbane* a few hours later, she was many miles southeast of Selemont. She wasn't moving. She was hovering in one spot, at an extremely low altitude, practically sitting upon the surface clouds. Tak had never seen a battleship do anything like that. It is, in fact, a difficult thing for a battleship to do. Tak couldn't help but wonder why. He took out his spyglass. Luff and Brieze did too.

Through their glasses, the three sky riders saw that the *Dragonbane* was dropping bombs.

The bombs were no more than powder kegs reinforced with extra steel bands and fitted with long fuses. They rolled from the deck with their fuses burning and quickly disappeared beneath the clouds. Tak heard muffled booms and caught brief flashes of explosions that lit up the surface clouds from below.

Tak's heart sank. Here they had promised the Gublin King that they would stop Scud's attacks, and the very next morning Scud was dropping bombs on them. At least, Tak assumed the bombs were meant for the Gublins. He exchanged a puzzled look with Luff. Gublins lived deep underground, safe from any explosions on the surface. Gublins came to the surface only at night. Trying to harm them by dropping bombs blindly beneath the clouds during the day seemed at best useless, at worst crazy. Had Scud somehow lost his mind?

What the boys didn't know was that several large gas bubbles had been seen yesterday afternoon emerging from the exact spot the *Dragonbane* currently hovered over. Scud had ordered all other ships out of the area, on the pretext of safety. He said the *Dragonbane* would remain in the vicinity, to observe. But once all other ships were gone, Scud maneuvered his battleship directly over the spot where the gas bubbles had emerged. Then he ordered that bombs be dropped. He reasoned, correctly, that a vent or vents to a Gublin mine must lie directly below. If he could get just one bomb to drop into one of those vents, it would cause a substantial amount of damage to the mine and miners below the surface.

It was also ridiculously dangerous. If another gas bubble emerged, it would hit and destroy the *Dragonbane* before the ship's crew would even have a chance to react.

Brieze seemed to understand what Scud was up to. She was beside herself with fury. As soon as the transport ship approached near enough to the *Dragonbane* to tie up she leapt from the railing onto the deck of the battleship. She took the men on board by surprise—no one tried to stop her as she stalked toward the command deck, flew up the ladder to it, and thrust her face up at Admiral Scud's as he stood watching the bombs rolling off the deck below.

"Stop what you are doing, *immediately!*" Brieze said.

Scud didn't bother looking at her. He shrugged and sucked his teeth thoughtfully. "I don't take orders from little girls," he said.

"But you take orders from the *King*," Brieze said. "Has he authorized this bombing...or your underground attacks? These are acts of war you know! You can't just take it upon yourself to do this!"

"I am not at liberty to divulge the King's orders to his Fleet Admiral to just anyone," Scud said. "And especially not to little girls who...how shall I say it...appear to be in close contact with the Gublins."

"My father sent me to talk to the Gublins in his place. *You* requested that he do so yourself. Don't you remember?"

"I remember your father said he would send *someone*. He didn't say anything about sending *you*. All I know about *you* is that you helped these two—" and here Scud gestured to Tak and Luff, who'd caught up to Brieze and stood to either side of her on the command deck, a little breathless and accompanied by many armed men, "spy on me and *then* you helped them escape when they'd been discovered."

The lieutenant from the transport ship had also reached the command deck. He whispered in Scud's ear.

"Aha!" Scud said. "And when we finally find the three of you, you are sneaking up the mountainside at night wearing Gublin emblems and carrying other Gublin devices."

"You think we are spies?" Brieze demanded.

Scud shrugged. He in fact did not believe they were spies. But that is exactly what he wanted others to think. In the city of Selestria, Scud's allies and accomplices were spreading this rumor on the streets, and in court. Scud suspected that the young sky riders might have information that would turn people against his plan of starting a war with the Gublins, so it was important to try to discredit them. "I think your recent activities are suspicious and warrant investigation," he said. Many of Scud's men, a large group of which had assembled on the command deck, murmured in agreement.

"My father sent *me* to talk with the Gublins and no one else," Brieze said. "I have discussed the matter with the Gublin King and have important information. These gas bubbles are not weapons. They have been released by accident and the Gublins have promised to stop—"

"They have, have they? Well, three more appeared yesterday afternoon at just this spot. Nearly took out another one of my ships. Does that sound like stopping to you?"

"Yesterday afternoon was when I was talking with the

Gublin King. It takes *time*. They have to shut down their mining operations and figure out a way to contain the gas. I promise you they are doing this."

"Hmm," Scud said. "So what am I supposed to do? On the word of a little girl?"

"On the word of an official emissary from the Kingdom of Spire, you must stop your hostilities immediately," Brieze said. "The deaths you've caused have made the Gublin people eager for war. The Gublin King does not want war. He will stop the gas bubbles. You will stop your attacks. Otherwise, *you* will have started another war with the Gublins. Do you really want that on your hands?"

Scud grinned a wicked grin, making his white scar twist and turn over the deep furrows of his cheek. He stuck his face close to Brieze's and said quietly, almost whispering to her, "Yes, missy, as a matter of fact I do. Nothing would make me happier."

Brieze held his eyes and didn't back up an inch. She squared her shoulders and gave him glare for glare. Tak had to admire her. First facing the Gublin King in the underworld, now going toe-to-toe with Admiral Scud on the deck of his own battleship. She was an extraordinary girl. One day she would be wizard. Already, she was not one to be crossed.

"Why?" Brieze asked, her eyes locked with Scud's. "Why do you hate them so much?"

"Why?" Scud echoed, mocking her tone. "Why do you *love* them so much? Do you know what they did to us thirty-seven years ago?"

Scud's men tensed. They knew the topic of Gublins was a sore point for their admiral and brought out the worst in him. They knew how to read his face, and they could tell he was about to strike. But to strike the wizard's daughter! That would be dangerous. Nevertheless, Scud's men were loyal, and they were used to facing danger on his behalf. Many of the men who surrounded the three young sky riders on the *Dragonbane*'s command deck were the same men who had ventured into the mines to kill Gublins at Scud's command.

"I know you are attacking the Gublins without the King's orders," Brieze said. "And I am going to tell him about it."

Scud struck—his hand snaked out and wrapped around Brieze's throat. "Oh you will, will you?" Scud's face had gone a deep red that was nearly purple, and it was so close to Brieze's face that their lips nearly touched. "Do you know what you are?" Scud asked. His voice had started out deadly calm and quiet, but it rose to a shout that sent flecks of spittle flying as he shook Brieze by the throat. "You're nothing but a little bastard girl from a backwater mountain who's gotten way too big for her britches. You're a damned Gublin lover! You've no business interfering with me!" He shoved Brieze so that she fell sprawling to the deck. "Seize her!" he shouted to his men. "Seize them all!"

Tak and Luff were grabbed by many pairs of strong hands. But Brieze, quick as an angry cat, twisted out of the grasp of Scud's men and leaped into the ship's rigging. In the space of two heartbeats, she'd climbed the ratlines of the main foremast shroud to a spot above their heads, out of their reach. She paused and looked down at Scud. Her long braid whipped in the wind. There were red finger marks on her throat. And there were tears on her cheeks, as much from Scud's hurtful words as from his painful choking grip.

"I'm going to see the King," she said, her voice hoarse.

"And then I'm going to summon my father."

Scud guffawed. Many of his men laughed with him. "And how exactly are you going to manage that, missy?" he asked. "Seems to me you're trapped on my ship. Caught in my rigging without a parachute. Like a fly in a web. Right men?"

To Tak and Luff, this seemed exactly true. More of the *Dragonbane's* crew were stationed in the rigging above Brieze. They made their way down toward her.

"Let's think of another fate for you," Scud said, his voice supremely confident. "You and your little rat friends are just going to disappear. Victims of the Gublins I'm afraid. Or some other violent and unfortunate end in the underworld. It's a dangerous place you know. Haven't you heard? No one who ventures beneath the clouds ever returns. I don't think many people will find it hard to believe that you did-n't, either."

"So you mean to kill us?" Brieze said.

"Oh no, not at all," Scud said, pretending to be shocked at the thought. Then he grinned his scar-twisting grin. "All we mean to do is tie a few cannon balls to your legs and toss you overboard. It's the fall that will kill you, I should think."

Brieze shut her eyes, and she chewed her lower lip as she did when she was thinking. A strand of her windblown hair had caught in the corner of her mouth. Then she opened her eyes and fixed them on Tak and Luff. "I need you to trust me," she told them. "No matter what he says, he won't do it." Then she squinted out into the wind, almost as if she were trying to read the nearby currents.

"Oh I'll do it all right," Scud said. "Don't you boys worry about that." The men in the rigging above Brieze had nearly climbed down to her.

And then, to everyone's surprise, Brieze leaned out far from the shroud, holding onto a ratline with only one hand, and she flexed her knees, preparing to jump.

"You are brave boys," she said to Tak and Luff. "You have been good friends to me. Thank you."

"Wait!" Tak shouted. "Stop!"

Brieze jumped into the sky.

She fell and disappeared below the deck rail. Everyone, Admiral Scud included, rushed to the rail and looked down, expecting to see her body slowly disappear beneath the clouds.

Instead, they saw a slim black figure gliding on the wind. Her arms and legs were outstretched, and what had been the loose folds of her robe had turned into wings, stretched taut and filled with air. Brieze executed a few experimental turns and loops, then she caught an updraft that took her above the *Dragonbane*. She rose upward in ever-widening spirals. When she'd risen so high that she looked like just another bird in the sky, she found a northward current and disappeared, headed in the direction of Selemont.

Tak and Luff, leaning on the rails of the *Dragonbane* and watching, exchanged wild grins.

"So *that's* how she landed on the *Arrow* from the floating island," Luff said.

Tak had no words. But if he could have said one at the time, it would have been, "*Extraordinary*."

After a moment or two, Admiral Scud recovered from his surprise. "Full about!" he shouted to his men. "After her! Back to Selemont. We can't have her telling tales to the King." The *Dragonbane's* crew scrambled across her decks to comply with the order. Scud leaned his elbows on the command deck rail. His mind was clearly racing. He folded his hands together and rubbed the stubble on his chin against his knuckles. Once again, Tak saw the wheels turning behind those stormcloud-gray eyes. Scud was trying to figure out his next move now that Brieze had changed the game with her surprise escape.

"You'll never catch her," Tak said.

Scud backhanded Tak across the face. So hard that Tak fell to his knees on the deck.

"You misbegotten fool of a boy," Scud said. "I don't *need* to catch her. I just need to get back to Selemont with you two, hand you over to the King, and tell him and the court that I caught the three of you giving information to the Gublins. Anything she says—or that you say—will seem like wild and guilty lies after that."

Tak glared up at the admiral, dabbing with his thumb at the blood on his lip. "Do you really think you can get away with this?"

Scud smiled another one of his unsightly smiles. "Why not? Half the lords at court are already eager for war and think that you're spies. It will be my word against yours. And when it comes to military matters and the kingdom's security, who do you think the court and the King will believe—the celebrated Admiral of the royal fleet or a freakish wizard-girl, a goatherd, and the famous spoiled Spinner brat?"

Tak didn't have an answer for that. Scud's men grabbed him and hauled him to his feet. They grabbed Luff, too.

"Take them to the brig," Scud ordered.

FIFTEEN

The high northward current Brieze had caught was not wide or strong enough to carry a battleship. So the *Dragonbane,* which had little coal to spare, had been forced to make its way home on a lower and slower current. In fact, by the time the *Dragonbane* tied up at castle Selestria's main dock that afternoon, Brieze had already had an audience with the King. She had told him what she knew, and she had been dispatched in one of the royal fleet's fastest courier ships—a sleek ship that could travel several times faster than the *Dragonbane*—to find her father on the floating island and summon him back to Selemont. Fireworks or no fireworks, the wizard would be needed if it came to war with the Gublins.

So when Admiral Scud entered the throne room atop the keep of castle Selestria with Tak, Luff, and a large group of his armed men in tow, he had some serious lying to do. Not only to the King, who was seated on the throne, but to the assembled group of advisors who were present. All eyes in the room fixed on Scud. All eyes but one pair, actually. These belonged to Tak's father. Tak's father looked at Tak with a mixture of relief to see that he appeared to be unharmed, shock and disbelief about his present situation, and an extra glint in his eyes that said *if you manage to get out of THIS trouble you will be in much MORE when you get home.* The artery in the hollow of Tak senior's throat pounded. Tak knew the only thing that kept his father from leaping off the dais and hauling him out of the room that instant was it would be an intolerable breach of protocol in the present situation and presence of the King.

At the foot of the dais to the throne, Admiral Scud and his men stopped. Scud made a low, courtly bow to the King. After that, he kept his chin up. His eyes blazed with sincerity and righteous anger. It was clear that he had important news for his Highness, but that he knew he could not speak until the King spoke first. The whispering advisors hushed.

"Admiral Scud," the King said, his voice echoing in the chamber. "Is it true what the wizard's daughter has told us? Have you taken it upon yourself to attack the Gublins without my permission?"

Scud blinked in surprise as if he could not quite believe he'd heard the King correctly. "Did she say that?" he asked.

The King frowned and narrowed his eyes at Scud. "She did," he said. "And more."

Admiral Scud appeared to be at a momentary loss for words. "I...I feared she might invent some sort of tale when she escaped my custody on the *Dragonbane*," he said, slipping into the fancy language and tone that members of the court used rather than his usual rough way of speaking. "That is why I came here as quickly as I was able. The sad truth is that the young girl and her companions, whom you see here with my men, were caught spying on my conference with the wizard. I tried to apprehend them then, but they escaped. When we caught them later, it was clear that they had ventured below the clouds to visit with the Gublins. They were bearing Gublin emblems and devices. Their actions seemed...suspicious to me. But I withheld my judgment. My only concern was to bring them here so that you could judge for yourself, your highness."

However, the carefully crafted look on Scud's face said that he believed the young sky riders to be spies, as much as it grieved him to have to admit such an unpleasant truth.

The advisors whispered among themselves. Tak stood up straight, as he had been taught to do at court. His hands were bound with rope in front of him, as were Luff's hands. He gave an apologetic look to his father, and an imploring look to the King. But he did not speak, as much as he would have liked to. This is because Scud had warned him not to. And because one of Scud's men stood behind him with a concealed dagger pressed against his back.

The King looked as if the past several days had been hard on him. In trying to figure out what to do about the exploding gas bubbles and the increasing call among his advisors to go to war with the Gublins, he had gotten little sleep. His normally neatly trimmed gray beard had grown shaggy, and there were dark circles and puffy bags under his eyes.

Still, the King's mind was clear, despite his lack of sleep. He was a good judge of men. He knew the truth, and a lie, when he heard it. And he was struggling with the fact that in his heart he knew that Brieze had told him the truth and that Scud was lying. It was a hard thing to swallow—that the Admiral had betrayed him and was trying to start a war behind his back. That many of his own advisors and military men were on Scud's side. The King knew what needed to be done about it. Still, he hesitated. To side with a young girl, even the wizard's daughter, against an Admiral whose service to the kingdom was nothing short of legendary—that would appear foolish. The fact the decision would be based on nothing more than his own gut instinct would make it seem that much more foolish. There would be outrage. There would be backlash. There would be many who would call his judgment into question and debate whether he was a fit ruler. It would not be easy.

The King pushed himself up from his throne with a sigh. "Admiral Scud," he said, "you and your men will kneel."

After a moment's hesitation, Scud knelt. His men knelt too, following his lead. Tak breathed a sigh of relief as the man who had been pressing the dagger into his back removed it and hid it up his sleeve in order to kneel.

The King put a hand on his sword hilt. As he did so, the chamber's squadrons of guardsmen moved forward out of the shadows, hands also on the hilts of their swords.

"Cutbartus Scud," the King said, using Scud's first name and not his military title, "You are hereby relieved of command of the royal fleet and of your captain and admiral's rank, pending an investigation into your recent activities. Your men are similarly removed of their rank and duties until further notice."

Just for a moment, Scud's face changed. It was clear that he hadn't been expecting those words, and that they cut him deeply. Being an admiral and ship captain was all he knew. His face filled with shock and sadness. For a moment, he looked like nothing more than a baffled old man.

A deadly silence settled over the chamber. The King's guardsmen moved in closer, eyeing Scud's men warily. Scud's men eyed them back. For the men on the *Dragonbane*, their first loyalty was to Scud, even before the King. They loved and respected their admiral that much. They put their hands near their weapons, and they tensed, ready to leap up from their kneeling positions and fight if ordered to. It seemed that the Kingdom of Spire teetered on the brink of a civil war.

Scud's face changed back to its usual hard, scarred mask. He stood up, defying the King's order to kneel. His men stood up with him. Scud glared at the King with contempt, sneering. "You are a weak king," he said. "The citizens of Spire will be shivering in their houses this winter from lack of coal. Our battleships will be at the mercy of the winds. But you don't have the guts to do what needs to be done about it. You're afraid of war with the Gublins, and you'd rather side with that Gublin-loving little girl than me."

At this point, Tak, now free of the dagger that had been keeping him silent, spoke up. "Your majesty, everything Brieze told you is true!" he cried. "I was there. I saw it! He was dropping bombs on them and he threatened to—"

"Silence you miscreant!" Scud shouted. He grabbed Tak by the back of the neck and forced him to his knees. Tak winced in pain. With his hands bound, he couldn't fight back. "*Here* is who you should be punishing," Scud said to the King, his hand squeezing so hard that Tak cried out. "This boy has been spying and prying his entire life. He spied on me at the wizard's island. And he went with that girl beneath the clouds to meet with the Gublins and who knows what they actually—"

That was as far as Scud got. There was the *shhhhhhnk* of a sword being drawn and Tak senior leapt off the dais with a growl and attacked. Scud barely had time to let go of Tak and draw his own sword to parry Tak senior's lunge. It would have skewered him through the heart. Then the two men were locked in combat, swords ringing and clashing.

"Filthy goat," Tak's father said. "That's the last time you'll mistreat or malign my son."

"Thieving wretch," Scud replied. "You've taken everything from me. And now you want my life, too? Well come get it if you can!"

Tak fully expected to see his father cut to bits by Scud's sword. In fact, he'd unconsciously rushed forward to help his father. But Scud's men grabbed him and held him back. As Tak struggled against their grip and watched the fight, he realized that his father was holding his own against Scud. He was matching Scud swordstroke for swordstroke. Each man was trying to make the other give ground, but neither would budge. Tak couldn't understand why his father was faring so well against the best fighter in the kingdom.

The reason was that one's mental state is a big part of any fight. If you are afraid of your opponent, you are likely to lose. Fear paralyzes a person, slows the reflexes, dulls the wits, makes one a poor fighter. Scud won fights not only because of his skill with weapons but because everyone in the kingdom was afraid of him. Everyone, that is, except Tak's father. Tak senior was one of the few people in the Kingdom of Spire who knew the boy who hid behind the old, scarred mask of Scud's face. And Tak senior was not afraid of him.

The fight threw the crowded chamber into an uproar. Some of the King's guard surrounded the dueling swordsmen, trying to find a chance to intervene in the fight and disarm the men without getting their hands or heads severed. Other guards surrounded the King protectively with drawn swords. The King's advisors of course started shouting, and then pushing, at one another. Those in favor of Scud's plan for war and hoping to see Scud best Tak's father in the duel strove against those who backed Tak's father and sought a more peaceful solution to the kingdom's fuel problems. It wasn't long before blades were drawn on both sides, and there were not enough of the King's guard in the chamber to keep the peace. Throughout the chaos, the King sat on the throne with his head in his hands, massaging his temples as if he had a terrible headache and, by the look on his face, re-thinking his policy of allowing advisors to bear weapons in the throne room.

Things would have gotten completely out of hand had not a deafening voice roared, "*That is enough!*"

It was a voice of command, the kind of voice that is clearly heard above the roar of cannon fire and the screams of wounded men. The kind of voice that is instantly obeyed. Everyone in the throne room—even Scud, Tak senior, and the King himself—froze at the sound of it. The words boomed back and forth in the chamber, echoing off the curved walls in that cavernous space. The birds and reptiles roosting in the ceiling quivered quietly in fear, not daring to move or make a sound. Not a feather or scale dropped.

Captain Adamus Strake, of the former battleship *Vigi-*

lance, stood framed in the huge doorway to the throne room, breathing heavily. He had just arrived upon the scene. He wore a fresh captain's uniform, and he had his sword out, though he leaned on it as if it were a cane or crutch rather than brandishing it. His hands were wrapped in bandages.

As it turned out, the young surgeon who first examined captain Strake after his rescue made a mistake. The surgeon had noted the terrible burns on Strake's hands and face and assumed the rest of his body must be covered with similar burns. What the inexperienced surgeon didn't know was that airmen' uniforms, like the hulls of their ships, were made to be fire resistant. The burns under captain Strake's uniform were not nearly as bad as the visible ones. He was recovering quickly.

Captain Strake had never been a handsome man. His features were rough-cut and fierce looking, even frightening to some, and having been caught in the fiery explosion that destroyed his ship had done nothing to improve them. As he leaned in the doorway to the throne room, people exclaimed in shock at seeing him. Strake still lacked hair and eyebrows, although some stubble had grown in here and there. The features of his face had survived the fire intact, but they were crisscrossed and pockmarked with burn scars—some still an angry red, others having faded to dead white. If his face had been frightening to some before, it was frightening to all now. No one said anything to challenge his intrusion into the chamber. Not even the King.

Strake took a few steps forward. He moved stiffly, as if every step hurt him. He fixed his eyes on those of Scud's men who were still gripping Tak. He raised his sword and pointed it at them. His next words he spoke quietly, and this was somehow more frightening than his roar of command had been. No one had trouble hearing him in the absolute quiet that had settled over the room.

"Anyone who does not wish to lose his hands immediately," Strake said. "Will remove them from that boy's person."

Scud's men let go. Strake moved stiffly to Tak's side and put a hand on this shoulder. He smiled down at Tak and said in a low voice, "I owe you my life, lad, and my thanks." His eyes were friendly and Tak found himself smiling back at Strake despite his fearsome appearance. Strake raised his voice and said aloud to the room, "One hears a lot of rumors and gossip while lying idle in an infirmary bed. I have heard this boy called a traitor and a spy. I have heard it said he lied about risking his life to save mine. I am here to say this boy is no liar. I've seen few acts of bravery that could match what he did that day. This boy deserves to be honored by you—not suspicious looks and whisperings behind his back. And he deserves to have his side of the story told, and told fully in front of all of us, *without* interruption,"and with that Strake looked meaningfully and not-too-kindly at Scud. Captain Strake had a good idea about where the nasty rumors concerning Tak had originated. Scud glowered back, looking as if he were chewing on a particularly sour lemon, but said nothing.

"So if it pleases your Majesty," said captain Strake, "let's hear this boy's story."

The King nodded his agreement. Scud and Tak senior were parted by guardsmen, though each glared at the other to say that their fight was by no means over. Swords were sheathed all around. The King ordered that Tak's bonds be cut and that a chair should be brought for him. Captain Strake ushered Tak to sit in a spot at the foot of the steps to the throne. Tak's father came and stood at his son's side. They exchanged a look of understanding, and forgiveness. Tak senior put a proud hand on his son's shoulder.

"All right lad," Strake said, "just take a calm breath. Tell them about the *Vigilance* and about everything you've been up to since then. And take your time."

So Tak told them the story. About seeing that giant bubble rise shimmering from the surface clouds. The explosion that destroyed the *Vigilance*. His rescue of captain Strake. He told about why he had decided to break his father's grounding and follow the *Dragonbane* to the wizard's floating island. About picking up Luff along the way and meeting the wizard's daughter Brieze—although he left out a few of the embarrassing details there. About how Brieze had helped him spy on the meeting between the wizard and Scud and his men. What the wizard had said about the gas bubbles—that they were natural phenomenon released by the Gublin mines and not Gublin weapons. How the wizard had designated Brieze to visit and talk with the Gublins in his place and about how he and Luff had ended up accompanying her.

He told them about meeting with the Gublin King, the cave filled with thousands and thousands of angry, armed Gublins. How the King had assured them the Gublins had not realized the bubbles would be harmful to the world above and his promise to halt the release of the flammable gas and contain it. About how the Gublin King had asked for their help in return to stop the underground surprise attacks.

He told them about the time they had spent in Deelok's cave. About the kindness of the Gublin wizard and the ingenious gifts he had given to them. About their trip back up the mountainside, being picked up by Scud's men and taken to the *Dragonbane*. About the bombs rolling from the deck and Scud's threat to throw him and his companions overboard with cannonballs tied to their legs so that the news from their diplomatic mission would not hinder his plans for war.

At that, Scud growled as if to interrupt, but he was silenced by glances from Strake, the King, and especially Tak senior, who looked as if he were using every ounce of his willpower not to draw his sword and attack the admiral again. The King looked as if he were adding up the criminal charges against Scud in his head, and had just added attempted murder to the long list that included treason and perjury.

When Tak had finished his story, ending with Brieze's leaping escape from the deck of the *Dragonbane*, the crowd in the audience chamber began to murmur. Many nodded approvingly, looking at Tak with a new respect in their eyes. Others glared angrily at Scud. At a nod from the King, his guards took Scud's sword and laid their hands on him. Many voices in the chamber called for the King to deal out punishment to Scud and his men on the spot.

The King held up a hand for silence. "We will deal with Cutbartus Scud soon enough," he said. "Right now, we have another important matter to discuss." The King turned to Tak junior. "The wizard's daughter," he said, "Before she left, she said that you had some sort of idea about how these gas bubbles might actually be…used as fuel? Is that correct?"

Tak swallowed, hesitating. He wasn't sure of the idea himself. He was no scholar or wizard. He'd barely had the courage to bring it up to Deelok and Brieze. To propose it in front of the King and his advisors! What if it was…stupid… or just plain wrong? He would look like a fool.

Terentius Liberverm, standing among the King's advisors, cleared his throat and gave Tak an encouraging smile. "Go ahead son," he said, nodding. "Brieze explained it a bit to me and I think you are on to something."

That gave Tak the courage he needed. He recounted how the wizard had said the flammable gas bubbles were like coal, but in a different form. He explained that Deelok said it was possible to store the gas in containers and release it carefully so that it would burn slowly. "I know the kingdom is running out of coal," Tak said. "It just occurred to me we might be able to use this gas instead. The Gublins say it can be contained and burned slowly, so maybe we could use it instead of coal to heat our houses. Maybe even to power our battleships?"

At that the King's advisors began talking animatedly among themselves, although many were not enthusiastic about the idea.

"And how are we supposed to obtain these flammable bubbles," Gasparus Miner asked. "Are we to somehow snatch them from the sky without blowing ourselves up?"

Tak reminded him that the Gublins said they could put

the gas into containers with valves attached that would release it slowly.

"I see," Gasparus said. "So I imagine we are just supposed to walk beneath the surface clouds and ask the Gublins nicely if they would give us these containers of fuel?"

Many in the chamber laughed at that notion.

"No," said Tak. "I'd suppose we'd have to trade them something for it."

At that, there was an outcry from many.

"Establish trade? With the Gublins?"

"Impossible! They're savage monsters. One can't trade with the likes of *them*."

"Just as soon spit and roast us as look at us, you know."

"They eat *children*, for heaven's sake!"

The King kept his eyes fixed on Tak, stroking his beard thoughtfully. Terentius Liberverm was at the King's side, bending to whisper in his ear. The King listened, then gestured for all to be silent.

"So Taktinius Spinner junior," the King said. "You propose trade with the Gublins. An astounding idea. My advisor Terentius informs me that old texts speak of trade long ago between men and Gublins. But the details have been lost. Gublins certainly have plenty of iron, gold, gems, and precious metals of their own. They need none of ours. What in heaven could we offer them that they would want?"

The answer came to Tak in an instant. He had only to remember the ravenous, greedy light in Deegor and Deelok's eyes at the sight and smell of...

"Goats," Tak said confidently. "We could offer them goats. They'll do just about anything for goat meat, and it's one thing we've got plenty of."

At that, a stunned silence settled over the crowd as each person pondered the possibility. To trade goats with the Gublins in exchange for a new fuel that would solve the kingdom's coal scarcity problem? It was an extraordinary idea. Could it really be made to work? As farfetched as it sounded, there was something that made sense about it, something that couldn't just be dismissed. It was an arrangement that would benefit both sides.

One of the most important benefits, in some people's minds, was that the proposed trade arrangement would avoid the war that had been brewing with the Gublins.

On that point, however, they were mistaken. No one in that room knew it yet, but, as they were about to find out, the possibility of avoiding war with the Gublins had passed. One of the bombs that rolled off the deck of the *Dragonbane* that morning had indeed found its way into a vent and down a deep mineshaft. The explosion had not only collapsed a tunnel, killing and wounding hundreds of Gublin miners, but it had reached caves adjacent to the tunnel that were occupied by Gublin women and children. Many of them had been killed and wounded as well. The Gublins were crazed with fury. The Gublin King could no longer hold back his vengeful hordes.

The thoughtful silence in the throne room turned into a buzz of discussion as advisors talked over details of the proposal. Could the kingdom's homes and ships really be modified to use the gas as fuel? How much gas was there to be had? How many goats could the kingdom afford to trade on an annual basis? How many goats did one suppose the Gublins would accept in exchange? Who would draw up details of the proposal, and how in heaven would it be presented to the Gublins? How could they negotiate terms when neither group spoke each other's language?

The King and his advisors were so engrossed in their talk that at first they didn't hear the alarm bells ringing. They were the distant bells on the city's outer walls at first. When the alarm bells on the castle's own walls and towers began to clang loudly, people looked up in confusion. Some rushed to the chamber's tall windows and looked out. No dragons or attacking ships were visible in the sky. But shouts could be heard from below. People were running through the streets in panic. Merchants in the marketplace were hastily packing up and closing their stalls.

"What is the meaning of this?" the King said, hand on his sword hilt, poised for action. But before he finished the question, Sir Galfridus Stone, the King's commander of ground forces who was in charge of the city's defenses, rushed into the chamber. He bowed hastily to the King and whispered in his ear. The King's face, which had been bright with interest and hope at this new idea of trade with the Gublins, darkened. He closed his eyes, and once again he looked weary and sad. Then he opened his eyes. A grim line of determination set in his jaw. All eyes in the chamber were upon him.

"Ladies and gentlemen of the court," the King announced, his voice taking on the hard edge of command. "My commander on the ground informs me that his scouts have seen a large Gublin army moving on the lower reaches of Selemont beneath the surface clouds. We must prepare the city for attack."

At first, everyone was too surprised to speak. They stood rooted where they were as the alarm bells continued to clang and the shouts and cries from the streets below drifted through the windows. Finally, one of the King's military advisors spoke up.

"How many your Majesty?" the general asked. "How many Gublin soldiers?"

The King looked to Sir Galfridus for an answer. The commander licked his lips and spoke his next words as if even he did not quite believe them. "My scouts report they number in the tens of thousands. Almost too many to count. Forty or fifty thousand at least. Possibly more."

The people in the chamber, Tak included, emitted a collective gasp. Tak and his father exchanged looks. Forty or fifty thousand? Why, the entire army of Spire amounted to only fifteen thousand men, and these were spread out among the kingdom's mountains. There were likely no more than half of these—seven or so thousand—on Selemont itself.

The King glared bitterly at Scud. "Well Cutbartus," he said. "It seems we will have your war after all."

Sir Galfridus cleared his throat. "It looks as if the attack will come tonight," he said.

SIXTEEN

The people of Selemont and the city of Selestria prepared frantically for war. In the mountainside villages outside the city wall, houses and buildings were boarded up. Everything of value—livestock, food stores, fuel, water, weapons, gold and personal possessions—were hauled or carted inside the city to the castle. The roads that spiraled or switchbacked gradually up the mountainside were crowded with donkey-drawn carts crammed to overflowing and with families who struggled up the mountain on foot carrying their possessions in sacks flung over their backs. Soldiers directed traffic, cleared jams, and broke up the squabbles that inevitably erupted among the mob of frightened people all trying to reach safety at the same time.

It was a mercy that the summer solstice, the longest day of the year, was only a few days away. That meant there were still several hours of daylight to prepare. The Gublins, because of their sensitive eyes, would not attack until the sun had fully set. Had this war started during the winter season, the sun would have been touching the horizon already and the situation would have been even more desperate.

Inside the city wall, houses and buildings were likewise being boarded up and food, water, and valuables also being transported to the castle. In fact, the plan was for the entire population of Selemont to crowd not just behind the city's outer wall, but inside the castle itself. This was not as impossible as it might sound. The builders of castle Selestria had prepared her well for a siege. Underneath the castle, vast underground storerooms and deep wells had been dug. The storerooms were designed to hold not only huge amounts of food, water, and supplies, but to accommodate the populace as well. There were even underground pens for livestock. And the castle's walls and towers were high and strong. She had been built to withstand a massive attack. The city streets were thick with refugees seeking her shelter.

The decision had been made to crowd everyone and everything inside the castle because the King and his military advisors agreed that the chances were slim they could hold the city's outer wall for long against tens of thousands of Gublins. The wall was more than six miles in circumference, and sections of it were weak and in need of repair. Even with streams of soldiers and volunteers flying in from every nearby mountain to help defend the city, it was unlikely there would be enough men to properly defend the city wall. The King and his advisors took into account, too, that one Gublin soldier was worth two human fighting men. That made the already bad odds doubly worse for the human defenders. But no one wanted to give up the city wall without a fight. Teams of masons were hard at work patching holes and cracks and shoring it up as best they could with fast-drying mortar. Generals and their staff strode along the top of the wall, inspecting it and discussing how best to defend it and its four gates.

The sky above Selemont swarmed with airships. Tak, who stood on the deck of his house with Luff gaping upward, had never seen so many ships in the air at once. It seemed to him as if every airship in the kingdom must be racing to or from Selemont. Those heading away from the mountain were carrying people who wished to leave Selemont for the safety of other mountains. The King's scouts had seen no evidence that other mountains were in danger of attack. That made sense. If you wanted to deal a devastating blow to the Kingdom of Spire, your best bet was to strike at its heart. The Gublins knew this. The King had not *ordered* anyone to leave Selemont. The people of Spire are very attached to their home mountain. Most would rather die defending it than flee to another. But still, some of the old, the sick, and families with young children had chosen to leave.

The ships arriving at Selemont carried supplies, weapons, and above all men. The King had called for all of his soldiers that could be spared from nearby mountains to hasten to the defense of Selemont. He had also called for able-bodied men eighteen or older to volunteer to fight. The King did not draft or force any man to fight against his will. But he didn't have to. Once the call went out for volunteers, the men of Selemont swarmed the castle to enlist as volunteer soldiers. And ships full of more volunteers from nearby mountains were arriving every minute. Already, in public parks throughout the city, professional soldiers were drilling these volunteers, giving them a crash course in the tactics of Gublin fighting, which required two-man teams working together.

Gublins are not right-handed or left-handed. They use

both hands equally well and completely independently of each other. They fight with a sword in either hand, no shields, and are perfectly capable of engaging two human swordsmen at once. A single human swordsman, even a good one, will find himself badly mismatched against a Gublin. They can parry an attacking stroke with one sword and strike back with the other sword simultaneously—and blindingly fast. It usually takes two and sometimes even three humans to outfight a Gublin.

Tak and Luff leaned on the deck rail of the Spinner house. Through their spyglasses, they watched one of these drilling sessions at a park not far from Tak's house. Some of the volunteer soldiers looked awfully young to Tak, many no taller or bigger than he was. Many had no armor, and most that did wore incomplete sets that had been cobbled together from here or there. Many also handled their weapons and shields clumsily. They were obviously men more comfortable with hammers or hoes in their hands than spears or swords.

Part of Tak yearned to be down there drilling with those men. To take up his sword and join the battle to defend his mountain. To be a man and not a mere boy. But another part of Tak, a very large part of him in fact, was secretly glad that he was not old enough to be allowed to do so. He'd seen Gublins fight with his own eyes. He knew firsthand how inhumanly fast their swords flew, how ingeniously their armor was made, how terrifying it was to come suddenly face-to-face with one in the dark. He didn't like to think about what was going to happen when those clumsy farmers and craftsmen faced off against Gublin soldiers.

Tak's father was out there somewhere, drilling a group of men of his own. As a high-ranking advisor of the kingdom and trained swordsman, he was charged with leading a group of men in the city's defense. Tak's father had given his wife and son a long, hard hug goodbye before being whisked off in a royal ship to undertake his duties. He'd told his wife and son that he loved them. Tak couldn't speak. He struggled to force down the rising lump in his throat as he watched his father go. He and his mother held hands tightly. They tried to give each other reassuring looks, but the fear that Tak Spinner senior might not return to them showed all too plainly in their faces.

Tak's mother was busy inside the house. Like most of those who were born and lived on Selemont, she had not even considered leaving the mountain. She was working to gather everything she could into a cart parked nearby on the Southern Spiral road. In a few hours, she and Tak would make their way up to castle Selestria and join the populace of Selemont in the castle's underground vaults to wait out the battle.

Tak's assignment during all this confusion was relatively ordinary and would have even been pleasant, under other circumstances. His job was to work with Luff to repair the *Ram* as best he could and to send Luff on his way in the ship back to his family on Gatmont. There are few things that the boys of Spire like better than tinkering with and fixing up their airships. Both the *Ram* and the *Arrow* were tied up at the Spinner household's dock. The boys' ships had been delivered there from the *Dragonbane*.

And speaking of the *Dragonbane*, Cutbartus Scud was no

longer in command of that ship. The command of the *Dragonbane*, and the entire royal fleet along with it, had been given to Adamus Strake. The King had wanted to throw Scud and the men loyal to him into the castle's dungeon. But several military advisors had convinced the King otherwise. Every experienced soldier and ship were going to be needed in defense of the city, they'd argued. Therefore, the King had agreed that Scud and his crew would command a smaller ship, the *Dragonscourge*. This ship would join the royal fleet in encircling the city from above and warding off the Gublin attack with cannon fire. However, before allowing Scud and his men a reprieve from the dungeon, the King had made each one kneel before him and swear an oath that he would return, after the battle, to stand trial at court. The look on Scud's face as he swore this oath was a truly memorable one—it was as if each word that came out of his mouth tasted like goat dung.

On close inspection, the *Ram* appeared to Tak even more questionable in terms of its design and construction than it had originally. And its hull had been chewed on by hungry grekks. Many of the planks along its hull and bulwarks had sprung loose from the nails holding them down. They stuck out in warped curves. The fore and aft masts, normally straight and perpendicular, leaned apart from each other. Tak and Luff would have been hard pressed to repair the ship by themselves in the short time they had. Fortunately, Tak's neighbors and best friends, Lucias and Marcus Wright, had agreed to come over and do what they could before they too would join their family in the vaults below the castle.

If you needed to fix up an airship in a hurry, you could do much, much worse than having the help of Lucias and Marcus Wright. Sons of the chief Shipwright of the realm, these boys had learned to use some of the simpler shipwright's tools before they'd learned to walk. And they had built and flown their own airships while most boys their age were still learning how to dress themselves. They arrived at the Spinner household deck in one of their neatly trim little ships, loaded with spare pine planks and spare parts, nails, hot pitch, and tools of every size and description. They tied up, leapt out, and dragged the *Ram* onto the deck for a close inspection, tying her down across her bow and stern so that she would stay still. Lucias ran his eyes along the uneven lines of the *Ram's* hull and keel. Marcus inspected the torn sail and leaning masts. Each boy seemed not to see the actual ship itself, but the *idea* of the ship that was present among the warped and broken parts.

"Hmm…" Marcus said. "See there?"

"Uh huh," Lucias said, "And there?"

"Right," Marcus said, then turned to Tak. "Grab some of those nails and hand them to me, will you?"

For the next two hours, Tak and Luff were relegated to the position of assistants, handing the brothers tools and whatever else they needed and then standing back as the brothers went to work. In a much shorter time than seemed possible, the sagging and broken *Ram* began to stand straighter and taller. The awkward lines of her hull smoothed out under Lucias's and Marcus's hands. Her masts straightened. Her patched-up sail flapped eagerly at the gusting wind, and she tugged against the ropes that tied her down to the dock.

Lucias and Marcus stood back and surveyed their work.

"That should do you," Marcus said to Luff. "She'll get you back to Gatmont, or I've never had my hand on a tiller before."

"She's really not a bad little ship," Lucias said, "If you look at her with one eye closed."

"I don't know how to thank you," Luff said. He ran a hand along his newly rebuilt ship. All his usual bluster was gone. He clearly felt awkward and out of his element on Selemont among the Wrights and Spinners, people who lived in big houses under the shadow of castle Selestria, rubbed shoulders with the King and his advisors, and could work miracles with wood and sailcloth.

What he didn't realize was that the Wright brothers were equally in awe of him.

"You're the boy that walked under the clouds with Tak here and the wizard's daughter to talk to the Gublins on the kingdom's behalf," Marcus said. "No thanks are necessary."

"We are at your service," Lucias said, with a courtly bow. "Should it ever be required again."

There was one improvement to the *Ram* left to make. Tak had it in his hands. He'd brought it from a storeroom in the back of the house. It was the *Arrow's* spare sail, made of pure spider silk. They boys unfolded it on the deck. Strong as steel, light as feathers, it rippled in the wind like liquid silver.

"It's too much," Luff said.

"It's not enough," Tak answered.

The boys took down the *Ram's* old, patched sail and rigged up the new one. With the new sail, the *Ram's* transformation was complete. She was a different ship. She pulled impatiently at the ropes holding her down, eager to leap into the sky.

Tak and Luff faced each other. Tak held out his hand. He didn't know what to say. There seemed to be too much to say to his new friend. "Let the winds be kind to you," he said. "When you come back to visit, I'll show you all of Selemont, and we'll race that bunch of sticks against the *Arrow* and see what she can really do."

The Herders of Gatmont are not formal folk. They go with their gut. Luff ignored Tak's outstretched hand and wrapped his arms around his new friend in a crushing bear hug, pounding him on the back. "Be safe and well my friend," he said. "When you come to Gatmont, we'll teach you how to shoot straight. Maybe then you'll keep the wolf bites off you."

The boys grinned at each other, and then that was it. Luff climbed into the newly-rebuilt *Ram*. Tak, Marcus, and Lucias untied her bow and stern. As the ship began to rise on the wind, Tak, Marcus, and Lucias grabbed hold of her and ran her off the deck, helping her to catch the wind and rise into the sky. Luff tightened the sail, adjusted the tiller, and soon the *Ram* was just another speck among the frenzy of ships around Selemont, disappearing off to the north.

* * *

Tak helped to push the donkey cart loaded with Spinner family goods up the Southern Spiral road toward the castle. Normally, if Tak and his family wanted to visit the castle, they would have taken one of their airships, and they would have tied up at the castle dock and been greeted by courteous attendants who would have unloaded their ship for them, carried their things, and escorted them wherever they wanted to go. But the castle dock was now off-limits to all but ships carrying men and weapons. Families of Selemont wishing to wait out the battle in the castle, even those of high-ranking advisors, had to make their way themselves by cart and foot.

Tak had strapped on his sword for the trip. His mother had noted this with her all-seeing eyes but said nothing. Boys of Selemont were usually not allowed to go about wearing their swords except on special occasions. But it seemed to be allowed today. In fact, not only most of the boys that Tak saw, but most everyone in that line of carts and plodding families on the spiral road—young or old, man or woman—had some sort of weapon on them. A long knife tucked into a belt here. A hatchet gripped there. It was a silent acknowledgement that things might turn for the worst. Something everybody was doing but nobody wanted to talk about.

As the cart wound up the road closer and closer to the castle, Tak couldn't help but turn his head and look back at his house. And what he was looking at in particular was not the house, but at the *Arrow* tied up at the deck of his house. He had wished there were someplace safe to put her, but there wasn't. In the end he patted her hull goodbye and left her tied up where she was. It hurt him to leave her like that.

"Take a good last look," a boy a year or two older than Tak said, seeing Tak look wistfully over his shoulder. "If the Gublins get over the city wall, everything you see will be gone."

"Shut your mouth Jerome!" the older boy's mother said. "Stop trying to frighten everyone. You don't know what you're talking about."

"If the Gublins get over the city wall, they'll burn every house and everything they get their hands on," Jerome said. "That's what they did in the Gublin War, granduncle Julius said."

"Nonsense lad!" an old man shouted. "The Gublins won't *burn* anything. If you knew anything about them, you'd know their eyes can't stand bright fire."

"And your granduncle Julius loved drink and a good story much more than the truth," the boy's mother said. "I wouldn't put stock in any of his tales. Now stop it with your dramatics and put a shoulder to this cart."

"Fine," Jerome said. "I'm sure when the Gublins come they'll tiptoe through our gardens and wipe their feet politely on the mats before they enter our houses. Maybe they'll even ring the front bells to make sure they're not disturbing anyone who's still at home."

Nobody said anything to that. It was true, they had to admit to themselves, that an angry invading army was not likely to be gentle with their homes or property.

The old man finally sighed, "No one likes a smart ass, lad. Put your shoulder to the wheel."

Tak watched his house and the *Arrow* grow smaller and smaller with each curve of the road around the mountain until the *Arrow* looked like a tiny red balloon bobbing above the dock at the end of a string. In his mind, Tak cut that string and let her rise free.

SEVENTEEN

When the lower edge of the setting sun touched the horizon in Etherium's purple sky, everyone on Selemont held their breath. The Gublin attack would come once the sun had set. Everyone knew it was coming. They could *feel* it coming. Out on the dusky mountainside, nothing moved. Nothing made a sound. No hawk screeched. No dog barked and no goat bleated. Even the wind had stilled. But the air felt somehow alive. It crackled with energy as it did just before a thunderstorm. Somehow, the people of Selemont could feel the energy of the Gublin army massing, the energy of countless angry, living souls just beneath the clouds. It communicated itself to them through the air, prickling the skin on their arms and the backs of their necks.

Every fighting ship of the royal fleet was gathered in a protective ring above the city's outer wall. It was an impressive and reassuring sight to see the entire fleet sitting nose-to-stern like that, each ship presenting the cannons along its outward side toward the enemy below.

The shadows of the pine trees stretched longer across the mountainside. The sun half disappeared. The first stars appeared in the sky. Soldiers on the city wall gripped their weapons more tightly and narrowed their eyes as they peered into the dimness of the countryside below. Torches were lit and placed in every available spot along the wall. The torches blazed brightly, and soon it looked as if the entire wall was topped with a ring of fire. The better to ward off the Gublins with their sensitive eyes. Soldiers said silent prayers to their ancestors in the realm above, asking that they, their families, and their city be spared the worst of what might happen.

The sun sank out of sight completely. The sky turned black. More stars came out. As people's eyes adjusted to the darkness, the trees, roads, villages, and pastures out on the mountainside became visible in the moonlight and starlight. Every eye, every spyglass, was trained on the edge of the cloud mist at the base of the mountain, the border between the human world and the underworld.

Finally, the Gublins emerged from the mist.

In the darkness, with their pale skin and silvery armor shimmering faintly in the moonlight and starlight, they looked like an army of ghosts. Columns of them marched up every major mountain road. Rank upon rank of them advanced through the fields and pastures. And what made them seem even more like ghosts was that they moved in utter silence. No orders were shouted, no signal horns blew or drums beat as the vast army moved into position around the city, massing and organizing itself just out of cannon range. Gublins have a kind of sixth sense, an instinct, that allows them to act effortlessly as a group. Each individual can sense what the group is doing and respond accordingly. It is the same kind of instinct that allows huge flocks of birds to suddenly change direction all at once in mid-flight, and it makes a Gublin army all that much more formidable. It can instantly take advantage of any opportunity, any weakness or breach in an enemy's defense, without orders having to be shouted or troops being re-organized and re-directed by generals.

An hour passed. And then another. And still the Gublins kept coming. It became clear that Sir Galfridus's scouts had been right. Human soldiers' hearts sank as they realized there were in fact tens upon tens of thousands of Gublins surrounding their city. Too many to count. In every direction one looked below, every field and pasture, every hollow and clearing was filling with orderly battalions of armor-clad Gublins. And still column after column and rank after rank of them marched out of the clouds. It was as if the underworld were emptying itself of every last Gublin.

What nobody had bothered to remember, in contemplating a new war with the Gublins, was the issue of numbers. The Kingdom of Spire was a fair-sized realm as human kingdoms went. But because humans could only live on the mountaintops, they had a limited amount of space and natural resources to support a population. The Gublins, who had the whole of the underworld in which to live and grow, had no such limits. The last census of the Kingdom of Spire put the population at just over two hundred thousand souls. The population of the Gublin kingdom they were at war with, which was not even the largest under Etherium, amounted to more than two million.

All at once, the Gublin army went still. Every last soldier was in place. The city was completely surrounded. Human and Gublin stared at each other across a steep, rough mile of open ground.

The Gublins charged.

At first, the sound that reached the men on the castle wall wasn't even a whisper. More like a tickling feeling inside of the ear. Then it grew. It sounded like the sigh of a breeze, like the wind stirring the trees. Except there was no wind. It was the Gublins hissing. As their charge gained speed and momentum, the hissing grew to the frenzied howl of wind in a storm. Men on the wall felt a distinct tremor in the soles of their boots—the rumbling caused by tens of thousands of churning Gublin feet. It was as if the mountain were trembling at is roots.

Every human soldier—even the ship captains and generals on the wall—simply stared for a moment with his mouth hanging open. They knew it was happening. Yet somehow they couldn't believe it. They expected the Gublins would attack the city wall in several places at once. They didn't expect the attack would come from *everywhere* at once. What they saw was like a swarm of insects eating up the mountainside. Like an ocean of swords and armor rising up to engulf them.

Finally, the ship captains came to their senses and started bellowing orders. The ring of battleships fanned out and moved as close to the ground as they could. The captains knew they had to act fast, had to fire as many cannon volleys as possible to try to even the odds before that army reached the wall. The thunder of those first volleys going off—nearly simultaneously from every ship in the fleet—challenged the roar of the Gublin army. The cannon blasts lit up the night like flashes of lightning.

Royal cannoneers train and train again until they are able to hit a dragon on the fly at two hundred yards or more. They do not miss. Firing point blank into the charging Gublin army was horribly easy for them. The cannon fire tore huge holes in the ranks of advancing Gublins. But as fast as those holes were made, they filled up again. The Gublins kept coming. The ring of battleships fired a second volley. Then a third. A fourth. The night became thick with the sulfurous smell of gunpowder. Gublins screamed and died in droves. But their fellow soldiers loped over their bodies and kept up the charge. Many of the Gublins who volunteered to be in the front ranks were those whose close friends or family had been killed in the human attacks.

One last cannon volley and then the Gublins were within striking distance of the city wall, too close for the ships to fire upon without risking hitting their own men. The battleships were forced to rise and back off. They had to content themselves now with firing into the rear portions of the ever-advancing Gublin army. The men on the city wall were on their own. The archers there had time for one volley of arrows before the Gublins reached the wall. Arrows rained down on the Gublins, but few found their way through Gublin armor. The Gublins fired no arrows back. Because they had such poor eyesight, they had never developed the knack for long-range weapons. They specialized in fighting up close and personal.

The Gublins had not brought any siege ladders or grappling lines with them for scaling the wall. They didn't need them. Gublins lived in stone, and they could climb anything made of stone, as easily as any sky rider could climb a tree.

Each Gublin was perfectly capable of climbing the wall himself, using only one hand and his feet. The old wall had plenty of cracks and spaces between the stones that Gublins could use as hand and toe holds. That left one hand free to wield a sword as they climbed. Gublins began scaling the wall like so many armored beetles. Their bulbous black eyes and sharp teeth became visible in the torchlight at close range. The men on the wall frantically hurled down stones at them. Cauldrons of scalding oil were tipped over the wall in places. The screams and the smells were awful. Some of the volunteer men in a panic even threw down their shields and weapons at the climbing Gublins. But it made no difference. Gublins reached the top of the wall and vaulted themselves over the battlements. Those who wished to test their swords against the swords of the humans now had their chance.

Tak and his mother sat on a cot in one of the vaults beneath the castle. They had Avelina Wright, wife of the Shipwright Giraldus, and her twelve-year-old daughter Dulcia for company, sitting on a cot across from them. Lucias and Marcus, as well as the other brothers of the Wright family, were also there. But the boys couldn't sit still. They kept jumping up and wandering about. Everyone had sensed the attack above when it came, faintly heard the howling charge of the Gublin army and the blasts of the royal fleet's cannon volleys. Gunpowder fumes had drifted underground through air vents, making people wrinkle their noses. As if the smell hadn't been bad enough already. Excellent ventilation had not been one of the chief concerns of the engineers who had designed and built the old vaults. Neither had been excellent toilet facilities. These amounted to a few deep holes which had been drilled in the floor at one end of the vault, which men, women, and children alike were to use as they were able, without the benefit of privacy. Even so, after only a few hours, the smell from the pits was more than noticeable and less than pleasant.

Tak couldn't sit still. He kept standing up and sitting down. He went to the toilet facilities several times just to be able to move and have something to do. His mother was attempting to distract Avelina and Dulcia with the story of how she and Tak senior had met during the first Gublin War, but Tak had already heard that story and now he couldn't concentrate on the words. Trying to distract someone from the fact that the city above them was being attacked by a Gublin army was pretty much a pointless task. But Dulcia Wright sat still on the cot across from Tak's mother with her hands in her lap and nodded politely as his mother spoke. She tried not to look up at the ceiling each time she heard one of the cannon volleys from the royal fleet. She leaned against her mother, and Avelina Wright put an arm around her daughter, stroked the girl's blond curls reassuringly.

Tak was worried sick about his father. Each time he thought about the fact his father was out in that battle somewhere, it became difficult to breathe and he felt as if he might throw up. The worst thing about it was that there was nothing—*nothing*—Tak could do about it. His father would either live or he would die. Tak was helpless to affect the outcome. So he did his best to not think about it because he knew those thoughts would drive him crazy if he let them.

Instead, Tak thought about the *Arrow* tied up helplessly at his family's dock. If the Gublins did get inside the city wall, what would they do to his ship? He remembered how angry and savage the Gublins had been in the underground chamber of the Gublin King. He imagined them hacking at the helpless *Arrow* with their curved swords for the pure pleasure of destroying her. Now, Tak wished he had untied her and let her rise free into the sky. That way, she would at least have had a chance of surviving. It wasn't impossible that she would drift to another nearby mountain. Or be discovered and recovered in the air, although the odds were slim. At the very least, she would live out the end of her days in the sky.

Tak stood up abruptly, his hands clenched, the sheathed sword at his belt knocking against the wooden frame of the cot.

"Going to the privy *again*?" his mother asked.

"No," he said. "I'm going to try to find Lucias and Marcus. They went off that way."

"All right," his mother said. "But don't be too long about it. I don't want you out of my sight for long."

Tak nodded and stalked off. Being down in that crowded vault was exasperating. Every which way he turned, someone was in his way, bumping up against him. The place stank of sweat and fear. He shouldered his way aimlessly through the crowd for a while. Then he moved toward the entrance to the vault. The air was a little fresher there, by the large stone archway that opened up onto a long, steep flight of stone steps that climbed to the surface. Tak and his mother had descended those steps just a few hours ago. The stone stairway was still packed with families making their way down to the vault. Without quite acknowledging to himself what he was doing, Tak began to climb those steps, setting his shoulder against the flow of human traffic.

After several minutes of climbing and jostling against everyone hurrying down the steps, Tak popped up into the castle's courtyard. It was filled with people and confusion. Most of the people were civilians like himself and they were hurrying to get down the stairs that Tak had just climbed, or other stairways that led to similar vaults beneath the castle. Some of the people were soldiers, rushing this way and that and shouting to each other. There was a warm wind that smelled like sulfur. Distantly came the thunder and flashes from the royal fleet's cannons over the city wall, the clash of swords and noise of battle.

Tak looked toward the castle's Eastern gate, through which he and his mother had come. The iron portcullis was half raised. The massive wooden doors—each made from tree-sized planks of *ironwood* carved from Ironwood pines, and reinforced with bands and plating of actual iron—stood ajar. People from the mountainside continued to stream in through the gate. But there were also people going out, Tak noticed. Mostly soldiers and royal messengers being sent to the city wall, but also one or two ordinary people like himself. Tak edged closer to the gate. Then a little closer. It seemed that everyone was still being allowed to come and go at will. He sidled a step closer.

"Hey there lad, what's your business?" called one of the

gate's guards, who had noticed him shuffling toward the massive doors.

"Umm," Tak thought fast. "I need to get something important from my house."

"Well be *quick* about it lad!" the guard said. "Don't stand there hanging about like a feather on a weak breeze! These gates won't be open forever. We're trying to let every last soul get into the castle. But I wouldn't go far or be gone long. If you hear the horns sounding loud blasts from the city wall, that means it has fallen and the retreat has started. You'll have no more than twenty or thirty minutes till all the castle gates close for good."

"Thanks," Tak said, and darted through the gate out onto the streets of Selestria.

The streets were dark and quiet, lit only by moonlight and starlight. Not a single glimmer of candle light shone from any windows. No streetlamps were lit. But Tak knew those streets as well as he knew every knot and line of grain in the wood of the *Arrow*. He could have found his way back to his house blindfolded as sure as a Gublin would have known his way back to his own cave in the dark. Tak's boots clattered on the cobblestones as he ran. Here and there, he ran past the shadowy figures of stragglers making their way up to the castle. If any of them wondered what a boy was doing dashing the wrong way down the streets toward the city wall, they didn't ask.

Tak's house lay in the city's Northeast Quadrant above the Southern Spiral, about midway between the castle and the city wall. Tak ran down the Eastern Straight Road, turned left onto the Western Spiral, then right onto the

Northeast Winding Way, then ducked down Bakers Lane until it hit the Southern Spiral near his house. It took him ten minutes of running to reach the house. He climbed up breathlessly onto the deck. The *Arrow*, still tied there, bobbed above him in the dark. But as glad as Tak was to see her, he had no eyes for her once he had reached the high vantage point of the deck and was given a clear view of the rest of the city, right down to the wall about a half mile below him. The wall was topped with fire and confusion. Tak could just make out figures fighting on the battlements, the firelight glinting off swords and armor. Tak took out his spy glass. Through it, he saw his worst fears confirmed. Gublins were firmly in place on top of the wall and fighting with the human defenders there.

Tak took out his knife and cut the lines that moored the *Arrow* to the deck. He looked up at her and held the last severed rope in his hand. The rope yanked as the *Arrow* began to rise on the gusting wind away from the mountain. Tak let the rope slither between his fingers, but squeezed hard enough that it burned the skin of his palm as the *Arrow* made her escape into the nighttime sky.

"Let the winds be kind to you," Tak said. "Be safe and well, my friend."

And then, from many places on the city wall below, horns blasted loud and long. The signal for retreat. The wall had fallen.

Tak scurried down the deck stairs. He decided to take the Northeast Winding Way all the way back up to the castle. It would be an easier climb than if he retraced his steps back the way he had come. No more than twenty or thirty minutes until the gates closed, the guard had said. He would have time. Tak tried not to think about the look on his mother's face and what she would say to him—or what he would say to her by way of explanation—when he returned.

Tak's heart thumped and his breath came in ragged gulps as he tried to run up the mountain, even though the road snaked back and forth as it rose to make the climb easier. His lungs burned and forced him to slow down. Going *up* the mountain was much, much harder than going down—something a city boy used to traveling by airship hadn't fully appreciated until now. Tak slowed to a trot, trying to catch his breath. As he made his way up the Northeast Winding Way, he noticed more and more people like himself on the street also making their way up toward the castle. These were civilians who had decided to remain in their homes until the last possible minute, hoping the city wall would not fall. Now they were hurrying for their lives.

Looking more closely at the people in the dark, Tak saw they were not all civilians. Many of them wore armor and carried weapons. They were soldiers. Wounded soldiers from the wall. The ones who could walk. They staggered together up the Winding Way in groups of twos and threes, doing their best to support one another. Tak realized that he was now caught up in the beginning of the army's retreat from the city wall. His heart hammered and he made himself move faster despite his protesting lungs. This was a little too close to the actual battle for comfort, not where he wanted to be at all. He wanted to be back in that safe, stifling vault with his mother.

Tak took a shortcut through a narrower, emptier street

that cut up and away toward the North castle gate. On this street, there was only one person up ahead of him. Tak passed him easily. As he passed the man, Tak guessed he was a young soldier, probably no more than eighteen or nineteen. The soldier wore no armor but had an old-fashioned wooden shield slung across his back, an empty scabbard at his belt. He must have dropped his sword. The young man wore fine-fitting clothes, as far as Tak could see in the dark, not a uniform. He was probably one of the new volunteers, the son of a wealthy family in the city. The volunteer staggered up the street as if dizzy or drunk. After Tak had gained a block on him, he looked back over his shoulder.

The young man had fallen to his hands and knees.

Tak slowed.

The young man got himself up onto one knee and tried to stand up. But he fell again with a grunt of pain.

Tak stopped.

The volunteer, after a few moments of breathing heavily, began to crawl up the street on his hands and knees.

Tak turned and ran back to him. He hauled the young man up onto his feet and got his arm under his shoulders, supporting him. "Are you all right?" Tak asked.

The young man leaned hard upon Tak and found his feet. He was quiet for a moment. "No," he said. "I don't think that I am."

"What's your name?" Tak asked.

"Justin Merchant," the young man said. "Of Selemont. Yours?"

"I'm Taktinius Spinner of Selemont," Tak said. "We'll

get you to the castle."

"*The* Tak Spinner?" the young man asked, voice brightening. "The one who rescued Captain Strake?"

"That's me," Tak said, a little taken aback that a stranger would know his name.

"I'm in good hands then," Justin said.

"Can you make it with me helping you?" Tak asked.

"I'll try."

But it was slow, heavy going. After only a few blocks it became clear that Justin Merchant would not make it to the castle, even with Tak's help. He begged Tak to let him rest. Tak lowered him and propped him up against the stone wall of a house on the narrow street. Tak got the shield off of Justin's back and tossed it aside.

"Are you badly wounded?" Tak asked. He knew the young man must be, but Tak couldn't *see* anything in the damned dark. He tried to search for the wound with his hands in order to staunch it, but he couldn't find it. Justin's entire shirt was warm, soaking wet, and sticky in places with what could only be blood.

"Yes," Justin said. "I'm thirsty too. Do you have water?"

Tak stood up. "I'll find you water. I'll find someone to help. Just stay here and I'll be back."

"No," Justin gripped Tak's hand fiercely. "Don't go. Just please sit and stay with me for a while. Not long."

Tak knelt. He knew what Justin meant by *not long.* They both knew. The boys rested in the quiet of the narrow street. Justin's breathing became slower and more relaxed. Tak's heart pounded.

"I'm sorry we let them over the wall," Justin said, his voice dreamy and far away, as if he were falling asleep.

"Nobody expected anything different," Tak said. "You did your best. Don't think about it."

"They were so *fast*," Justin said, squeezing Tak's hand.

"I know," Tak said. "It's all right."

"There were so *many* of them," Justin said. "And their armor is *good*."

"I know," Tak said.

Justin closed his eyes. His breathing became shallower. More and more noise came to them from nearby streets. The sounds of hurrying footsteps and shouting men. The main body of soldiers was making its retreat through the city streets to the castle. It sounded like there were civilians too. Tak heard women's voices in the crowd.

Justin opened his eyes with a start and fixed them over Tak's shoulder. "Grandmother!" he said with surprise. "What are you doing here?"

Tak looked over his shoulder, expecting to see an old woman standing in the street behind him with a sack slung over her back. Another late-coming refugee seeking the castle's shelter. But the street was empty. No one was there. Tak looked back at Justin. His eyes had become unfocused. Then Tak understood. It was said that when one was about to pass over to the realm above, the spirits of loved ones came to greet you.

Justin smiled. His grip on Tak's hand relaxed. "Grandfather," he said, his voice fading, "I haven't seen you in so long..."

Justin Merchant of Selemont closed his eyes, let go of Tak's hand, and went with his grandparents to the realm above.

* * *

Tak didn't know how long he knelt there by the body of the young man. He had never seen anyone die before. It seemed an impossible thing, that a person could be there one moment and gone the next. Seemed impossible, too, that someone so young could be gone. Tak didn't know what he should do. He felt that he should stay with Justin Merchant of Selemont. Felt that leaving him would be wrong somehow. He arranged the boy's hands into a peaceful position in his lap, brushed the hair out of his face. He considered breaking into one of the nearby houses to find a sheet to lay over his body. It seemed like that might be a proper thing to do.

Tak's thoughts were interrupted by heavy footsteps behind him and a rough voice calling, "Hey there, volunteer! Get up! We need every available sword on the castle wall, now."

A squad of ten or twelve volunteer soldiers stood in the street behind him, breathing heavily. They were headed by an actual soldier, a sergeant, in uniform. This is the one who had spoken to him.

Tak turned and blinked at them. "What...?" he said. Most of the men looked much the worse for wear. Some were dazed and wide-eyed, in shock. Others' eyes blazed fiercely with anger at the defeat they had suffered.

The sergeant bent down and hauled Tak to his feet. "This isn't the time for mourning, soldier. I need you to get up and fall in. Every last one of us is needed at the castle."

Then Tak understood. The man had called him volunteer. Soldier. It was an easy enough mistake to make in the dark and confusion. Tak was wearing a sword, after all. And he was tall enough to look older in the dark. And he had been kneeling next to the body of a soldier. Who else could he be? Certainly not the young son of the kingdom's chief Sailspinner. Someone like that would not be out in the streets at a time like this.

A large part of Tak—a very, very large part—wanted to explain that the sergeant had made a mistake. That he was not a volunteer soldier. That he was in fact a fifteen-year-old boy who needed to get back to his mother, who was no doubt frantic with worry by now.

But something the sergeant had said made Tak hesitate. *We need every available sword on the castle wall, now.* It was clear the battle was going badly. The city wall had fallen even more quickly than anyone expected. Tak had seen some of those volunteers drilling in the park by his house. He was much better with a sword than they were. It seemed likely that the city really *did* need every available sword. What if just one person like himself could make a difference in this battle? Didn't that obligate him to try? And if he tried and it made no difference, well, he would have ended up facing the Gublins with his sword anyway, in the vaults below the castle rather than on its walls.

"All right," Tak wiped his hands on his shirt, adjusted his sword belt. "All right. I'm ready."

"Got armor?" the sergeant asked.

Tak pulled aside his shirt collar to show the chain mail underneath. In the dark it looked about the same as any other chain mail.

"Grab that shield," the sergeant said.

Tak picked up Justin Merchant's shield and slung it over his back.

Even in the dark, the sergeant could tell that Tak was young and uncertain and afraid. His voice softened. "I'm sorry," he said. "Did you know that man?"

"No," Tak said. "We'd just met. Do we have to leave him here like that?"

"I'm afraid we do," the sergeant said. "There's nothing more we can do for him right now."

Tak nodded and hung his head.

"All right then," the sergeant said, and shouted to his men. "Squad, fall in!"

Tak joined the squad of men as they jogged up through the streets to the castle, his sword bouncing against his hip. Just like that—a case of mistaken identity, a few words exchanged in the dark—and he was no longer Taktinius Spinner, fifteen-year-old son of the kingdom's chief Sailspinner and notorious bother to castle sentries and battleship lookouts. He was a volunteer in the royal army now, a soldier, and he was going to war against the Gublins.

EIGHTEEN

To Tak, who stood with his squad on a section of the castle wall near the Eastern gate, many of the city's main streets seemed to be on fire. The sergeant explained that huge piles of wood had been stacked at strategic intersections, to be set alight in case the Gublins overran the city wall. The giant bonfires were intended to discourage the Gublins from using the Straights, Spirals, and Winding Ways and to force them into the confusing tangle of side streets, slowing their advance to the castle. Much of the wood that would have kept the people of Selestria warm during the winter burned in those bonfires, but the King and his advisors reasoned that the sacrifice would be worth it if it hindered the Gublins.

The ever-present mountain wind atop castle Selestria dried the sweat soaking Tak's clothes and chilled him. As he watched through his spyglass, shivering, he saw thousands and thousands of Gublins clambering over the city's wall and pouring into its streets. They didn't bother to try to break down the gates. It appeared that climbing over the thirty-foot wall was easier for them. Their armor flashed in the firelight and starlight.

The bonfires were more or less successful in keeping the Gublins out of the main streets. Through his spyglass, Tak also caught sight of human soldiers with crossbows on some of the rooftops. Those heavy crossbows were fitted with armor piercing bolts. The brave men were also there to slow the Gublin advance, allowing the rest of the army and civilians to reach the castle in safety. The castle's four huge ironwood gates were being shut, locked, barred, and reinforced with thick wooden beams. Most of the crossbowmen out on those rooftops would not make it back alive. A few might survive the night hiding in cellars or up in trees, the sergeant explained, if the Gublin's keen noses did not find them.

As the wind whipped the bonfires below, sparks flew and soon the tarred, pine-shingled roofs of nearby houses caught fire. Thick columns of smoke billowed up into the night sky, lit up by the fires below so that they rose in garish shades of orange and red.

Cannons blasted directly above Tak's head, making him jump. He looked up. The fleet had formed into several tight circles above the castle. They were also trying to slow the Gublin advance. The cannon fire blasted holes in some of the bigger streets where ranks of Gublins could be seen making their way forward and upward. The Gublins hid inside houses and buildings to avoid the cannon fire, and the fleet blasted these, too.

Tak's heart sank as he saw a building he knew come under fire. It was one of the city's libraries, the one closest to his house that he visited most often. The old stone, ivy-covered building had a balcony on the third floor. In the summer, comfortable armchairs were placed out on this balcony and Tak had spent many a quiet afternoon there, engrossed in books about flying or tales of adventure, his only distraction the buzz of an occasional fat fly wandering by. He'd hoped to take Brieze there, sometime.

In a matter of minutes, the old building was nothing but rubble.

Tak groaned, and, as he did so, he became aware of other men on the walls groaning in shock and disappointment. They, like he, were seeing places they loved—some of them their own neighborhoods and homes—being destroyed by the fleet.

Soon, though, the cannons ceased firing. Word spread among the men on the wall that the King himself had ordered them to stop.

"That's a wise order," said the man standing to Tak's left. "You could level every house in the city and they'd still come. Might as well leave something for us to save. And might as well let them come and have a look at my axe."

The man's name was Jon Cutter of Pinemont. He was a newcomer to the squad, and Tak's fighting partner. All the men had been paired up. They had been told that under no circumstances should any of them attempt to take on a Gublin alone. Extra men, runners, roamed the walls to take the place of any man that fell. Jon Cutter was a lumberjack, one of many that had flown in from nearby mountains to help defend the city. Tak knew of the Cutter family, although he had never met Jon before. The Cutters of Pinemont were well known for their size, their ability to fell prodigious amounts of trees, and their bad tempers when crossed.

Jon Cutter was a huge man, seemingly tree-sized himself. He stood a foot-and-a-half taller than Tak. His arms and legs were as thick as Tak's waist and his waist was thicker than many trees. His curly hair and wild beard were fiery red. He looked maybe forty years old. He wore no armor save a stiff leather jerkin dotted with iron studs. Mismatched vambraces—one leather, one steel—covered his forearms. The muscles of his arms bulged; they had grown thick and knotted from years of swinging an axe to fell trees.

Tak had never seen an axe as large as Jon's. The well-worn wooden handle was nearly as long as Tak was tall, and the double blades that topped it were three feet long from end to curved end if they were an inch. The gleaming edges had been honed razor sharp. It had been made for chopping trees, but it looked as if it could more than handle Gublins as well.

Tak was comforted to be paired with a fighting partner that was so large and formidable-looking. If Jon Cutter was unhappy about being paired with someone so young and slight by comparison, he didn't show it. He twirled the blade of his axe and growled as he and Tak watched the Gublins making their way through the streets up to the castle.

"Did you fight on the city wall?" Jon asked Tak.

Tak shook his head. His mouth was too dry to speak.

"Me neither," Jon said. "Didn't get here in time. Had to calm the wife down before I left, you know. She wasn't keen on me leaving her and the kids. You know what it's like."

Tak looked Jon in the eyes, then looked quickly away. He gave a nod as if, yes, he knew what it was like.

Jon squinted at Tak, seeming to study him more closely in the dark. Tak, who was having second thoughts, hoped Jon would ask, how old are you anyway? Then he could confess to being fifteen, explain the mistake that had landed him on the castle wall among the volunteers. Maybe then

Jon would call out to someone in charge, the sergeant perhaps, and insist that Tak be taken back down to the vault with the other civilians. But Jon only chewed thoughtfully at the wiry beard under his lower lip, cleared his throat with another growl, and spit over the ramparts. It seemed that anyone standing with a weapon on the castle wall would be allowed to stay there, no questions asked.

Tak and his fellow volunteers had been told, however—and this again by the sergeant—that anyone deserting his post at the wall would be shot down with arrows. "Nothing personal," the sergeant had said, "but I'll do it myself if I have to. We can't have anyone deserting their posts." The sergeant wore a bow and quiver of arrows slung across his back, and he looked like he meant to use them if he had to.

Runners on the wall began placing torches in every available spot, lighting them. The wall blazed brightly with firelight. The men stirred. Word was going round—Gublins had reached the base of the castle wall! Tak poked his head out over the edge. Sure enough, in the dimness far below at the base of the wall, he caught the greenish glint of countless pairs of eyes. It was the moonlight and starlight reflecting off the Gublins' giant retinas as they looked upward. Tak also caught flashes of swords and armor in the moonlight, shimmering and winking as the first Gublins started to climb.

Jon yanked Tak roughly back from the edge of the wall. "Don't show yourselves to them!" he growled, echoing the last-minute instructions they had received. "Get a grip on yourself and wait for them to come to us. And draw your sword, for heaven's sake!"

Tak drew his sword and held it as steadily as he could. He forced himself to breathe slowly. His mind tried to make sense of the situation. There are thousands of Gublins down there, he told himself. They are climbing up here. When they get here, they are going to try to kill me. If I don't want to die, I am going to have to kill them. In his fear, Tak had forgotten all about the shield slung over his back. He should have unslung it and set it on his left arm. But he did not. Instead, with his free left hand, Tak grabbed hold of one of the iron brackets set into the stone wall that held a torch. He gripped it tightly. He did this because his legs were trying to run away, and he felt that if he did not hold onto something he would let them.

Tak and his fellows were fortunate in that the walls of Castle Selestria were widely considered to be unassailable, at least by any method known to humans. They stood three times higher than the city wall—nearly one hundred feet high in most places. Climbing up their sheer face was like climbing into the sky itself. The walls where whipped by a steady, unforgiving wind that did its best to tear any climber away. The Gublins scaling that wall were having a hard time of it. Most were already tired from fighting their way over the city wall and forging their way up the mountain. And even for those who were not—Gublins are used to the warmth and dampness of their caves. The cold, dry wind and the difficult climb took much of the fight out of them—it dried their eyes, making them blink and hardly able to see, and it constricted their lungs, making them gasp for air.

Still, even a half-blind and wheezing Gublin was a dangerous enemy.

When a helmeted Gublin head appeared above the castle wall—not three feet from where Tak was standing—he struck at it with his sword before he knew what he was doing. It was a lucky blow, finding its way into the narrow un-armored space at the Gublin's neck, between the lower edge of his helmet and the armor covering his shoulder. Tak felt the sword blade bite deep into flesh, into bone. He didn't realize how hard he had struck. He felt the blade hit something deeper than bone, felt a jerk that transmitted itself all the way up the blade to his hand. He knew instantly that he had killed the Gublin. He felt life leaving the creature as sure as if his hand were on the Gublin's heart.

The Gublin fell back into the darkness without a sound and Tak's sword came free, slick with Gublin blood. The blood was black.

"Nice hit!" Jon roared, standing at Tak's side with his massive axe at the ready, face red with fighting fury. "Let's give them some more, boys!" he called to the men around them.

The men cheered Tak's blow and readied their own weapons to strike.

I've just killed someone, Tak thought.

It was an overwhelming thought. Tak knew that for the rest of the men on the wall the Gublins were nothing but bug-eyed monsters from the underworld. He couldn't blame the men for that. But Tak had spent time in the Gublins' caves as their guest. He'd shared a meal with them. He knew they were capable of kindness. They could serve you a cup of tea and hope that you liked it. They wrote lullabies for their children. They gave gifts. Tak thought of Deelok and Deegor, reveling in the joy of goat meat. He remembered Deelok's nimble fingers tailoring the chain mail shirt he wore. He found himself hoping that Deelok and Deegor were safe in their cave tonight, not out in this battle somewhere.

I've just killed someone, Tak thought again. And then he had no more time for thinking because another Gublin appeared, leaping over the wall in front of him, and he had to kill this one too.

This Gublin had vaulted himself over the battlements with one hand, a sword raised high in the other. In doing so, the Gublin had exposed his underarm for a moment. There was no armor there. Tak stabbed at it. His sword hit home and sank deep. The Gublin gasped in pain, landing on his knees on the walkway between Tak and Jon. The Gublin dropped the sword in his one hand. His other hand scrabbled weakly for the second sword at his belt, trying to draw it. A crushing blow from Jon's axe finished him before he could do so. Tak had to plant his foot on the Gublin's ribs and yank hard, then harder, to pull his sword free.

Then Gublins were trying to get over the wall everywhere. There was nothing but shrieking and shouting and the clash of weapons.

Tak knew where he was. He was on the walls of castle Selestria. He had lived much of his life on these walls. They were a wonderful place to watch airship races with friends, to have picnics, to lure girls up to at night under the pretext of watching stars and try to steal kisses. He had carved his initials into these walls somewhere with the blade of the knife at his belt. But that night, even though Tak knew exactly where he was, the clash of swords on shields and armor, the blasts of cannon fire lighting up the night, the screams of the wounded, the flames eating up the houses below and the red and orange columns of smoke rising into the sky all combined to put him into a kind of trance. He didn't know himself any longer. He felt that he had left his body and was watching himself from someplace outside as he hacked and stabbed with his sword. He could not have felt farther from himself, his home, and everything he knew than if he were standing on the surface of the moon.

* * *

The assault seemed to go on forever. In fact, it lasted about an hour. Then the Gublins simply stopped coming. The men on the castle wall lowered their weapons, breathing heavily. There were noticeably fewer of them standing upright than there had been before. The dead and the wounded lay scattered on the stone walkway among them, the wounded groaning with pain. Immediately, men began to kneel and attend to their fallen comrades. Many shouted for surgeons. Others heaved the bodies of dead and wounded Gublins over the castle wall. Tak risked a look over the parapet. He saw no sign of climbing Gublins, no flashes of eyes or armor below.

A cheer went up from the defenders of the castle. They had done it! They had protected their castle and their families from the Gublin attack!

Jon Cutter leaned unsteadily on his axe. There was a gash in his neck. One of the Gublins had nearly taken off Jon's head with a sweeping sword blow. The lumberjack had dodged the blow, but not completely. The tip of the Gublin blade had caught the side of his neck. It didn't look as if an artery had been cut; there was no spurting blood. Still, the dark blood flowed freely down Jon's shoulder and arm and he blinked as if drowsy. His held his head at an odd angle, and his face was much closer to white now than fiery red.

"Surgeon!" Tak called as he had been instructed to do if a comrade were wounded. "We need a surgeon here!"

Soon enough a surgeon and his assistant came running. They made Jon sit down and examined the wound by torch-light.

"This could be a serious wound," the surgeon said. "You should come to the field hospital in the courtyard. We'll get this taken care of."

"Nonsense!" Jon growled. The Cutters of Pinemont were notoriously tough. Some had been known to lose a toe or two to a poorly aimed axe strike and still finish their day's work. "I'm not leaving my post for a scratch. Just sew it up here and I'll be fine."

"Suit yourself," the surgeon said. Someone else was already calling for him and he didn't have time to argue. He and his assistant sewed the wound up on the spot, more hastily than they would have done under ideal circumstances. Jon Cutter barely grimaced as the needle went in and out. When the surgeon was done he wrapped a bandage around Jon's neck and said, "Drink some water. And try to keep the wound clean. Have it tended to properly when you are able."

"Sure thing, doc," Jon said. "Thanks."

"So what do we do now?" one of the volunteers in Tak's squad asked, to nobody in particular.

"We wait," the sergeant said. "If we can last the night, the Gublins will have to retreat come sunrise."

"And then we'll have won?" Tak asked. He still felt as if he were watching himself from the outside. Nothing seemed real. His arms and shoulders trembled with the exertion of swinging his sword nonstop for an hour. His hand ached from gripping the hilt. Some of the men were cleaning the Gublin blood off their weapons, but Tak didn't even have the heart to look down at his. He shoved the sword back in its scabbard. Once again the wind dried the sweat soaking his shirt and chilled him. The metal rings of his chain mail felt icy against his skin.

The sergeant shrugged. "They could renew the attack tomorrow night if they want to. But I don't know. They would have to take the city wall all over again, and they've already suffered heavy casualties. Maybe we've taken the fight out of them."

"I hope so," somebody said.

Tak looked up at the moon. It must be well past midnight, he guessed. Just a matter of hours and they would be safe.

Then someone farther down the line cried "Look!" The man pointed out over the wall to the city below.

They all looked, eyes squinting, trying to make out what was happening by moonlight and starlight and the firelight from burning houses. The Gublins had withdrawn beyond bowshot range of the castle wall. But they were not milling about in the city's streets and squares. And they were definitely not retreating. They had climbed up onto the roofs of the city's buildings and houses. Wherever one looked, as far as the eye could see, every rooftop in Selestria was crowded with Gublin soldiers.

"By heavens, how many Gublins can there *be* in the underworld?" someone bawled.

Nobody felt like trying to answer that.

The Gublins were eerily quiet. To Tak, they seemed to

perch on the city's roofs the way vultures might perch near a dying donkey.

"What are they doing up there?" Tak asked.

"Damned if I know," Jon Cutter growled, and spit over the wall.

Then the Gublins began to clash their swords together over their heads. Rhythmically.

Clash. Clash-clash.

Clash. Clash-clash.

Just a few at first, but more and more joined in. Soon, with that eerie Gublin sixth sense, all of them were clashing their swords above their heads to the same rhythm. The clamor of blades echoed off the castle walls.

Clash! Clash-clash!

Clash! Clash-clash!

Once they had a rhythm going, the Gublins chanted in time to it. The words they chanted sounded to the humans something like:

Ah! Rock-nog!

Ah! Rock-nog!

"What's a rock-nog?" one of Tak's squad asked.

"I don't know," the sergeant said. "But I doubt it's anything good. Keep your eyes open, men. Let's be prepared for some action."

The Gublins were chanting the very old Gublin word *Arachnagh.* It referred to a type of machine the Gublins used for digging and mining.

One of the Gublins out in that host improvised a short song which he sang over the sword clashing and rhythmic chant. Gublins are good at coming up with that sort of thing on the spot. The Gublin's fellows on his rooftop liked the song and they all took it up. Soon, the song spread to other rooftops. After a while, much of the Gublin horde was singing it, over and over, while the rest kept up the clashing and chanting underneath. Translated into the human tongue, the song went something like this:

Fly away little flies!
How high can you fly?
Can you fly beyond the spider's claws?
I think you better try.

Fly away little flies!
How high can you fly?
Can you fly beyond the spider's jaws?
I think you're gonna die.

Ah! Rach-nagh!
Ah! Rach-nagh!

The humans didn't understand the words, of course, but the song was frightening enough anyway. The nasty, mocking tone of it came through unmistakably. And tens of thousands of Gublins crowded onto the rooftops of the burning city, all singing and chanting and banging their swords together, was an intimidating sight. The actions were clearly not that of a defeated army ready to retreat. The Gublins seemed to be waiting for something.

The humans didn't know it, but that first assault on the castle was nothing but a preliminary, probing attack. It was intended to assess the state of the castle's defense, nothing more. The real assault was about to come.

Soon, even over the Gublin singing and sword clashing, the men on the castle wall heard a deep rumbling and clanking. The sound was so low that at times it seemed to make the ground and the walls shake, just a little. It was the rumbling and clanking of a giant machine. But sky riders had no experience with such machines and had no idea what they were hearing.

Then they heard the cracking and splintering of huge amounts of wood and stone, loud as an avalanche. Everyone looked in the direction of the noise just in time to see the city wall's Eastern gate destroyed. Chunks of wood and stone flew in every direction. An entire section of wall on both sides of the gate collapsed, the giant blocks of carved mountain stone falling inward as if something were pushing against them from the outside. A huge cloud of dust rose. The dust and darkness obscured whatever it was that had destroyed the gate.

"Was that some kind of bomb?" someone on the wall asked.

"Damned if I know," the sergeant said, gritting his teeth.

There was the sense of a giant, dark shape in that cloud of dust, moving forward. As the dust cleared, what looked for all the world like two glowing red eyes appeared where the gate had been. If they were in fact eyes, the creature they belonged to must be huge. The eyes were twenty or thirty feet off the ground, nearly level with the top of the remaining wall. The rumbling and clanking grew louder. The castle walls trembled.

Then the thing emerged fully from the dust and darkness into the firelight from the burning houses and bonfires along the Eastern Straight road. The men saw what it was.

Up until this point, the men on the castle walls had been brave. Even those who were wounded and who'd lost friends or family. They had believed they could win this fight. But when the gigantic machine below emerged through the ruinous hole it had made of the city's Eastern gate and started crawling up the Eastern Straight road toward the castle, Tak saw the men lose their courage. They had the shaken look of men trying to face defeat and death as best they could. One man fell to his knees and pressed his forehead to the stone of the castle wall. Then he began to knock his head against the stone. Gently at first, then harder and harder. "Wake up," he pleaded to himself. "Wake up, wake up, wake *up*..."

The thing looked like one of Deelok's *animatrons*. But on a huge, nightmarish scale. Deelok in fact had no part in the creation of this machine. It was devised by Gublin wizards with darker hearts.

It was a giant spider, the size of several houses put together, made of gleaming black metal. Its body filled the width of the Eastern Straight Road and brushed against the houses and buildings on either side. Each of its eight jointed legs were as thick as a large tree trunk. The legs, each ending in a massive claw, moved in a lifelike way, crunching through the walls and roofs along the road. The Gublins called the thing an *Arachnagh*. It was a machine modeled on a spider's body that they used for digging huge tunnels underground. But they had realized the powerful machine could be used for war as well. Especially if there happened to be a tough castle that needed breaking into.

Built into the spider's head were what looked to Tak like windows or portholes. Tak guessed that Gublins must be inside the machine, controlling it somehow. He was right. The two glowing red eyes on the spider's head cast a wavelength of light that helped the Gublin operators see especially well aboveground.

The thing belched smoke from vents on its back. It was powered by steam, and deep in its belly a team of sweating Gublins shoveled coal furiously into the furnace of its boiler.

The most frightening thing about the *Arachnagh*, other than its size and power, were the two fanglike objects projecting from its head. They were industrial-sized, diamond-studded drill bits. The kind used to bore into bedrock. To the men on the castle wall, they simply looked like terrible weapons. The kind that would make short work of the castle's gate the way they had done with the city gate. If any of the castle's four gates were breached, the battle was over.

For some of the men on the wall, those whose courage had been hanging by a thread anyway, this new threat was too much. They dropped their weapons and ran. The sergeant barely turned his eyes away from the giant machine to watch them go. His expression was a mixture of shock and disbelief. His bow and quiver were still slung across his back, but he clearly wasn't going to make good on his threat to shoot anyone who deserted his post. It seemed that with the arrival of this giant mechanical spider, the battle had reached some surreal state where the normal rules no longer applied. Those who wanted to stay and fight could. Those who did not would be excused.

Now's your chance! a part of Tak shouted in his head. *Get out of here. Run! No one will blame you. No one even knows who you are. Get back to your mother.*

Jon Cutter leaned on his axe and eyed Tak. He seemed to

know what Tak was thinking. He cocked an eyebrow, and his eyes asked, *you running too?* He looked weak and weary, but determined, rooted to his post.

They had each saved each other's lives several times in the past hour. If I run, Tak thought, will someone come to take my place? Or will Jon have to fight alone? Tak looked around. There were precious few men left to defend the wall.

The giant spider continued to climb up the Eastern Straight road. If the Gublins had built a machine with the express purpose of squashing Tak's spirit with terror, they could not have done a better job. Tak dropped to his knees and clasped his hands together, and this time when he sang the spider song under his breath, it came out more like a prayer.

Spider, spider it may be true
That I'm a hundred times bigger than you
But I'll not mash you, or smash you, or turn you into goo
So don't fear me, and I won't fear you

The words were all wrong. Reality had shifted underneath them. Tak was no longer the giant. He was the bug, the one in danger of being mashed and smashed. Still, the old song worked as it always had. Tak's fear no longer controlled him. It had become a lump of cold steel in his chest, centering him. Giving him weight. Tak stood up.

He and Jon Cutter exchanged glances, then nodded.

Tak was staying.

NINETEEN

In their dismay at the appearance of the *Arachnagh*, the men on the castle walls had forgotten all about the royal fleet protecting them from above. On the deck of the *Dragonbane*, a momentarily silent Admiral Adamus Strake threw off his shock and started issuing orders for the fleet to attack.

One by one, each of the fighting ships made a low attacking run at the *Arachnagh*, firing a broadside of cannons at it. Again they were firing nearly point blank, and again royal cannoneers do not miss. But whatever the huge machine was made of, it was stronger than any metal known to humans. The *Arachnagh* withstood a cumulative barrage from the entire fleet, every shot a direct hit. The cannonballs dented the spider's skin, ricocheting off with an eerie, shrieking, ringing sound. Some of the ricochets took out Gublins on nearby rooftops. But the royal fleet's cannons didn't punch a single hole through the giant spider—or even slow it down. The thing continued to crawl. It plowed through the giant bonfires set up to block the Gublin advance, scattering the burning logs, firelight gleaming off its sleek black metal flanks and fangs. Gublin soldiers climbed down from the rooftops and followed in its wake.

The *Arachnagh* was halfway up the Eastern Straight Road

to the castle gate. The fleet's fighting ships made a second pass at it, again one by one, but this time their aim was more calculating. Admiral Strake had seen that the skin of the creature was invulnerable, but he reasoned that its eyes and the joints of its legs might be damaged by cannon fire. He directed his fleet captains accordingly. The first ship in, the *Avenger*, twenty guns to a side, took aim at the glowing eyes and smashed them both with ease, putting them out. A hopeful cheer went up from the castle walls. The ships that followed the *Avenger* aimed at the leg joints. However, the eight globe-like leg joints, each no more than about fifteen feet in diameter and each constantly moving up and down and back and forth as the spider crawled, proved hard to hit in the dark, even for royal cannoneers.

The cannoneers managed to snap one leg off completely and badly twist another so that it dragged on the ground. The *Arachnagh* slowed. But it did not stop. It was able to claw its way forward with only six legs and was somehow still able to see without its red eyes. It was less than a hundred yards from the castle gate.

There was yet one fighting ship left to make an attacking run. It was the *Dragonfly*. The *Dragonfly* was one of the smallest ships in the fleet. Crewed by only thirty-eight men, the ship had only six guns per side. It was roughly the size of the *Arachnagh* itself. No one had any real hope that the *Dragonfly* would disable the giant spider after the rest of the fleet had failed. Still, a faint hope is better than none. Every eye was on the *Dragonfly* as she prepared to make her attack run.

But the tiny ship seemed to hesitate. It just hung there in the sky, its sails glowing in the moonlight.

"What are you waiting for?" the men on the castle walls shouted. "Go! *Go now!*"

But the ship didn't move. Soon, it became clear that she was furling her sails up and switching to steam power. Smoke poured from her stern as her propellers fired up. However, her propellers had fired up in reverse. The *Dragonfly* began to back away.

"No! *No!*" the men on the walls called. "You cowards! Don't run away! *Fight!*"

Had the men on the walls known about the brief conference the *Dragonfly*'s captain had taken with his crew, and the decision they had unanimously reached, they would have been kinder.

The *Dragonfly* backed about twice as far away from the *Arachnagh* as she had originally been. Her propellers stopped for a moment. Then they fired up again. This time she moved forward. The steam power allowed her to gain much more speed than her sails would have. It appeared that she was now finally making her attack run. She headed straight for the *Arachnagh*. But she was gaining speed too swiftly. In a short time, it became clear that she was moving much too fast and flying much too low for her cannoneers to have any hope of an accurate shot.

Admiral Strake watched from the deck of the *Dragonbane*. He realized what the captain of the *Dragonfly* was doing. He cursed furiously and ordered his men to signal her to stop.

She didn't.

Soon it became clear to the men on the castle walls that the *Dragonfly* was not on an attack run.

She was on a collision course.

The *Dragonfly* streaked low enough and close enough past the castle walls that Tak caught a glimpse of her captain on the command deck, at the wheel, his eyes fixed on his target. Tak saw the kegs of powder that the men had brought up from below decks and lashed to the rails. He saw the men standing by with lit torches guttering in their hands, ready to ignite the powder at the moment of—

The ship hit the *Arachnagh* and disintegrated into a shower of splinters and flame.

The men on the castle walls ducked. There was an enormous cloud of sulfurous smoke that blinded them and made them cough. Chunks of burning wood rained down on them. The men brushed the burning wood out of their hair and clothes.

When they looked over the walls again, they saw nothing recognizable of the *Dragonfly*. The *Arachnagh* had been knocked off the road by the force of the impact. Nearby buildings had collapsed onto it. The machine was covered with rubble. The men could see it had been badly damaged. All four legs on the side where the *Dragonfly* had impacted were broken. They stuck out of the rubble, their severed ends only twisted shards of metal. The men on the walls cheered the sight.

Gublins swarmed over the spider's body, clearing rubble from it. Some opened the portals in the *Arachnagh's* head and climbed into the machine. They tossed the dead bodies of Gublins out the portals. They were trying to get the machine working again, and replacing the machine's operators who had been killed. The *Arachnagh* was within easy bowshot of the walls now. The castle's defenders sent a steady hail of arrows at the Gublins there. But, once again, few penetrated Gublin armor.

With a creaking and grinding metallic sound, the spider's legs twitched. There were still three unharmed legs on the side of the machine where the *Dragonfly* had not impacted. With these, the *Arachnagh* managed to heave itself up and sideways out of the rubble and push itself back onto the road, piles of stone and wood sliding off its back. It tilted at a wobbling, unsteady angle, the four broken legs on its one flank much shorter than the others, and of uneven lengths.

And then, with a lurching, listing, sickly and twisted gait, the *Arachnagh* crawled forward. Its belly dragged on the paving stones of the street. It moved forward slowly and torturously. But it moved. There was nothing now to prevent it from reaching the castle gate. Its drilling fangs were intact. They fired up and started spinning with a shrieking whine. Their diamond studs flashed wickedly in the moonlight.

Tak and his squad were told to maintain their position on the wall. But many other squads were ordered down from the walls into the castle courtyard. A last-ditch defense was being organized there. Rows and rows of tightly packed men on the cobblestones faced the gate. But nobody had any real hope now. If the gate were breached, there were not enough defenders in the castle to fight off the Gublin horde that would pour through. And the walls now were thinly defended.

The *Arachnagh's* fangs bit into the ironwood and steel bands of the gate—and shredded them as if they were no more than old, rotten pine. In a matter of minutes, the gate was gone. Then the spider turned its attention to the heavy iron portcullis behind the gate. The bars of the portcullis were so thick that a man could not circle both of his hands around them. But the iron bars twisted and splintered and gave way as if they were no more than weak green saplings under the *Arachnagh's* attack. Once the gate and portcullis were gone, the *Arachnagh* shoved its huge body into the stone archway of the gate, breaking and crumbling the stones around its edges and making a larger hole. The castle wall itself held. The massive blocks of mountain stone groaned but did not collapse and fall inward as the city's wall had. Still, as the *Arachnagh* lurched and hobbled backward away from the ruins of the gate to make way for the Gublin army, it had left a large ragged hole.

The Gublins let out a hissing cheer. Tak and his fellows on the wall watched in horror as an endless stream of them swarmed through the breached gate, each one brandishing two swords. The men in the courtyard surged forward to meet them. The two groups crashed together. There were hisses and curses, shrieks and screams and the all-too-familiar clanging of metal on metal.

Then, from the sky above, came human shouts and roars of challenge. Tak looked up. Hundreds and hundreds of men were parachuting from the fighting ships of the fleet above, their swords drawn. Admiral Adamus Strake had ordered that skeleton crews be left behind on the ships and that every available man should jump from his vessel and join the defense in the courtyard below. Admiral Strake was the foremost among these men. His voice roared above the noise of battle as he swooped down toward the Gublins below, hanging in his parachute harness and steering with one hand, his sword raised in the other. His scarred face was twisted with fury. He cursed and swore at the Gublins. If they thought they were going to take his city and his castle, they would do it over his dead body, and at a great price.

The men of the royal fleet trained for this kind of parachute drop maneuver. Admiral Strake swung his body forward and backward in the parachute harness, the arc of his swing growing longer and longer. And then, at the high point of a forward swing, he flipped a mechanism that released his chute. Just as his chute came free, he used his swinging momentum to flip in midair and come down headfirst at the Gublins below with his sword pointing straight down at them. The maneuver was called the falling spear. Each of the parachuting men who followed Strake executed the same maneuver. They fell upon the Gublins like a rain of spears.

The attack from above confused the Gublins and drove them back. But only for a short time. Had thousands and thousands of fighting men parachuted down upon the Gublins, there might have been a chance of successfully defending the breached gate. But the hundreds of men from the royal fleet who dropped into the courtyard, many of them to lose their lives there, only delayed the inevitable. The Gublins pushed the humans steadily back toward the castle keep.

And then a man on the wall a short way down from Tak screamed in surprise and pain.

A Gublin had climbed over the wall and stuck both swords into him. Nobody on the walls had been watching for an attack. Everyone had been preoccupied with the fighting below. But Gublins had once again scaled the castle walls and were trying to get over. Whether these Gublins were just too impatient to wait their turn at the breached gate or whether they had been ordered to scale the walls again to distract the few remaining defenders, nobody knew. It didn't matter. Once again, Gublins were everywhere. The sergeant bellowed orders. Jon Cutter roared and swung his axe. Tak stabbed and hacked with his sword.

These Gublins were not the Gublins who had first tried to assault the castle. They were fresher. They had not fought their way over the city wall. And they had rested from their climb up the mountain while the *Arachnagh* did its work. Their swords flew faster and they didn't leave themselves exposed as often. Still, the two-man defense that Tak and Jon Cutter had been taught was working. If they couldn't kill a Gublin before he got over the wall, they would get one on each side of him, force the Gublin to take on the both of them. It wasn't long before either Jon or Tak managed to get a deadly blow in.

But with the vigorous swinging of his axe, Jon Cutter's bandage had unwrapped from his neck and his hastily sewn stitches had pulled free. Blood once again poured from the gash in his neck. The massive lumberjack's eyelids fluttered. His face had gone pale again. The swings of his axe became weaker and wilder. His dodges and parries of Gublin sword strikes became slower and clumsier.

"Surgeon!" Tak screamed breathlessly as he fought. "Surgeon here!"

But no surgeon came. Tak became aware that men were screaming for surgeons all along the wall.

There was a pause in the fighting. For whatever reason,

the Gublins held off their attack on the wall. Once again, Jon Cutter leaned unsteadily on his axe, breathing heavily. He held a hand to the gash on his neck. Once again, Tak shouted futilely for a surgeon. He put a hand on Jon's arm. "Are you all right?" Tak said. "Hold steady, Jon."

Jon waved off Tak's concern with a bloody hand. "Fine," he gasped. "I'm fine. Just need...just need a bit of a rest." And then, the drowsy Jon Cutter smiled to himself as if he had come up with a wonderful idea. He set down his axe, leaning it against the stone wall. Then he laid his body down on the stones of the walkway, curled himself up with his arms under his head, and closed his eyes for a nap. Blood began to pool underneath his head.

"Get up!" Tak shouted, kneeling next to Jon and shaking him as hard as he could. Tak knew he couldn't afford to take his eyes off the wall for long. The Gublins could renew their attack at any moment. "Wake up, Jon, please!"

But Jon Cutter of Pinemont had closed his eyes for good. A major vein in his neck had been nicked by the Gublin sword, and he had lost too much blood. He would not wake from the sleep he had taken.

Tak was all by himself on the wall. He had no fighting partner.

The Gublins chose that moment to attack again. They vaulted or clambered over the wall in countless places.

"Hole in the wall!" Tak cried. This is what he had been instructed to do if his fighting partner fell. "Hole in the wall!"

A runner was supposed to come and take Jon Cutter's place. But none did. Tak became aware that men everywhere were shouting for replacements as he was. Gublins were over the wall in many places now, standing confidently on the stone walkway with both swords in hand, dealing death blows. Tak glanced down at the courtyard below. It was littered with bodies. The Gublins had pushed back the human defenders there to the gates of the castle keep.

And then there was a Gublin soldier standing on the walkway before him, both swords drawn, blinking at him and breathing heavily.

Tak raised his sword. He and his fellow volunteers had been instructed never to take on a Gublin alone. One volunteer had asked the sergeant what to do if they were forced to fight a Gublin one-on-one. The sergeant had given this advice:

Keep your shield up.

Don't strike first.

Call for help.

Finally, Tak remembered the shield slung across his back. He unslung it quickly and set it on his left arm. There was no point in calling for help. And there seemed no point in waiting for the Gublin to strike first. The Gublin was tired and slow from his climb up the wall. His eyes were dry and blurry, his lungs wheezing. If Tak struck first, before the Gublin had a chance to recover from his climb, it might be his only chance. Tak lunged forward, attempting to knock the Gublin's right hand sword aside with his shield and to thrust his own blade in low and quick under the Gublin's left hand sword.

Tak felt as if he were hit by four or five swords at once. On his left, multiple strikes rained down on his shield and shattered the old wood. On his right, his thrusting sword was knocked out of his hand. A blade jammed into the center of his chest. If it had been anyone else but Tak, wearing Deelok's chain mail shirt under his clothes, that blade would have pierced his heart. As it was, the Gublin's sword shoved him backward and drove the metal rings into his skin. Tak staggered and toppled over a body behind him on the walkway, landing on his back.

The Gublin stood over him, his eyes momentarily perplexed. His sword strike should have killed the human defender. But the Gublin didn't waste time wondering. He saw plenty of exposed, unarmored flesh on the man below him. He raised both his swords and picked his next targets carefully.

Tak closed his eyes. He wondered what it would feel like to die, how badly the sword strikes would hurt.

He wished he could apologize to his mother, explain why they would find him on the castle walls, if there was anyone left to find him.

He wished he could see her one last time, and say goodbye.

TWENTY

Floating islands are awfully hard to see in the dark. In the nighttime sky, a floating island, even a big one, is nothing but an ever-changing absence of stars. If you happen to be distracted by a horde of angry Gublins overrunning your city, floating islands are pretty much impossible to see at night.

Nobody, not even the lookouts of the royal fleet, saw the wizard's island glide silently into place above the city of Selestria. It had been making for Selemont as swiftly as possible ever since Brieze had arrived in the fast courier ship and informed her father that war with the Gublins was growing more and more likely by the hour. The wizard, Brieze, and the rest of the island community were making frantic last-minute preparations even as the island slowed to a stop. The wizard had sized up the situation and decided there was only one chance of saving the city.

This year's summer solstice fireworks display would be coming early. And, given the circumstances, the wizard had decided to skip the first part. There would be no artistry, no painting the nighttime sky with iridescent birds and shimmering airships.

The wizard was skipping right to the finale.

From the floating island, rockets whistled upward and outward in every direction into the dark, trailing sparks. They flew in graceful arcs. Nobody below heard or saw them.

The nighttime sky above Selestria burst into a bewildering series of colored explosions—red, orange, yellow, green, blue, purple—each one brighter than the sun. The wizard had sent the fireworks in low. The blasts rattled the castle walls. They could be seen from every part of the kingdom. When it was over, the echoes ran back and forth between the mountains and the atmosphere above Selemont churned so that the stars appeared to be jumping up and down.

The men on the castle walls were momentarily stunned. Their ears rang. They staggered and shook their heads, blinking. Yellow and blue spots swam before their eyes. Then they shook their heads again and their vision cleared. They found themselves still on their feet and gripping their weapons.

The Gublins did not fare so well.

Not nearly as well.

Every Gublin in that army of tens of thousands dropped his swords and clawed at his eyes. He had no thought but for the lancing pain of light in his head. To a human, it would have been as if someone had thrust a dagger in each eye. They fell to their knees. They rolled on the ground, writhing and hissing in an agony none of them had known before.

The human defenders of castle Selestria had trouble making sense of the situation. It didn't seem possible that the Gublin army that had been about to defeat them was now helpless at their feet. No one knew what to do. But the King and his generals, directing the battle from their position atop the castle keep, soon grasped the situation. With a prayer of thanks to the wizard, they sent out orders. *Open all gates and advance. No mercy, no prisoners. Kill them and drive them off the mountain.*

A huge shout of triumph and relief went up from the castle's defenders. Many of them were only too happy to obey those orders. On the section of wall that Tak's squad had been defending, his fellows quickly dispatched the helpless Gublins there. The Gublin soldier that had been about to kill Tak had fallen on top of him instead, his swords clattering to the stone walkway. Tak struggled to push the writhing Gublin off him. Two men grabbed the Gublin, one by each arm, and wrenched him off Tak. They shoved the Gublin up against the wall and pressed the points of their swords to his throat.

"You want him?" one of the men asked Tak.

Tak shook his head, and lowered his eyes as they killed him.

Castle Selestria had been besieged many times in the nearly one-thousand years of its history. It had survived every one of those sieges. But never in its history had its defenders been ordered out of the castle to slaughter the besieging army. Every Gublin in the courtyard by the Eastern gate died quickly, their bodies heaping into piles. Black blood pooled in the spaces between the cobblestones. Then the human soldiers charged out of the Eastern gate into the streets of the city. The castle's other three gates opened and men charged out of them, too, roaring for blood and revenge.

On the wall, Tak's squad made ready to descend the steps to the courtyard and join the rout of the Gublins. But

Tak sat with his back against the wall, near the body of Jon Cutter. He didn't know where his sword was. It was somewhere nearby in the dark. But he didn't feel like looking for it, or touching it. He had wrapped his arms around his knees. He was shaking, and he couldn't make himself stop.

"You coming?" the sergeant asked. It was a question, not a veiled order. The sergeant was an experienced warrior, and he knew a man with no fight left in him when he saw one. The young volunteer had acquitted himself well. With victory assured, there would be no harm in leaving him behind.

Tak shook his head. He wasn't coming.

"Then stay here and maintain a watch on this section of wall," the sergeant said. "You are not yet dismissed from your service. When we return, there will be plenty of work to do." Tak nodded his understanding. His squad left.

Tak sat there for a long time in the dark with his head on his knees, trembling. He had been about to die and then....he hadn't died. Or had he? As he sat by himself in the dark with only the slumbering form of Jon Cutter for company, the torches on the walls guttering down to mere flickers and the night closing in, he felt more like a ghost than a real person. Like a spirit haunting the castle wall. But no. Tak remembered. The sergeant had spoken to him. Asked him a question. He had shook his head in response, and the sergeant had replied. So he was not a ghost. He was real. Why then, did everything seem so unreal? Why did he feel so utterly empty and numb? Part of him, a rather large part of him, felt like curling up next to Jon Cutter and joining his former fighting partner in that endless, oblivious sleep.

* * *

One might suppose that most of the Gublins in the attacking army died that night. In fact, they did not. Most escaped. There were several reasons for this. For one thing, the human soldiers were bone weary. After the initial surge of adrenaline from their victory had worn off, they slowed down. Their legs and their swords worked heavily. And the heat of battle cooled in them. Soon, even the most enraged and bloodthirsty had his fill of killing. For another thing, a blind and agonized Gublin is still a fast Gublin, and still knows his way downhill. Most managed to flee unharmed down to the city wall, climb over it, and disappear into the farms and fields, eventually finding their way under the surface clouds and back to their homes again. Most of the Gublins recovered their eyesight after a few hours. For some, it took a few days or weeks. Some never did.

The Gublins operating the *Arachnagh* were only briefly blinded by the fireworks. The light from the explosions had entered the interior of the machine only indirectly through the heavy glass of its portals. But it didn't take them long to realize the battle was over and that they had better get themselves to safety. Men hurled rocks and rubble that clunked against the machine. Others were hacking at the portals with axes, cracking the glass. The frightened, dismayed Gublins inside turned the machine around as quickly as they could. The *Arachnagh* limped and dragged itself back down the Eastern Straight road, eventually disappearing through the hole it had made of the Eastern gate.

TWENTY-ONE

Dawn broke with a pale and sickly green, smoke-streaked sky above the city of Selestria. The fires in the city had gone out, but black smoke continued to curl up from the smoldering remains of bonfires and houses. People walked the streets in stunned silence, seeming not to recognize where they were. With the light of day, the battle of the night before—the hordes of Gublins, the fires, the *Arachnagh*—seemed like a dream. It would have seemed more like a dream had it not been for the rubble clogging the city's streets, the ruined buildings and houses.

And the bodies. Gublin and human. They lay everywhere.

When he was younger, in the library near his home that was now just a pile of broken stones, Tak had read accounts of important battles. There could be no doubt that the story of last night's battle would also be written down in a book and read and re-read. In the accounts Tak had read, there was much about strategy and maneuvers, about split-second decisions that won or lost the day, about heroics—brave charges and determined defenses.

There was nothing in those accounts about cleaning up afterward.

When Tak's sergeant had told him to stay at his post, that he was not dismissed from service, that there was still plenty of work to do, it was the cleaning up afterward that the sergeant had been talking about. Tak's squad returned to their section of the wall an hour before dawn. Tak found himself glad for their company. The men were given a meal. Bowls of warm mush. Water skins were passed around. The men ate and drank greedily. Blankets were also passed around—one was laid over Jon Cutter, no one had the strength to try to move him—and the men took a few hours of sleep right there on the wall, laying on the cold stone. Tak's blanket was stiff and smelled like old donkey. Still, at that moment, it felt like the most wonderful blanket he'd ever known. He wrapped it around himself and closed his eyes. He was more thoroughly exhausted than he had ever been in his life. But still, somehow, sleep eluded him. Every time he started to nod off he woke with a start, his heart pounding. The best he was able to manage, after a few hours, was a fitful doze. When he was shaken awake by the sergeant, his muscles felt even stiffer and sorer than they had before. It hurt to move.

He couldn't believe that he and his fellow volunteers were being asked to do more. It seemed to him that what they had done last night should be much, much more than enough. Some of the men grumbled. They were anxious to get back to their homes and families. But there was much to be done, and the kingdom needed strong arms to do it. The terms of service had been spelled out in the agreement each man had signed when he volunteered.

The first task was to clear the bodies.

Gublin bodies lay thickest in the castle courtyard by the ruined Eastern castle gate. They lay tangled together, heaped into piles, their limbs stiff. Their big black eyes were sunken and wrinkled, sightless and dry. The men were ordered to load the Gublins onto carts. The sergeant directed the men to work in pairs. One man grabbed the arms and the other grabbed the legs, and they swung the bodies into the carts. The grim irony of this was not lost on the men. "Even when they're dead, it's still two to one," a man said. A few men grimaced at the joke. Nobody laughed. Tak didn't want to touch the Gublins with his bare hands. But then he remembered his reluctance to shake Deelok's hand, and he made himself do it. This time, the flesh was cold and clammy. The dead Gublins were heavier than they looked. Tak's muscles ached and protested as he worked. Soon they grew numb with the effort.

In the light of day, some of the men gave Tak sidelong looks. The sergeant did too. Even with his face streaked with soot and blood and grime, this volunteer looked awfully young. One of the men sidled up to Tak and whispered, "Hey lad, are you really eighteen?"

Tak shrugged. "Does it really matter now?"

The volunteers marched behind the carts as they wound their way down the city's Spirals, then out one of the gates in the city wall, and finally down through the fields and pastures to the cloud mist at the base of Selemont. The Gublin bodies were unloaded and deposited there. The wizard, who was helping to direct the cleanup, had assured the King that if the bodies were laid down close to the cloud mist that the Gublins would come peaceably in the night and retrieve them. At first, the men just tipped the carts and left the Gublin bodies in piles. But the wizard, seeing this, ordered that each Gublin body be laid out respectfully with two swords crossed over his chest. The King sanctioned this order. The men complained among themselves. It was a *lot* more work. But no one dared disobey the wizard. He had, after all, saved them all by laying a horde of tens of thousands of Gublins helpless at their feet—nearly single-handedly and in a matter of minutes.

The human bodies were laid out in neat rows in courtyards, parks, and open public spaces near to where they fell so that their families could come and identify and retrieve them. In death, their skin had gone a waxy white similar to Gublin skin. Tak tried not to look at their faces, especially their eyes. Blankets were arranged over the ones in the worst shape. Gublin swords could certainly make a mess of someone. Some surgeons and nurses, no longer needed to tend to the living, tended to the dead instead. They sewed up the worst of the wounds, washed away the blood so that the families wouldn't have to see their loved ones like that. To Tak, that seemed a brave act of kindness. He didn't think he would be able to do that if asked.

It took Tak and three others to carry Jon Cutter's body down from the wall and lay him in the rows on the castle courtyard reserved for those not of Selemont. They laid his axe beside him. The sergeant scrawled *Jon Cutter, Pinemont* on a slip of paper and pinned it to the lumberjack's chest. He would be loaded onto an airship and taken back to his home mountain. Tak looked down at his former fighting partner. He thought of his wife and his children, and the shock they would feel when he was returned to them. There must be something he could do to soften the blow. He borrowed the sergeant's quill and wrote on the paper, *He was a brave man. He loved you all. I am sorry. Tak Spinner.*

Already, families from Selestria and the outlying villages of Selemont were coming to search the bodies that lay in the castle courtyard. When Tak first heard the sounds they made, he lowered his head and put his fingers in his ears. He had never heard anyone make a noise like that. It was the sound people make when their hearts and their lives have been broken beyond any hope of repair. The sound of people finding their fathers, husbands, and sons among the rows of the dead.

Tak couldn't bear those cries of anguish, so he closed not only his ears but his heart to them. He moved. He worked. He did what he was told. He sank deeper into a numbness of body and spirit. Somewhere, dimly, in the back of his mind, Tak was aware that he could simply walk away from all this. He could confess to being underage. He could mention his father's name. Wipe the blood and grime off his family ring and show it to them. They would have to let him go. But Tak was still in a kind of trance. It was better, now, *not* to think. If he stopped doing what he was doing now, he would have to think about what he had done last night—about the Gublins he had killed. There had been a lot of them. He didn't want to do that. It was better now to move, to work, to obey orders.

Around midday, Tak's squad was ordered out to the base of the castle walls to help with the clearing of the Gublin bodies there. As his squad marched out of the broken Eastern gate, they passed a man and woman heading into the castle. The man was badly wounded in the leg. His thigh was bandaged and he limped and leaned heavily against the woman. Their faces were white and stricken with worry. Tak and his squad barely spared them a glance as they passed. They were clearly a mother and father searching for a lost son. Tak and his squad had seen many such couples already. They knew what was likely to happen once the mother and father searched the rows of bodies in the castle courtyard.

But something about the woman made Tak look again. It was her brown eyes. They were familiar. The woman looked back at him. She didn't recognize him at first. She saw only another weary solider marching with his squad, his shoulders slumped, his face covered with soot and grime. From the depths of his numbness and exhaustion, Tak saw only another frightened mother, her face lined with worry and pain, about to discover that her son was dead.

Then Tak realized that this woman was *his* mother.

And she, blinking, recognized him. The wounded man leaning upon her was Tak's father. The moment they recognized each other, the spell that had been holding Tak broke. He knew himself again. He abandoned his squad and was in his parents' arms. They all three gripped each other tightly, there in the street by the gate. None of them said anything at first. They just held onto each other as hard as they could. It was hard to say whose arms were whose, whose breath was whose, whose tears were whose. For once in his life, Tak senior allowed himself to weep openly. He didn't care who saw. His chest heaved. "Heavens...," he sputtered, over and over again, "Heavens...I thought we'd lost you." Marghoret-tia of Selemont was beyond words. She clung to her son as if her life depended on it.

She smelled like home.

* * *

People in the street couldn't help but stop to witness Tak's reunion with his parents. There were few such happy scenes in the city that day. Tak's squad had also stopped. The sergeant stepped forward, cleared his throat, and said, "Volunteer, I hate to break up your reunion, but you are still not dismissed from service. I need you to fall back in."

At this, Tak's father let go of his family and turned to face the sergeant. "What are *you* talking about?" Tak senior growled, wiping hastily at his reddened eyes and looking the sergeant up and down. "Who are *you*, and what have you been doing with my son?"

The sergeant took a step backward. He recognized Tak senior. The sergeant was a smart man. His eyes darted back and forth between the face of Tak senior and that of his son. The sergeant began to realize that he was in a lot of trouble. He stammered. "I policed him up last night...near the Northeast Winding Way...I thought he was a volunteer."

"A volunteer?" Tak senior shouted. "The boy is fifteen! Are you blind?"

"It was dark...he wore a sword..." the sergeant stammered, "...we needed everyone to defend...to defend the castle wall."

"You made my boy fight on the castle walls last night?"

Tak senior said, the artery in the little hollow above his collarbone thumping as if it would break through his skin.

More people gathered to witness the unfolding scene. They couldn't help but overhear the shouting. Many of them recognized the kingdom's chief Sailspinner, and, in the clear light of day, his son. Most had heard of Tak junior's rescue of captain Strake. Now the boy had been fighting in last night's battle on the castle walls? And had come through alive. Even unhurt, apparently. People jostled against each other to get a glimpse of the reckless young Spinner boy who had joined last night's battle.

Tak senior turned to his son. "Tell me this isn't true."

"Yes," Marghorettia of Selemont said, now holding her son at arm's length, looking as if she were about to either kiss him or strike him. "What in the world were you doing out in the city last night? You told me you were going to find Lucias and Marcus in the vault. Do you know how sick with worry I've been...?"

Tak tried to explain. He explained that he had just wanted to run down to the house and free the *Arrow*. And that he had done that. But that things afterward had gotten...complicated. That's the best way he could put it. He couldn't tell them about meeting Justin Merchant, about trying to get the young man back to the castle. That Justin Merchant was probably still propped up against a house in a narrow street off the Northeast Winding Way. Or the things that had happened afterward. It was just too much to try to put into words. He was too exhausted and overwhelmed by it all.

But Tak senior felt that he had heard and understood

enough. He took one hobbling step toward the sergeant, grabbed the man by the collar, and shook him. "You idiot! If he had been killed, if he had been hurt, I would....I would have killed you myself. I would have gutted you and hung you from—"

"Father," Tak interrupted softly, but in a different tone of voice than he had ever used with Tak senior before. It was an older, weightier tone of voice.

Tak senior loosened his grip on the sergeant and looked at his son.

"Let him go, father. It wasn't his fault. It was a mistake. I let him believe I was a volunteer."

"And why in the name of all the clouds and currents would you do that?" Tak senior said, letting go of the sergeant. Tak's mother was also looking at her son, her eyes echoing the question.

Tak sighed. "It seemed like the right thing to do at the time."

TWENTY-TWO

That evening, at dusk, the humans and Gublins met to discuss a treaty. They met at the very iron gate and crumbling wall near the old apple orchard where Tak, Luff, and Brieze had descended beneath the clouds on their diplomatic mission. The wizard and Deelok, who had a special means of communicating known only to them, had arranged the meeting, hastily negotiating details back and forth.

The King and a group of advisors flew down to the orchard by airship. A company of one-hundred armed men had marched down the mountain and met them there. Tak and his father were among the advisors accompanying the King. Tak had been asked to come by the King himself. The King had not forgotten that it was Tak who had gone on the first diplomatic visit to the Gublins, or that Tak had come up with the idea of trade that would be discussed and negotiated that evening as part of the treaty. It was a great honor. Tak had bathed and eaten and rested, sort of. He wore his best clothes. But he still wore his sword at his side.

The King stood before the wrought-iron gate, one hand on his sword hilt, his chin out, his back straight. The wizard stood to his right. Tak, who stood with his father and other advisors on the King's left hand side, couldn't help but notice Brieze at the wizard's side. She seemed to feel him looking at her, and her eyes met his. They flashed briefly with pleasure at seeing him. That made Tak's heart pound warmly. But there was no question of speaking to each other, or even of waving or smiling. This was as formal an occasion as occasions get, and it demanded they face forward, eyes front, silently, with solemn expressions.

As they had on the night of the battle, the Gublins emerged from the cloud mist below like silvery ghosts. The Gublin King walked in front as they made their way up the path. He walked slowly and stiffly, supported by Deelok on one side and an attendant on the other. But he kept his head held high. The *Fayex*, wound about him, flashed and shimmered. It soon became apparent that Deelok and the other attendant were not just supporting the old King—they were guiding him. The Gublin King was blind. He was not the kind of King to stay safe in his cave while his people went to battle. He was too old to fight, but he had been on the field, directing his troops from the rear, when the wizard's fireworks went off. For his old eyes, the blasts had been too much. He would never see again.

The Gublins numbered about one hundred as well, including advisors and soldiers. Tak was pleased to see Deelok looking apparently safe and sound. But he wondered about Deegor. Tak didn't see him anywhere in the crowd as the Gublins drew close and gathered about the gate. Tak didn't know it at the time, but Deegor, along with much of his clan, were among the first victims of the battle. Deegor had been killed by the royal fleet's cannon fire during the storming of the city wall.

The human King and Gublin King faced each other across the wrought iron gate. There was no shaking of hands, no exchange of gifts as there might have been on another diplomatic occasion. The human King merely cleared his throat and said, "So, let us begin."

The two Kings talked for hours. The wizard and Deelok served as translators. Scribes on both sides took notes. Tak noticed that the Gublins did not write on paper. Of course they would not have anything to make paper with. But they had figured out how to use metal to meet their needs. The Gublin scribes held books that contained sheets of metal as thin and flexible as paper. If Tak had looked more closely at the books and scrolls in Deelok's cave, he would have seen that many of them were made from the same material. The Gublin scribes scratched into their metal leaves with sharp writing implements. As the sun went down, the humans lit lamps and torches but made sure they were not too bright and kept them away from the Gublins' eyes.

The first topic discussed was the terms of ending hostilities between the two kingdoms. The human King demanded payment for the damage done to Selestria, for the cost of rebuilding the city wall, the ruined houses, the Eastern Gate. The Gublin King countered by demanding payment for the damage to their mining facilities inflicted by the human sneak attacks and bombs. In the end, after much haggling, they agreed to call it even. In truth, much of the arguing was done for show. The human and Gublin Kings signed an agreement that stated neither would take military action against the other, from that day forward and indefinitely. It was an unprecedented agreement between the two peoples.

Then the two Kings moved on to the trade agreement—goats for fuel. This took much longer than the ending of hostilities. There were so many details to iron out. How much of each commodity each kingdom had to trade. What they were worth in relation to each other. How they would be delivered and when. But one thing became clear as the talk wore on—humans and Gublins would be in close contact and communication with each other for the foreseeable future. More of them would have to learn each other's language if the agreement was to work out.

Tak's mind soon became lost in the details of negotiation. Although he had climbed into bed that afternoon intending on a long nap, more exhausted than he ever thought a person could be, he was not able to sleep for any length of time. He kept having strange dreams, disturbing dreams, that woke him up again and again. As the negotiations wore on, Tak's eyelids—his whole head in fact—felt heavier and heavier. He blinked and nodded. His father had to elbow him in the ribs to keep him alert.

Finally, with the moon high in the sky, the two Kings agreed to halt negotiations for the night. They agreed to take them up again at the same time and place tomorrow. The scribes closed their books and put away their writing instruments. Humans and Gublins made ready to turn toward home.

Tak shook himself awake. He saw the Gublin King turning to head back down the path beneath the clouds, Deelok at his side.

"Your Highness!" Tak called to the Gublin King. "Please...wait."

Everyone stopped what they were doing and looked at Tak. The human King and his advisors exchanged surprised glances. The boy had broken protocol. But it was also clear he had something he thought was important to say to the Gublin King. Given that the boy had been among their first diplomats to the Gublins, and that he had come up with the trade agreement idea in the first place, and that he had risked his life in the battle to defend Selestria, and, finally, that nobody knew what the correct protocol would have been exactly, anyway, they let him speak. They all looked at him expectantly, Tak senior included.

The Gublin King turned back towards Tak's voice. Deelok translated Tak's words. "Who is that?" the King said. Deelok whispered in his ear, explaining who had addressed him.

"Well met, Tak Spinner of Selemont," the Gublin King said through Deelok. "I am pleased that you are here. What would you say to me?"

Tak dug into a pocket and pulled out the medallion of friendship the King had given him, the silver medal worked into the shape of a Gublin hand held out in a gesture of peace. Tak held it out to the Gublin King, forgetting the blind King could not see it. "I feel I must return this to you," Tak said. "I request that you take it back."

The Gublin King was puzzled. He could not see what Tak was trying to give to him. Deelok again whispered in the King's ear, explaining.

The Gublin King's eyes may have been blind, but they were not without emotion. An expression of sadness and regret flitted across them. "And why would you return this gift to me?" he asked.

"I promised you that I would stop the attacks against your people. I did not. I failed to uphold our agreement, your Highness."

The Gublin King considered Tak's words. "Did you try your best?" he asked.

"I did," Tak said.

"Then keep it," the Gublin King said.

Tak shook his head. "There is more, your Highness..." His voice began to quaver as he realized that everyone, human and Gublin alike, was looking at him. But he wanted so very badly to say what he had to say. He pressed on. "I...I defended the walls of my castle last night. In doing so I..." But Tak couldn't finish the thought. It was too hard. There were too many people looking at him.

A look of understanding dawned on the Gublin King's face. "You fought with and killed my subjects last night?" the King asked.

"Yes," Tak said, the word coming out in an agonized whisper. "I don't deserve this any longer."

The Gublin King was quiet for a long time. Then he and Deelok whispered together. Finally, Deelok approached Tak. Deelok took the medallion from Tak's outstretched right hand. With his other hand, Deelok took Tak's left hand and turned it so that it faced palm upward. Then Deelok put the medallion in Tak's left palm, placed Tak's right hand on top of it, and enclosed both of Tak's hands in his.

Deelok spoke softly. "My King feels that this is not the time to sever what few bonds of friendship we have between our kingdoms," he said. "Rather, it is a time to strive to renew them. He prays that you will keep this gift. He knows what he asks is difficult, but he prays that you will try." Deelok's black eyes once again seemed to look directly into Tak's mind, and again they were infinitely deep, like the night sky.

Tak bowed his head. "I will try," he said.

Deelok whispered into Tak's ear, so quietly only the two of them could hear, "Did you wear my chain mail shirt last night?"

"I did," Tak whispered back. "It saved my life. Thank you."

"I am glad," Deelok said. "Be at peace, young one. Don't let last night's battle weigh so heavily on your heart."

"I will try," Tak said.

TWENTY-THREE

Tak, Lucias, and Marcus spent all of the next day searching for the *Arrow*. The Wright brothers had lent Tak one of their own ships, a pretty little thing called the *Dwarf Dragon*, and the three had split up. They scoured the mountains north and south of Selemont, flying low and searching the trees with their spyglasses. They stopped and asked villagers for any sign of a lost and drifting ship. They also searched the sky, training their spyglasses on every glint of sail they saw.

For Tak, it was good to be in the sky again. But he couldn't get comfortable in the *Dwarf Dragon*. She was much smaller than the *Arrow*, a true one-person ship, and she rocked unnecessarily every time Tak moved. The handle of her tiller felt oddly-shaped to Tak's hand. And she was definitely not built for speed. To Tak, she seemed to glide frustratingly slowly through the sky.

When the sun began to set and the purple sky dimmed, the three boys met at a rendezvous point above Selemont. Their three ships bobbed together in a close formation.

"Anything?" Tak called to them. He'd seen no sign of the *Arrow*.

"Nothing," Marcus said.

"Me either," Lucias said. "I am sorry my friend."

"We'll try again," Marcus said. "But for now let's turn our bows toward home. It's getting late."

Tak sighed. "You two go on ahead. I'll follow soon."

Lucias and Marcus dipped the bows of their crafts as a sign of farewell and turned toward home. Soon Tak was alone in the sky, bobbing in his tiny ship. He stared down at Selemont. The features of the mountain were growing dim and blurred in the failing light. He knew he should go home, but he just couldn't make himself. He cursed the sun for setting and not giving him more time to search for his lost ship.

Without the *Arrow*, he was nothing more than a bird with borrowed wings.

When the first funeral balloon rose from Selemont, it caught Tak's eye. It rose from somewhere in Selestria, near the top of the mountain. The large balloon glowed warmly orange, lit up by the funeral pyre burning on the platform beneath it. It rose swiftly but gracefully, and when it had dwindled to a dot in the night sky it blossomed into a flower of fire.

Sky riders don't bury their dead. They couldn't bear to think of their spirits locked in the mountains. They give their dead to the sky. Their ashes drift on the wind forever.

As Tak watched, another funeral balloon rose from Selemont. Then another and another. Soon, there were too many for him to count—like a slow, stately shower of meteors in reverse, all rising and blooming into bursts of fire high up in the sky. Countless balloons began to rise from nearby mountains as well.

Tak sank down into the belly of the little ship and leaned his head on the gunwale. At that moment, he felt the entire world was upside-down, and the mountains were weeping tears of fire that fell and splashed against the stars.

TWENTY-FOUR

The next day was the summer solstice. Few in the city felt like celebrating, but it seemed wrong to let the holiday go by without a festival. So the residents of Selestria tried. Brightly colored pennants were raised from every tower and high roof. The pennants flapped smartly in the wind. Vendors lined the streets with their stalls, selling sweet-smelling, freshly baked pastries, roasted meats, pies, jewelry, perfume, clothing—anything a Selestrian could want or decide to indulge in. Musicians gathered on street corners in gaudy outfits, playing jigs and waltzes and reels. In public parks and squares, tumblers and acrobats performed, and there were games of chance and skill in which a young man could win pretty trinkets for a young lady, or vice versa, by knocking milk bottles off a stool with a ball, or by popping a balloon target with a toy bow and arrow.

Tak walked the streets of Selestria with Brieze at his side. He wore his best clothes, his sword hanging from his belt in its sheath. Instead of her black flying suit, Brieze wore a green summer dress. She had done her hair up in the traditional manner of the women of Spire, with a deep green scarf wound intricately around her dark braid, and the whole of the swirling creation held fast to the top of her head with sparkling pins. As they walked, Tak's hand had found its way into hers—or hers into his. But for some reason, Tak's hand couldn't fit comfortably with hers. His fingers fidgeted. His palm sweated.

As he'd promised Brieze the night he gave her a ride to Selemont across the Ocean of Clouds, Tak so much wanted to show her the beauty of his city. Its parks and gardens, venerable old buildings and lively marketplaces. Like the rest of the citizens of Selestria, he tried that day. He tried to win Brieze a trinket at carnival games, but failed. He bought sweet pastries for them, but he couldn't taste them as he chewed. They stopped to listen to a trio of musicians on a street corner, then took each other's hands and tried to dance a simple jig to their tune. But the merry piping of the musicians sounded false and hollow, and their feet tangled up in trying to do the dance. Tak cursed in frustration.

"You're not yourself today, are you?" Brieze asked.

No, Tak was not himself. Neither was his city. It was everyone in Selestria. The soul of the city. Despite the bright pennants, the games, the music, everything was wrong. Nearly every family had lost someone in the battle, and it was hard not to see reminders of it everywhere. It was hard not to notice the ruined buildings and houses, the bits of broken stone and glass that crunched under your feet. In the parks, it was hard not to notice all the flowers had been trampled into the ground by the feet of Gublin soldiers. It was hard not to see that most of the trees were nothing but rough stumps, having been hastily hacked down to fuel the battle's bonfires. And Tak, like many residents of Selestria, didn't think he would ever be able to walk in a city park again without seeing the rows of freshly laid dead there. In fact, for a generation or two to come, there would be Selestrians who couldn't walk through certain parks or public squares, who would take the long way around, to avoid the memories lurking there.

It was all ruined somehow, Tak felt. Dirtied. Spoiled.

And Tak had begun to realize he'd lost the *Arrow* for good. She would never return or be found. His own personal connection to the sky was gone. He felt hopelessly, helplessly stuck to the ground.

And on top of that, Tak still hadn't gotten any decent sleep. For the past two nights, the dreams that haunted him grew worse. Tak wasn't sure if he should call them nightmares or visions. They seemed to happen while he was still partly awake, while he was drifting off to sleep, in that twilight time in-between reality and the dream world...

＊　＊　＊

What would happen, as Tak was drifting off to sleep, was he would sense someone was in the room with him.

He would open his eyes, and he would see Gublins.

At first, it was just one Gublin. The first one he'd killed. The Gublin soldier stood at the foot of his bed. The Gublin's head lay at an odd angle upon his shoulders—the wound in his neck was horrible—but his eyes still managed to fix on Tak's eyes. They looked sad and accusing. *Why?* the Gublin's eyes seemed to ask. *Why did you do this to me?* And then there were more of them, crowding into his room, crowding around his bed. They all looked down at him with the same, sad, accusing expression. Black blood leaked from some of their mouths and noses, from wounds in their chests and bellies. They hissed at him in their Gublin language, but Tak understood. *I had a wife and family*, one said. *What are they to do now?* Another said, *I was so young. I had so many years of life ahead of me. Why did you take them from me?*

"You attacked *us*!" Tak shouted. He sat up and gripped his blanket with white knuckles.

The Gublins fell silent. But their eyes still accused.

"You would have killed *me*!" he screamed.

Their eyes were infinitely deep, like the nighttime sky.

The shouting and screaming woke his parents, who rushed into his room, Tak's father hobbling as fast as he could behind Tak's mother on his injured leg. The first time, Tak's mother gathered him into her arms. "It's all right, it's just a bad dream," she said, stroking his hair like she did when he was little. "Everything is all right now." But her efforts to soothe him had no effect. Tak's body remained tense. The Gublins had vanished but, still, Tak's eyes looked straight ahead at something his parents couldn't see. It was as if he were there with them in the room, but not there at the same time. Tak's mother and father exchanged glances. His mother's look told his father that he needed to say something.

Tak senior sat heavily on the foot of the bed, grimacing at the pain in his leg, searching for words. "I fought on the wall, too," Tak's father said. "I know what it was like."

Tak nodded, not meeting his father's eyes.

"Oh curse that damned sergeant!" Tak senior pounded the mattress. "I should have throttled him when I had the chance. I should have—"

Tak's mother laid a hand on his father's good leg with a meaningful look. Tak senior brought himself under control. He cleared his throat and searched for words again.

"I remember..." he said, in a calmer voice, "I remember back during the Gublin War. There were many soldiers who couldn't sleep afterward. They had bad dreams...bad memories..."

Tak still couldn't meet his father's eyes. Tak senior faltered. He looked to Tak's mother for help.

"If you want to talk to us about what happened," Tak's mother said. "You can. You can tell us anything."

But Tak only shook his head. He had still not told his parents much about what happened the night of the battle. It was all too much to get out, somehow. Too much for words. He wanted desperately to tell someone, but he couldn't tell his parents...

* * *

Brieze's black, almond-shaped eyes looked into Tak's with concern. She and Tak had abandoned trying to do the dance, but they still faced each other and held each other's hands. The musicians on the corner droned on. "I think it might be good for you to get out of this city for a while," Brieze said. "Come with me to my father's island. We can have a picnic by the pond."

The wizard's island no longer hovered directly over Selemont. It had moved a quarter-mile off, so as not to block the sunlight. Tak looked up at it, hanging there in the sky. It looked green and inviting.

A glimmer of a smile lit Tak's face. "I think I would like that," he said.

"Let's go then," Brieze said.

But at that moment, clocks throughout the city rang the hour of eleven, and Tak and Brieze groaned. They couldn't leave the city now. They had to attend a ceremony in the castle in an hour. The ceremony had been hastily set up for the day of the festival to honor those who had distinguished themselves in the battle of Selestria, and to remember those who had fallen. Tak had been told that he would be receiving some kind of honor from the King himself and that he had better be there, and dressed in his best.

"I guess we lost track of time," Tak said.

"We'll leave for the island right after the ceremony," Brieze said. "How does that sound?"

"I'd rather skip the ceremony," Tak said. "But it can't be helped."

✳ ✳ ✳

By noon, the throne room of castle Selestria was packed tightly with visitors. People stood shoulder to shoulder. Guards kept an aisle clear in the center of the room. The windows were opened to let in the cool mountain air, but even so the room was warm with the heat of so many bodies. The sound of so many voices echoing in that vast marble space disturbed the birds and flying reptiles roosting above. Their screeches and squawks added to the general hubbub. Many of the women held parasols above their heads to protect their elaborate hairstyles from droppings from above. The men were less protective of themselves, shrugging and mopping up droppings with a handkerchief if they happened to get hit.

Handkerchiefs were in demand that day, as there were plenty of tears. The King, flanked by his military advisors, made a short speech from the dais. He praised the courage of everyone who'd served in the battle and talked about one's duty to one's kingdom. He spoke words of condolence to those who had lost loved ones. He told them that the kingdom would be forever in their debt and that every family that had lost a breadwinner would be taken care of. Then a list of those who had lost their lives in the battle was read aloud. After each name was read, a bell tolled, and, if the man was from Selemont, a representative of the family was brought up to be presented with a posthumous medal of valor.

It took a long time.

Tak, standing between his parents in one of the middle rows of the audience, began to blink and nod his head. But he jerked awake when the name Justin Merchant of Selemont was read aloud. He craned his neck to watch a mother and father about the age of his own parents climb the dais and receive the medal. They leaned upon each other and moved slowly, as if in a daze. Tak's mother and father looked at him questioningly. He avoided their eyes.

Tak snapped awake again when the name John Cutter of Pinemont was read. But as the Cutters are not of Selemont, no one from his family came to claim his medal. It would be sent to them.

Special mention was made of the captain and crew of the *Dragonfly*. The King praised their courage and sacrifice. The name of each man and the history of his military service, the names of his wives and children, mother and father, were read aloud. Each man was awarded a posthumous medal of valor, which was presented to his family.

It should be noted that the kingdom lost one other ship during the night of battle. It was the *Dragonscourge*, the ship that had been given to Cutbartus Scud and his men. When the smoke and confusion of battle had cleared, the ship was gone. Admiral Adamus Strake puzzled about this, listing the ship and crew as *Missing* in the official records. Every look-out in the fleet was questioned, but none could remember seeing the *Dragonscourge* once the battle had started. None of the ships had come under any kind of enemy fire, so it seemed unlikely she'd been hit and sunk beneath the surface clouds. Could there have been some sort of accident or malfunction that caused the ship to sink or drift away? A search and rescue operation was initiated.

Then it was discovered that on the night of the battle, while everyone's attention was distracted, a group of men had broken into the kingdom's treasury and removed seven hundred and fifty pounds of gold and silver bars. Seven hundred and fifty pounds was exactly as much spare weight as the *Dragonscourge* could have carried, according to her last manifest. Nobody thought this was a coincidence. Especially not Admiral Strake. The status of the captain and crew of the *Dragonscourge* was changed from *Missing* to *Deserters*.

Oathbreakers, Thieves, and *Enemies of the Kingdom* were added for good measure. A large price was put on each of their heads, the largest on the head of Cutbartus Scud.

Every wounded man who was well enough was brought up to the dais and received a red emblem from the King. The crowd cheered as each medal was pinned to each man's chest. This also took a long time. Tak's legs were beginning to grow tingly and numb from so many hours of standing. But he forgot his discomfort when his father's name was called and Tak Spinner senior climbed the ten steps to the dais to receive his medal. Tak's father, aided by a walking stick, seemed to move more slowly and with even more pain than he had the day after the battle. Still, as he climbed down the dais and embraced his family with the medal on his chest, his face was alight with solemn pride. He felt excessively warm, and there was a sheen of sweat on his face. Tak supposed this was due to the warmth of the room and the exertion of climbing the steps to the throne.

There were also many wounded men not well enough to attend the ceremony. They lay in beds in infirmaries throughout Selestria. Red emblems were presented to representatives from the families of these men. Though in the days, weeks, and months that followed the battle, as many of these men died from their wounds, their families were given posthumous medals of valor as well. Most of the men died from infection—germs that entered their bodies through their wounds. The sky riders knew nothing of germs or ways to combat them, although the wizard had been trying to teach them.

The wizard of course received his share of reward and praise as well from the King.

With that, it seemed as if the ceremony were finally

drawing to a close. The hot, uncomfortable Selestrians in the crowd started fidgeting and murmuring, anticipating their release. But the King held up a hand for silence.

"We have yet one more honor to bestow," the King said. "The last but I hope not the least."

At that, the crowd quieted expectantly.

"Taktinius Spinner junior," the King said. "Approach."

Tak's drooping head snapped up. He was instantly awake, his heart pounding. His father gave him a gentle nudge in the ribs. His mother squeezed his hand. Tak felt that he floated, rather than walked, down the aisle and up the ten steps to the dais. He couldn't feel his numb legs. He could feel every eye in that room on him well enough, though. It made his face blaze hotly. Tak knelt before the King, as was required, but the King bid him rise. The King pinned a medal of valor to his chest, then turned Tak to face the crowd. With one arm across Tak's shoulder, the King recounted to the crowd Tak's service to the kingdom during its conflict with the Gublins.

There wasn't anyone in that room who didn't already know the story—word travels fast in Selestria. But a recounting was required during an official ceremony. The King began with Tak's rescue of Adamus Strake, then mentioned the initiative the boy had taken in following Cutbartus Scud to the wizard's island and discovering the former admiral's traitorous actions. The King praised the boy's courage in escorting the wizard's daughter beneath the clouds on her diplomatic mission to the Gublins. He praised Tak's intellect for coming up with the seed of the trade agreement that was now in place with the Gublins and which might have averted the war if things had gone differently. Finally, the King praised Tak's courage in "volunteering" to fight for castle Selestria on the night of the battle.

The King did not mention Tak's frequent royal reprimands for buzzing the castle walls with the *Arrow* and stalking his majesty's battleships.

"It is well known that Taktinius Spinner junior desires to enter the royal airman's academy upon the age of sixteen and to pursue a career in the royal fleet," the King said. "In consideration of his recent extraordinary service to realm, it has been decided that Tak's application to the academy shall be immediately accepted. No trials or further process will be required. He has already proved his skill and worth."

This was a significant honor. The application and evaluation process for the royal academy was grueling, and the academy accepted no more than one out of every fifty or so applicants. One's family name or connections, one's wealth and influence, meant nothing to the admissions officers. Applicants were judged solely on their merit. For the King to order that someone be admitted without going through this process was unheard of.

"In addition," the King said, "After his initial year at the academy, given that his performance is satisfactory—and I have every belief that it will be much more than satisfactory—Tak junior will be entered into the course for officers' training. No further process will be necessary."

This was also unheard of. After their first year at the academy, cadets were considered for officer's training. Only the best were picked, and these were few.

"A cheer for Taktinius Spinner junior and his service to

the realm!" the King shouted.

The room erupted into cheers.

Tak would have thought that he was dreaming, except that in his most extravagant dreams he'd never imagined such honors. To stand facing the citizens of Selestria with the King's arm around his shoulder, having the King recount his brave deeds to the crowd. Being awarded a medal of valor, the youngest person to ever receive such a medal for combat service. To be given entry into the airman's academy, entrance into officer's training. Tak scanned the faces in the crowd gazing up at him. His parent's faces were beaming. Tak found the faces of Marcus and Lucias Wright. They clapped and cheered fervently, and there were genuine looks of gladness on their faces. But as for the other boys in the crowd, their faces were nakedly envious, excruciatingly jealous even. Every boy near his age in that crowd looked up at him and couldn't help but wish he were there in Tak's place.

It was ironic, because Tak was thinking he would give just about anything to change places with any one of them. He would give anything to be an ordinary boy again, unhaunted by his ghosts. A boy who could sleep.

TWENTY-FIVE

Finally, Tak and Brieze reached the wizard's island. Brieze took them in one of her father's small airships. They sat by the pond in back of the wizard's house. They took off their shoes. Tak rolled up his trousers and Brieze rolled up her skirt so they could dip their feet in the cool, clean pond water. They leaned back on their arms and enjoyed the feel of sunlight on their faces, the rustle of wind in the grass, the music of the island's birds. Tak could not see Selestria from where they sat or even anything of Selemont. There was nothing but rosy purple evening sky, pure white clouds, and glittering flocks of flying creatures.

A scuttle of sailweaver spiders drifted overhead, their silken chutes shimmering. One of the low-flying creatures snagged in Brieze's hair, its parachute caught on the end of a hairpin. Tak reached out and scooped the spider into his palm. He and Brieze watched as it collected itself and assessed its chute. They smiled as it turned this way and that in Tak's palm, orienting itself.

"I thought you were afraid of spiders," Brieze said.

Tak offered her a look of wide-eyed innocence. "Why would you think that?"

"Oh, the way you screamed when you saw that spider on

the path beneath the clouds. And the way you tried to hide behind me when you saw the spider in the Gublin King's lap."

"I don't know what you're talking about," Tak helped the spider lift off his palm with a gentle breath, and watched as it drifted away. "They don't bother me at all."

Brieze regarded him skeptically. "Umm hmm."

The path of white gravel that meandered from the back of the wizard's house, past the pond, and out to the dock at the edge of the island caught Tak's eye. He smiled.

"Remember when we were running down that path?" Tak asked. "With Scud's men behind us?"

Brieze's eyes sparkled. "I remember trying to help some fool of a boy who didn't know when to keep his mouth shut," she said.

"I remember *you* put an arrow in my ship at our very first meeting," Tak said. "That was incredibly rude. You made a very bad first impression on me."

"Speaking of first impressions," Brieze said, "I remember *you* fell like a sack of turnips off your ship onto the dock at my feet. And you had jellyfish rings on your face. That was quite a...memorable impression."

They laughed at that.

"Oh well," Tak said, taking her hand, "All's well if it ends well, I suppose."

Brieze was quiet for a while, the spark of humor slowly fading from her eyes. "Except that you're not well," she said.

Tak's smile faded. There were dark circles under his eyes. "I haven't been sleeping," he said.

"I don't blame you," she said. "What happened?"

Tak sighed. In response to her question, he picked up his sword, which he had removed from his belt and set aside so he could stretch out and relax more comfortably. He drew the sword from its scabbard and set it on the grass between them.

From tip to hilt, it was caked and smeared with black Gublin blood. Other men on the walls had wiped their swords down with rags that night, but Tak, once he'd located his, could barely bring himself to look at it or touch it. He had shoved it in its scabbard. And there it had stayed until this moment. It was beginning to smell bad. And there were bits of things worse than blood stuck to it. The black, sticky mess had even dripped past the hilt guard, smearing the pommel and grip.

"Oh my heavens," Brieze exclaimed.

Tak shrugged. "I can't clean it. I don't know why, I just can't. In fact, I don't even want the damned thing anymore. Maybe I'll just chuck it into the pond," he reached for the sword, "That way I won't have to—"

Brieze laid a hand on his arm. "You can't throw away the sword your family gave you," she said. "And even if you did, they'd just give you another one." Tak's arm was trembling. Brieze looked into his eyes. He didn't look away.

"Tell me," Brieze said.

Tak was quiet for a long time, then he said, "I really can't remember much about it, it all happened so fast. But even so I can't forget it. How can you want so badly to forget things you can't even properly remember in the first place?"

Brieze let go of Tak's arm. With both hands, she pulled

pins out of her hair, letting her wound-up braid free, undoing her elaborate hairstyle. She stuck the pins in the ground so as not to lose them. She unwound the green scarf from her long black braid. The weighted braid fell straight down the back of her neck. She rolled the scarf up in one hand and soaked it in the pond water. Then, wringing it out a little, she began to use it to wipe the blood from Tak's sword.

"Don't," Tak said. "You'll ruin your scarf."

"It's all right," Brieze said. "I have other scarves. Now, tell me everything about that night. Begin at the beginning, end at the end, and leave nothing out in between."

It was partly a request, partly an order. Tak started talking. He told her about slinking away from his mother in the vault underneath the castle. About his mad dash down to his house and freeing the *Arrow*, seeing the fight on the city wall. About the horns blasting news of the wall's fall and his struggle to climb the streets and reach the castle again. Meeting Justin Merchant and his unsuccessful efforts to save the boy. Letting the sergeant believe he was a volunteer and joining his squad. John Cutter and the first assault on the castle wall, the first Gublin he killed. And the second. And the others, as well as he could remember—they blurred together in his mind. Then the second assault with the *Arachnagh*, the royal battleships' attack runs, the *Dragonfly*, the breached gate, the renewed attack on the walls, John Cutter sinking into sleep with blood pooling underneath his head, and finally the Gublin soldier that stood above him, swords poised for killing blows, before fireworks lit up the night sky.

Tak also told Brieze about the Gublins that haunted his dreams.

As Tak talked, Brieze worked calmly with her scarf, dipping it into the pond and wringing out the blood when necessary. She worked from the tip of the sword down to the pommel with slow, steady movements of her hand, making sure every spot and stain was sponged away. She didn't look at Tak or ask him questions. She let him speak.

When Tak finished his story, his sword gleamed bright silver in the evening sun.

"There," Brieze said, handing it to him, "It's scratched and notched-up a bit, but it's clean."

Tak sheathed the sword, giving Brieze a profound look of gratitude. He had no words to thank her.

They could never say who leaned in toward whom first. But their eyes closed, their lips met, and they kissed. Tak was surprised by how soft her lips were. She smelled like warm skin and island air and a smell all her own that Tak had never known before. Not like home, but still like someplace he would very much like to be.

She stroked his hair. His eyelids fluttered. "You're tired," she whispered into his ear. "Lay your head down in my lap and sleep."

He fell asleep with her hands in his hair. As his chest rose and fell, Brieze stroked his head and whispered soft words into his ear, over and over, like a spell. "All is well. You are forgiven. Be at peace." It was the first deep, untroubled sleep for Tak in a long time. No ghosts came to visit him.

✳ ✳ ✳

When Tak woke, he thought he must be dreaming, because he heard his friend Luff's voice.

"Hey there! Ho there!" Luff shouted from someplace above him. "Can I have permission to come aboard your island, my lady Brieze? I don't want to risk any more of your arrows."

Tak sat up and rubbed his eyes. The sun was much lower in the sky than when he'd fallen asleep. It was almost dusk. But Tak felt awake in a way that he hadn't been since the night of the battle. A fresh energy coursed through his limbs and his mind. He felt lighter, freer, than he had in days.

Brieze must have fallen asleep, too. Her voice was groggy as she squinted into the sky, shielding her eyes, and called, "Lufftik Herder of Gatmont? Is that you?"

The *Ram* idled on a current above them, its hull bobbing, the edges of its sail fluttering. Luff stuck his head out over the side. "Indeed it is, my lady Brieze," he said, doing his best to imitate courtly speech. "But what's this? I've journeyed most of today to reach you, on a mission of a very important nature. I've heard stories of the dire goings on here. But when I get here I find the two of you fast asleep by the pond, idling and picnicking no doubt, and who knows what *else* by the look of it, as if you were on an ordinary summer's holiday."

Tak shook himself fully awake. "Luff!" he said. "What in the heavens are you talking about? Why are you here? What mission?"

Luff's voice took on a tone of self-importance. "Well," he said, "as it happens, two of my second cousins, on my mother's side, who are really of no account in and of themselves as they happen to be sluggards and dunderheads of the worst kind, happened to discover a certain large bundle of sticks caught up in the beech trees on the lower south side of Gatmont yesterday afternoon. And as it's well known that Selestria will be short of firewood this winter, and as this bundle of sticks appeared to come from Selestria originally, I thought I would return it to you in case you wanted to burn it to help keep yourselves warm this winter."

"What...?" Tak said, gazing up at Luff and the *Ram*. Then he noticed the *Ram* was towing another airship behind it, a ship about its own size. This ship was badly damaged. Its aftmast had snapped about two-thirds of the way up and its sail hung over its side in tatters. A small temporary sail had been rigged to keep it aloft. All of the other rigging was a tangled mess. The ship's keel and rudder were badly gouged. It listed heavily to one side as it bobbed behind the *Ram*.

But there was no mistaking it. It was the *Arrow*.

Tak could hardly bring himself to believe his eyes. "Bring it down," he said.

"Certainly," Luff said. "My lady Brieze, may I have permission to dock?"

Brieze was about to answer, but Tak interrupted. "Don't bother with the dock," he said. "Bring her down right here, right now, ground landing."

Luff looked at Brieze. Brieze nodded. A ground landing is more difficult than a docking, and it was not Luff's specialty. Still, he managed to pull this one off nicely. He gave the *Ram* some lift, then circled slowly over their heads, lowering his ship, and the *Arrow* in tow, closer to the ground with each turn, slower and slower, lower and lower, angling the sail back to create drag, until the keel of the *Ram* hit the ground and dug a long curving divot into the grass. The *Ram* came to a stop, heeling over, balancing on its keel and sidewing. The *Arrow* settled into a similar position behind.

Tak leapt into the *Arrow* before the ship had stopped moving. He ran his hands along her gunwales, through her ragged sails. He sat in the stern and put his hand on the tiller, tried the pedals. It was really her. He could scarcely believe his senses. He grinned like crazy up at the sky. He had his ship back. Thanks to his friend Luff, he had his ship back. And he had some peace of mind back, too, thanks to Brieze. He was fairly sure the Gublin ghosts would visit him again, but he was also sure he would be better able to face them now. The world seemed like a much better place than it had been a few hours ago. He felt like his old self again. Well, not quite like his *old* self, but as close to that boy as he was ever likely to get again.

Tak leapt from the *Arrow* and shot straight at Luff. He'd intended to give Luff an enthusiastic bear hug, but it ended up being more of a tackle, knocking Luff back over the side and into the rigging of the *Ram*. "Lufftik Herder of Gatmont!" Tak said. "You are the truest friend a boy could have. I am forever in your debt. From this day on I call you brother. I'm at your service. If there is any way I might ever serve you or your family, you have only to name it."

Luff had the breath knocked out of him. It was a moment before he could speak. "Well," he finally said, "you could get *off* me and let me up for starters."

Tak helped Luff to his feet.

"And I'm hungry and I'm tired," Luff said. "Some Spinner hospitality couldn't hurt. A fancy dinner and a nice soft bed?"

"Dinner?" Tak said, snorting. "We are going to throw you a *feast*!" Tak turned to Brieze. "Would you give us the pleasure of your company tonight as well?"

Brieze's black eyes glittered. "I wouldn't miss it."

"You know what else?" Luff said, brushing himself off. "I was thinking that tomorrow—after a suitable feast and good night's sleep—we might visit our shipwright friends Lucias and Marcus. They could probably turn this broken down bunch of sticks into something flyable. Then we could race it against the *Ram* and see what she can really do."

Tak grinned. "You're on," he said.

APPENDIX
Some Notes on Etherium

Airships

It is thought that the first "airship" of Etherium was probably nothing more than a blanket or animal hide, gripped by its corners and held overhead by some adventurous person thousands of years ago who then stepped off a cliff or jumped out of a tree with it and found that, yes, indeed he or she could float away on the wind. There is even a theory that the principle of air travel was discovered by one or more people trying to hold down a tent on an especially windy day.

In any case, improvements were soon made. An especially important one was the addition of a wooden seat or platform below the parachute. As the years and technology progressed, this simple platform grew larger and more elaborate until it resembled the hull of a sailing ship, although these hulls were much wider and shallower. The simple hide parachute that kept the contraption aloft also developed into something that looked and functioned much more like a wing or the sail of a hang glider, supported by yards attached to a fore and aft mast. Then multiple sails and masts were added.

Although the airships of Etherium resemble sailing ships,

in principle they operate differently. Sailing ships float in water and are propelled by the wind. Airships of Etherium both float in and are propelled by the wind. Therefore, they operate much more like hang gliders. Unless they are powered by steam-driven propellers (a recent wizard innovation) sky rider airships move with the current they are floating in. Sky riders must be extremely knowledgeable about the complex, ever-changing system of air currents that stream around their mountains. (And around the entire surface of their world, in fact.) To get where you want to go, you have to find a current to take you there. And you had better have a good plan for getting home as well.

Floating Islands

All in all, there are less than a dozen known floating islands on Etherium. They are all made from a type of volcanic rock that is extremely light and porous, filled with holes and pockets of air. However, it is important to note the air trapped in the volcanic stone of these floating islands is many millions of years older than Etherium's current air. It came from a time when the atmosphere was less dense.

All of Etherium's floating islands are thought to have originated from a single, ancient cataclysmic event. Many tens of thousands of years ago, it is believed, a large meteorite smashed into part of the surface of Etherium composed of volcanic rock. The impact threw giant chunks of stone up into the sky. And because Etherium's atmosphere is so dense, and because many of these slabs of stone were extremely light and filled with pockets of air less dense than the air around them, many of them, well...just stayed up there. They refused to sink. Instead, they were taken up by the currents and began cruising around in their new home in the sky.

At first, these islands were nothing but bare stone. But soon the spores of lichen and mosses drifted onto them, and these organisms began to live on the islands and cover their surfaces. Over thousands of years, the lichens and mosses digested the stone and turned the top layer into soil. Flocks of birds and other flying creatures roosted on the islands, and they fertilized and added to the new soil with their droppings. The bird droppings also contained seeds from many different plants. The porous and pitted surface of the islands trapped and held much of the rain that fell upon them, so that the seeds that had been brought by birds or on the wind were able to sprout and grow.

Sadly, floating islands have short lives, geologically speaking. Even the toughest mountain stone is susceptible to erosion by wind and rain. The relatively soft stone of floating islands is even more susceptible. It is though that in a few million years, these once majestic and awe-inspiring natural wonders will be nothing but dust on the wind.

The Geography of Spire (And a Pretty Mountain View)

If you stood on the walls of castle Selestria, which sits atop Selemont, the highest mountain in the Kingdom of Spire, and looked around, here's what you would see:

Far below you, an endless expanse of flat surface clouds would stretch from horizon to horizon. Depending on the time of day and season, they might look gray and threatening, or they might be tinged with purple and gold from the sun. Rising out of these clouds would be a range of tall sharp green mountains, their slopes terraced with fields and dotted with houses, orchards, pastures, and pine groves. Cities would crown the tops of the largest mountains. On the nearest, you could make out the branches of the pines swaying in the ever-present wind, the roof tiles of the houses. The further mountains would be less distinct, fading off into blue shapes in the distance as they stretched away to the north and south. This mountain range, called the Highspire Mountains, forms the main part of the Kingdom of Spire.

If you looked to the east, you would see nothing but clouds and sky all the way to the horizon. (If you traveled east by airship, it would take you a month before your spotted the mountains of the Eastern Kingdoms.) Turning around and looking westward would provide a more interesting view. There, in the far distance, across a sizable stretch of surface clouds known as the Ocean of Clouds, would rise the razor-like Dragonback Mountains, which are also a part of the Kingdom of Spire. The Dragonback Mountains are still a wild, untamed place. Nobody lives there year round. Miners and lumberjacks work the mountains in the spring and summer, living in temporary settlements, but they retreat in the fall before the heavy snows—and migrating polar dragons—settle in for the winter.

Looking far to the south, you would barely make out the Twins, a pair of mountains south of the Dragonbacks but much closer to the east. Finally, if you used a spyglass and squinted southward past the Twins, you would see the last tiny, southernmost outpost of the Kingdom of Spire, a small isolated mountain called Lonemont. Whether this name was intended to be poetic or simply accurate, nobody knows.

If you looked skyward, the real fun would begin. The sky of Etherium is alive with flying and floating creatures. There would be flocks of colorful creatures that you would recognize as birds, schools of darting, glittering creatures that you would call fish, and large groups of other creatures that would look to you as if they couldn't make up their minds which of the two they wanted to be. Flying fish are a rarity and oddity in most worlds. Not so in Etherium. And many birds of Etherium have managed to sprout a fin or two from their backs or tails. Etherium also has no shortage of flying reptiles, from the dwarf dragons—rare and harmless and beautiful as peacocks—to the much less rare and much more harmful grekks.

As exotic and beautiful as it might be, if you were to actually visit Etherium, you wouldn't enjoy it at all. For one thing, you would barely be able to move because of the weight of the atmosphere. And breathing that air would be like trying to breathe pea soup. You wouldn't be able to talk. Oh, and for another thing, your eardrums would rupture and your eyes would bulge out of your head because of the extra pressure squishing down on you. And that would probably distract you from the pretty mountain views.

Gublins

The humans and Gublins of Etherium are distantly related, sharing a common hominid ancestor from millions of years ago. However, Gublins evolved to live in the realm beneath the clouds, in caverns and caves without sunlight, and like many creatures who learn to live without the sun, their skin is an unearthly, corpse-like white. And their eyes have grown huge from the effort of trying to see. Gublin eyes are big and bulbous, mostly black pupil and set so far apart that they're almost on either side of their heads, but not quite. Their noses are mere nostril slits below their eyes, although their sense of smell is good. Their chins tend to be pointed, and their mouths are rimmed with thin colorless lips and filled with sharp teeth, the better to tear and rend the tough creatures they find to eat underground.

Gublins are smaller than men on average, about five feet tall. Their arms and legs are longer in proportion to their bodies and appear thin and spindly, but they are powered by tough, lean muscle. Gublins usually walk upright, but when they want to move fast they can lope apelike on their hands and feet. Though smaller than humans, they are in fact stronger and faster.

Gublins are not right-handed or left-handed. They use both hands equally well and can use them completely independently of each other if they wish. Gublins' hands are in fact their most unique physical feature. Humans have evolved one opposable thumb on each hand, and they've found this extremely useful for grasping and manipulating objects and making tools. Gublins have two opposable thumbs on each hand. What used to be a pinky evolved into another thumb, opposable to their three long, dexterous middle fingers and the other thumb. Gublins are very good with their hands. They delight in making clever objects with springs and gears and moving parts. They love to make intricate jewelry from gold and silver and gems—bracelets and armbands, necklaces and rings. They are also extremely skilled at making weapons and armor.

The Streets of Selestria

The streets of Selestria tend to confuse newcomers. It is easy to become disoriented and lost among them. If you were standing on one of these streets near the base of the city, looking upward and trying to figure out how to get where you were going, there would be a bewildering variety of options—and so few of them even remotely straightforward or logical-seeming that you would have little confidence any route could bring you to your destination. There would be no sensible grid of north-south and east-west running streets as you tend to find in other cities. You might discern a number of main roads all going upward to the right and downward to the left. But there would be a greater number of smaller roads going every possible way, and some ways that seemed impossible—or at least distinctly improbable—as well.

The complexity of Selestria's streets is due to the difficulty of getting things up and down the steep mountainside. Straight roads make the shortest distance between point A and point B, but they tend to be extremely hard to climb. Spiraling and winding roads are much easier. If you were to get in an airship and hover directly over the city, the overall pattern of Selestria's main streets would become apparent to you. You might even think their symmetry was beautiful.

The city is circular, and the wall that encircles it is a little more than six miles in circumference. One of the city's main roads runs the entire length around the inside of this wall. It is called, unimaginatively enough, the Wall Road. Now, there are four gates in the city wall at points due North, South, East, and West. They are of course called the Northern, Southern, Eastern, and Western gates. From each of these gates, a broad, straight, paved road climbs directly up to the castle, which sits in the exact center of the city. These roads are called the Northern, Southern, Eastern, and Western Straight Roads, or Straights for short. However, the straight roads are so steep that they are closed to all but foot traffic. It would be too easy for a heavy cart to break loose on one of these roads and come rolling and crashing down with disastrous results. In addition, many people of Selestria, especially those who like to eat more than they like to exercise, find these direct roads much too taxing to climb. A few of them have also lost their footing on these roads and come crashing down with disastrous results.

So here is where things get more interesting. There are also four main spiraling roads that run through the city of Selestria. These roads, called the Spirals, are much easier to walk up and to push or pull a cart upon. Each of the Spirals begins at one of the city's four gates and winds its way counter-clockwise up and around the mountainside, eventually reaching the castle directly above the point where it started. So the Southern Spiral, for example, starts at the city's Southern gate. It curves up and away from the Southern Straight, climbing eastward. It intersects with the Eastern Straight Road a quarter of the way up the mountain, then with the Northern Straight Road halfway up the mountain, the Western Straight Road at three-quarters of the way up, and it finally makes its last quarter turn and reunites with the Southern Straight Road at the castle's Southern gate. The other three Spirals follow the same pattern, starting at their respective gates and intersecting with the straight roads at points one-quarter, one-half, and three-quarters of the way up the mountain, finally reaching the castle gate directly above the city gate where they started.

Lastly, if you are not too confused already, there are also four main winding roads, called the Winding Ways. They are not as hard to climb as the Straight Roads, but not as easy as the Spirals. Each of these starts out down at the Wall Road at a point midway between the city gates. They take a lazy, back-and forth path up through the city. The Winding Ways never intersect with the straight roads, always staying about midway between them. But the Winding Ways intersect with each of the Spirals at some point during their climb.

Mixed into this logical and symmetrical pattern of Straight Roads, Spirals, and Winding Ways are a myriad of other smaller avenues, side streets, thoroughfares, lanes, and alleys. These have no discernible structure or pattern. They were built haphazardly, as need dictated. No city resident knows them all. Still, each Selestrian has very definite opinions on how to best navigate the city.

If you were to arrive at the Southern gate and ask a guard there how to get to the Spinner household, he would likely say, "Take the Wall Road here to your right until you get to the Eastern Gate. Climb the Eastern Straight Road there and take your first right onto the Southern Spiral. The Spinner house will be on your left above the road just before you reach Northeast Winding Way."

You would be about the thank the guard and be on your way when another guard would clear his throat and interject, "Well, you *could* go that way, if you're not in a hurry, but if you wanted to get there a little faster you could climb the Southern Straight Road here, take your first right onto the Western Spiral, cross the Eastern Straight Road, take a downward right onto the Northeast Winding Way, then take a downward right onto Bakers Lane and that will put you out at the Southern Spiral right by the Spinner house."

You would just be trying to commit this second set of directions to memory when a third guard would say, "Nonsense! Now, the *fastest* way would be to climb the South Straight Road here, then take your *second* right onto the *Northern* Spiral. After you cross the Eastern Straight Road, take a downward right at the Northeast Winding Way. That will take you down to the Southern Spiral just a stone's throw from the Spinner house."

At this point you would become completely confused, and the three guards would start to argue the merits and demerits of the various directions they had proposed. That is another reason people travel by airship when they can in the city of Selestria. In addition to being much easier, there is a lot less arguing.

Wizards

Without wizards, the sky riders of Etherium would not

have cannons, which come in extremely handy for fending off dragons, or steam-powered airships, or many other technological innovations they have come to rely on. Wizards are not the *only* creators of new technology in Etherium—there are also university scholars and the occasional random inventor—but wizards tend to be the smartest and the best at it.

Every kingdom of Etherium has a wizard or two associated with it. These wizards consider themselves citizens of their respective kingdoms. However, the wizards are also a nation unto themselves. They meet once a year at the Wizard Summit to share ideas, make rules, and generally discuss how best to govern themselves. One of the chief discussions at these summits is the introduction of new technology to the general population. This is handled very carefully so as not to tip the balance of power in favor of any one kingdom of Etherium. One of the wizards' main rules is that if a new technology is to be shared with the general population, it must be shared equally with all. There is plenty of technology the wizards possess which they have decided not to share.

As you can imagine, there are times when individual wizards find themselves torn between the wizards' rules and their own interests or the interests of their kingdom, especially if their kingdom happens to be losing in a war. Every so often a wizard breaks with the wizard nation and becomes a rogue wizard. These rogue wizards generally have bad, or at least extremely self-centered, intentions. They also generally don't get too far in pursuing their intentions because the rest of the wizard nation makes it a priority to subdue or eliminate them.

The only way to become a wizard is to have a current wizard choose you as an apprentice. After an initiation period of seven years, the apprentice must pass a test of knowledge and of character administered by the wizard nation. The apprentice becomes a legal son or daughter of the wizard, inheriting all of his or her property, both material and intellectual, upon the wizard's death.

Some wizards prefer to live on isolated, solitary mountains where they can work and think in peace. Others like to locate themselves in the middle of the action and hubbub of major cities. Since the wizard Radolphus of the Kingdom of Spire claimed and settled a floating island as his home, these rare bits of real estate are starting to become fashionable among the wizard community.

THE SKY RIDERS OF ETHERIUM

Continues in...

The Wizard's Daughter

Jeff Minerd's soaring series continues as Tak and Brieze are taken on a new adventure.

Brieze's mother is still hung up on her father, a man from the East who loved her and left her seventeen years ago. Brieze, the apprentice and legally adopted daughter of the local wizard, never met her biological father. But when she turns sixteen, Brieze decides to pay the man a visit and get some answers for her mother's sake. Brieze journeys half-way around the world, to the Eastern Kingdoms, confronting dragons, pirates, and the nocturnal ship-crushing beast known as the Nagmor. She discovers why her father disappeared, and in the process learns the truth of her own story.

Tak is still haunted by ghosts from the siege of Selestria. And there might soon be a new ghost—Tak's father is dying from his battle wound. He slips into a coma as his body struggles to fight off infection. Tak is powerless to save his father's life, and his thoughts turn to revenge against the man ultimately to blame, the notorious and traitorous Admiral Scud. Scud is now an outlaw on the run, his whereabouts unknown. But when Tak receives word that Brieze is in danger in the East, he sets out to rescue her—and he just might find the chance for revenge as well.

For more details and information,
visit www.SilverLeafBooks.com

ABOUT THE AUTHOR

Jeff Minerd thought he stopped writing fiction a long time ago until the story for *The Sailweaver's Son* came to him not in a dream, but after a dream. He is grateful for that, and for the opportunity to explore the world of Etherium and entertain others with what he finds there.

Minerd has a son, Noah, who is also a writer and avid reader. Minerd hopes to one day place in the top ten—or maybe even top 5—of Noah's favorite authors. But the competition is pretty stiff.

In a previous lifetime, Minerd published short fiction in literary journals, where one of his stories won the F. Scott Fitzgerald short story contest, judged by novelist and NPR book reviewer Alan Cheuse.

More recently, Minerd has worked as a science and medical writer for publications and organizations including the National Institutes of Health, MedPage Today, The Futurist Magazine, and the Scientist Magazine.

Minerd lives in Rochester, NY.

www.JeffMinerd.com